AF334966

THE LETTERS OF ABSOLON

The Letters of Absolon

a novel

Jack Mahoney

KNOX ROBINSON
PUBLISHING
London & New York

**KNOX ROBINSON
PUBLISHING**

34 New House
67-68 Hatton Garden
London, EC1N 8JY
&
244 5th Avenue, Suite 1861
New York, New York 10001

First published in Great Britain and the United States in 2014 by
Knox Robinson Publishing

A CIP catalogue record for this book is available from the British
Library.

ISBN HC 978-1-908483-92-8
ISBN PB 978-1-908483-93-5

Typeset in Trump Mediaeval

Printed in the United States of America and the United Kingdom

www.knoxrobinsonpublishing.com

The Letters of
Absolon

PROLOGUE

Dorothy Handleman's death came as no surprise to anyone. That seems almost disrespectful but be assured she was missed for every possible reason. Her demise had been anticipated for some time. Her doctor told her when she turned eighty that she'd never see eighty-two if she didn't stop smoking. She didn't stop. "Whatever's supposed to happen at eighty-two, I've seen it." She puffed and wheezed through another sixteen years over which time she attended that doctor's funeral. Finally, at ninety-six, Dorothy went to bed and stopped breathing. No cancer. No pneumonia. A touch of emphysema and a load of arthritis but nothing fatal. She was simply done.

I genuinely liked Dorothy. I liked how she referred to herself as Dot though no one else did. She thought they did. She would tell a story about something and say, "They said to me...Dot? Why can't you get some exercise?" I liked how she made a cup of tea for anyone who came to see her and always put out a few cakes or cookies. Very old world but so was she. She loved to tell stories and had a seemingly endless bank from which to draw. And I love how she made her own rules. This was evident in her fashion sense which ranged from colorfully flamboyant to ridiculous. She dressed as she lived. Whatever seemed like the most fun at the time. Her life had always been hers. She wasn't openly defiant of any established conventions and was perfectly willing to let the world spin happily along as it pleases. She never complained about rap music or nuclear weapons or human cloning. None of it seemed to matter to Dorothy.

I was not shocked when I heard that she had passed away, but truly remorseful. She was a great lady and the world was lessened by her passing. It came as a much greater surprise to learn that I was executor of her will. It somehow fell to me to inventory and dispose of her worldly goods. This surprised me as I had only married into her family. Four generations of blood relatives had been circling for years. They had heard and spread the rumors about her gold and jewelry. They tried to discount the myth of her shoving wads of cash into the walls of her modest Arizona home.

I'm sure it was all gossip, but I'll never know for sure. By the time I got to her home, it had already been visited by most of them. They swooped in the day she died and went through everything. "Cleaning up," they said. And clean up they did. Not a single item of worth was left in the house. Her jewelry box had a few pairs of gaudy junk earrings and a couple of heavy broaches. The drawers were turned and the closets tossed. Everything shiny was mysteriously missing. Vultures the lot of them.

Little was left of Dorothy's life for me to distribute. I did find some old magazines from the war era and a few collectables. Most of the paper and personal effects were impersonally tossed into one of the waste baskets in every room of the small house. Few homes in the valley had basements but the attic seemed relatively untouched. As her step ladder had already been adopted by one of the vultures, I balanced a box on the seat of a kitchen chair and hauled myself up through the ceiling portal. The attic was dark and cluttered, but not as thoroughly ransacked as the rest of the house. The fat relatives seemed to have trouble climbing up through the small hatch. From the looks of things, Dorothy managed from time to time though she didn't linger up here long. The smell of cigarettes which blanketed everything below was absent here, replaced by the dry, musty odor of dust and age.

It was interesting in a way. I liked the old Anhauser Busch bottles with the raised emblems and glass stoppers. Dot liked a private bottle in the old days, apparently. Some broken picture frames with photos of people I didn't assume I ever knew. Some of them seemed like last century images. Some soldiers in indeterminate uniforms and some aristocratically attired people posed as if time would return for them. The historic worth might exceed that of the memory of the forgotten subjects.

A few plastic trash bags of old clothes had been pushed up through the hatchway in recent years. As I looked past them, cardboard boxes and cloth sacks suggested older storage. Funny how we can date things by what we stored them in. I loved coffee cans. Tough, reusable and free. They're getting harder to find as most brands are switching to bags or plastic containers. Soon the coffee can will go the way of cigar box, the universal storage receptacle of past generations. Free and easily obtainable, everyone kept precious things in cigar boxes at the turn of the century and up through the Second World War. I spotted one in a pile near the tiny window at the end of the attic. It was sitting on a larger box and was thick on top with dust. As things are in Arizona, the dust meant it could have been sitting there all morning. Things here can be dry and dusty while still on the shelf in the store.

I opened the cigar box to find a few old coins, a small postcard from Charlotte, North Carolina and a bundle of letters. They were tied together with a fine silk ribbon and yellowed with age. With almost as much time as curiosity, I opened one letter and read. It was oddly formatted. Written in rough longhand, the lines coursed the page both horizontally and vertically. It took me a second to realize I had to read across, ignoring the vertical lines. Then I turned the page sideways and continued reading. Like two letters in one. Too simple to be a code, I surmised it was merely a means of getting the most out of a piece of paper.

Not all of the letters were from this creative soul. These were written from a soldier to his girl. The more eloquent notes were her replies. And some were from a mutual friend. My curiosity thoroughly peaked, I gathered them in chronological order as best I could determine and read. It was not historical, but I was genuinely touched. As I read, the lives and emotions of these spirits torn apart by a century past war came back to life for a fleeting instant. Their pain and devotion was all here. The sacrifice had survived in these written accounts. I felt the soldier's honesty and humility despite his poor literary skills. Her letters were of the refined dignity and courtesy expected of a young lady of the south, almost too reserved to be from the heart, yet they conveyed true love. The friend's letters revealed the words of a loyal and devoted friend but clearly masked deeper, repressed feelings. In all of them, I felt pain.

As I read the words and responses of these unheralded souls, their ghosts awoke in me. I felt them and for this moment, they were not forgotten. Through Dorothy's legacy, their sacrifices, fears and courage were again alive and shared. While the letters survived, so did these toppled pillars of a war long ago fought.

1

Durham, North Carolina
September, 1860

The party planned was for Captain Lucas DuPonte, a local hero of Durham. He survived the Mexican-American War and had returned to his hometown to reap the benefits of the tall and improvable tales of heroism that preceded him. It was the biggest thing to happen of late and everyone needed an excuse to be happy. The arrival of the captain was needed.

Like any town of consequence in the Carolinas, the mood here was blanketed with talks of war. The pompous property owners saw no reason not to secede and seemed to look forward to the profits to be had. It was the silent majority of the population, the mothers and sisters and young men with more to lose than gain that were forced by local politics to hold their tongues and smile like good confederates whenever the talks of separating from the Union were raised. Rarely was there an uttering of reluctance with the encroachment of defending their rights with force. It simply wasn't done.

The old south was a glorious time of chivalry and dignity. Echoing the blue-blooded influences of British and French nobility, the aristocrats of the south had evolved into a unique brand of time honored codes of conduct and homespun casual manners. Their roots, long and short could be measured in the eloquence of the dialect. The town hall was a typical Georgian style mansion with massive pillars supporting only enough roof to justify their noble presence. Inside, the grand ballroom was alive with elegant chamber music, flowing gowns and tuxedoes and lavishly braided uniforms. Amid the dancing and wine and overall conservative merriment, the guest of honor stood proudly in the center of a mixed group and basked in the limelight.

"They fought well, I suppose," Captain DuPonte said, pausing to sip his wine. "The Mexican army was well drilled and dressed, but they had no stomach for the hardships of war. They fought in fear of losing. This was their undoing."

"Don't you fear losing?" asked one of the young girls in the circle.

The pompous old soldier stroked his long handlebar mustache. "It was never a consideration, my dear. Like any good leader, my every thought was on winning and how best to go about it. Once we put the fear in them, the conclusion was inevitable."

A brash young man spoke up. "So how do we put that fear in the Yankees?"

"We hope that won't be necessary, Mister Beaumont," DuPonte replied. "That's not what I would consider a good war."

John Beaumont smiled and gained in assertiveness. "Any war you win is a good one, I say."

"No sir. The way to measure a war is by weighing what is to be gained or lost in the outcome. There is the true worth of a well-founded war. Take California. It was clearly in the realm of the union and a land rich in all manner of resources. I don't think I've ever seen a more beautiful country. By going there to fight, we risked little and stopped the encroachment of the Mexican Army on our own soil. The result was a fruitful bounty and a sovereign union."

"And a war hero all the richer," a young lady added.

The captain turned solemn. "No, my dear. We left the real heroes there on the battlefields, buried in both uniforms. The brave men who fought and died for what they believed in are the heroes. Not some pompous old windbag who watched from a hillside."

"Now that I'll drink to," said a young man entering the circle. Absolon Wilkes raised his glass. "To the glorious dead. May they never be forgotten."

The Captain raised a glass and the entourage followed suit. "To the glorious dead."

John Beaumont seemed to take exception to Absolon's comment. "You drinking to battle, Absolon? I would expect you to be toasting the cowards who sat back to let others do their fighting for them."

Absolon was righteously calm amid the murmuring crowd. "I'll always drink to anyone who can find an alternative to bloodshed."

DuPonte tried to intercede. "Here, here. Well said. War should be the last resort of civilized people."

Absolon continued. "I prefer to see it off the table completely. I find when violence is an option at any level, there are many that reach for it first. Do away with it and watch men find a peaceful solution to their differences."

"A coward's solution," said John, his tone more challenging.

"A civilized solution," said DuPonte. "Kindly give the man his due, Sir."

John bowed subtly toward the captain without diverting his stare from Absolon. "I yield, sir. I've become accustomed to seeing Mister Wilkes let the others fight his battles for him."

As Absolon was on the verge of rebuttal, a young lady entered the circle and took his arm. The beautiful, honey-blonde haired girl looked to the Captain. "Were you planning on holding the whole party hostage, Uncle?"

Captain DuPonte smiled. "Well I am the guest of honor, you know."

Anne Carmichael responded with light-hearted assertiveness. "You're a liar and an incorrigible instigator. I want to dance and I'm stealing a man now. I advise all ladies do the same or this night will be lost."

John Beaumont was clearly agitated by Anne's intervention, though chivalry forbid he speak ill at this moment, at least to a great extent.

"If you're intent on stealing a man, fair Anne, might I suggest a real one?"

"Might I keep that with your other suggestions, Mister Beaumont?" she quipped. "I promise to give it no less consideration." With that, she turned and led a reluctant Absolon from the circle. Several ladies nearby followed suit and the tension was effectively broken for the moment.

The violins gave a timely waltz that brought many couples to the broadening dance floor. Absolon took Anne to the center and whirled her in unison with the others. Lovers young and old gazed into each other's eyes and all wrong with the world vanished for the moment. The magic in the air was to make a memory kept a lifetime. Anne gazed wistfully into the dark eyes of her lover. Absolon looked deeply into the green pools and mentally rehearsed his first line. He knew the rest would follow with her reaction but the first line was as critical as the moment chosen to speak it. He danced and planned and realized the time was upon him.

From the edge of the room, a group of men stood in casual banter. One of them seemed unable to divert his stare from the dancers, though he did his best to keep up with the conversation. Royal Pollard watched Anne dancing in the arms of his closest friend. They looked so perfect together. Absolon looked so happy that the question he had rehearsed and spoken to Royal about seemed inevitable. He looked hard to see if there was any hope evident that his best friend might not ask her this night. Seeing none, he sighed with reserved disheartenment and tried again to be part of the present conversation.

"Well there'll be a need for men here as well come a war," said the red haired man opposite Royal.

Royal shook himself back into the here and now. "Indeed there will, Josh. Despite the political demands, life goes on."

Josh Carmichael nodded as he sipped his drink. "Crops still need tending. Cattle need milking. Homes and families need protecting. Some men have to stay back for that kind of work."

Another man added, "That's what the old and weak are for." Sam Gottwick had clearly had a drink too many but remained coherent.

"And the cripples?" Josh tapped his leg, indicating it was less than perfect.

Sam immediately relaxed his position. "Sorry, Josh. I didn't mean…"

"It's all right, Sam. I know my limitations."

Royal spoke up. "You're hardly a cripple, Josh. You're the hardest working man I know."

"But I can't march. Means I can't fight the Yankees."

"You can walk, but you can't run. I can talk, but I can't sing. That's why I stand next to you in church."

Josh smiled. "I used to think it was so's you could sit next to Anne."

"Maybe it was. But there's your point. With the bulk of the men out, your place will be to see to her safety."

Sam spoke up again. "Won't we have a militia for that? We'll need to train a local garrison for our own protection."

"Yes of course," Royal agreed. "But we still need to take care of our own. Anne deserves to know she's safe in her own..."

He stopped in mid sentence upon seeing Absolon dance his fair Anne out the door to the presumed seclusion of the balcony. With this, he found himself unable to feign interest or contentment in else. He politely excused himself to get a fresh drink.

The balcony was large enough that the two lovers were able to walk past the other moon gazing couples to find their own small corner and a suggestion of privacy.

"It appeared John was on the verge of provoking you," she said with an accusing smile.

"To respond only," Absolon calmly replied. "My position on violence is easily defended."

"But to what end? John wants to fight. He'll never listen to reason that takes away his chance to fool himself into thinking he's a man of some sort."

"I wonder if you know me so well as to know where my thoughts lie tonight."

"I must say your obvious preoccupation is a mystery to me," she smiled coyly. "I'm used to being the only thing on your mind."

"I assure you that you are." He began to fidget nervously. "There is something I want to ask you. It's no small thing and I fear the answer though I must hear it from your own lips. Please prepare yourself to crush me with honesty rather than loft me to the heavens on false hopes borne of pity. Are you so prepared?"

Despite his well practiced eloquence, she knew that the bulk of Absolon's formal education had been acquired over the past two years and only a small portion of his lessons had been devoted to the arts. He had never truly been intimidated by her cultural refinement, though he knew his local accent and appearance contradicted the lifestyle to which she was accustomed. He endeavored to socially elevate himself purely for her sake. His statement was so clearly rehearsed that Anne began to feel the uneasiness of the moment. "I can't imagine a word I could utter in honesty that would do you harm, Absolon. Still, you have my word. I will crush you, should the need arise."

With that, Absolon drew a deep breath and slowly lowered himself to one knee. Holding her delicate hand in his, he looked up at her. The moonlight bathed her beauty in a glow that warmed his heart by the heavenly vision and thus strengthened his resolve.

"I know that I can't make you happy every day of your life. I can't promise I will give you cause to smile every day from this day forth, as you so richly deserve. But if you see fit to grace me with the opportunity to try, I swear to you with my life that I will devote myself to that very task by any means possible. Your absolute happiness will forever be my sole purpose in life. My darling Anne. May I have your hand in marriage?"

Royal had mingled his way to a more interesting group and was trying to enjoy the attention of three young ladies. Though in his late twenties, Royal had never taken a bride. His land was rich in mineral and livestock and his family wealth left him to a life of opulence and relative leisure. Still he avoided such social gatherings and preferred the casual company of a few well chosen friends. His presence here made him a target for the ladies in waiting, as he was the most eligible bachelor in the county.

"Unescorted again, Mister Pollard?" asked Sara Moore.

Royal smiled and tried to ignore the exaggerated eyelash fluttering. "I came with a friend."

"Absolon Wilkes," Belinda Sikeston responded, "can hardly be considered a date. That is whom you came with. Is it not?"

Royal retained a confident smile. "He is my best friend. And he needed a bit of encouragement just to come."

"Perhaps he knew his place," the third woman said in a low tone. "I mean, he hardly fits in with true aristocrats."

"Doubtful he ever will," Belinda added.

"I doubt he'll ever try," Royal said. "He's quite confident in his station."

Sara, still holding Royal's arm and pretending she was closer to him than were the others, did her best to side with Royal. "Now let's be fair. Mister Wilkes may not be as blue-blooded as the rest of us but he's done quite well for himself. That little farm Royal sold him seems quite prosperous."

Chelsea Underwood, the third woman, leaned in and placed a hand to her mouth, feigning discretion. "I heard he doesn't own a single servant, house or field. How prosperous can that be?"

Royal again spoke in his defense. "Absolon has very strong feelings about some things. Slavery is one of them."

Sara looked up at Royal. "Well it's easy to see why he's still single. But you remain a mystery. I'm inclined to wonder what we might have done to drive the most desirable bachelor in the county to take a vow of celibacy."

The other girls giggled at the brazen referral.

"My goodness, Sara," Belinda gasped. "You're positively shameless."

"Oh don't pretend you're not equally curious." She looked again to Royal. "You must think the worst of me but my curiosity has gotten the best of me again."

Chelsea looked seductively between her lowered brow and the raised rim of her glass. "I must say I'm a bit interested myself."

Royal felt that some sort of response was in order. He contemplated the truth for a second before securing his answer. "I could say I haven't met the right girl yet." He glanced from one set of eyes to another. "Anyone believing that?"

Chelsea laughed. "You're a terrible liar, Mister Pollard."

"Oh on the contrary," he quipped. "I've lied to you many times without a hint of suspicion. I'd say I'm quite proficient at it."

Absolon and Anne came into the ballroom arm in arm. He led her excitedly through the crowd until he spotted his friend. Royal had successfully changed the subject and was in the middle of a story when he felt a forceful tug on his arm and Absolon whispered in his ear.

"I got … I mean I *have* news, Royal. And I need a favor."

Royal excused himself amid the rolling eyes of the unforgiving ladies and turned to Absolon and Anne. "What is it?" he asked. "What happened?"

"I did it!" Absolon whispered. "I asked her!"

Royal looked at him in shock, then at Anne. Her glowing smile told him all to be known. Still he probed. "I didn't think you'd... You said you had to wait for the right time. What prompted you to...?"

"I don't know. The moonlight. The wine. The overwhelming love. The point is I asked her."

Royal looked again to Anne. "No need to ask what she said. Congratulations." Shaking Absolon's hand vigorously, he forced a smile and feigned the mandatory enthusiasm. "Congratulations, Absolon. You lucky, lucky soul. Congratulations." Then he turned to Anne and extended an arm. "And you," he said as he pulled her in for an embrace. "You could do a lot worse than him, you know." The hug was deliberately brief as he withdrew. Smiling, "You could have had me."

Anne's broad smile was true elation. "In the company of you two, I couldn't have gone wrong. I love you both so much. Thank you, Royal. Thank you for your friendship, your loyalty and your guidance. But mostly I thank you for bringing him here this night."

Royal, normally among the most eloquent of men, could offer no more than, "Indeed." He prayed his smiled looked sincere.

"Will you make the announcement?" Absolon asked him.

"Now? Here?"

"Oh yes, yes," Anne insisted. "We can't wait."

"Don't you feel it would be hasty? Perhaps give it the night to plan a few details. Dates and the like."

"No, no," Absolon pressed. "It has to be now."

"Then so be it," Royal said. "But it would be rude to steal the attention from our honored guest with an eclipsing event. Don't you think? Do this. Allow Anne's uncle to make the formal announcement. The wonderful news is out and he gets the praise for it."

"You're right," Absolon agreed. "That would be the right thing to do." He turned to Anne. "Let's go ask him now."

"Yes lets," she heartily agreed and they turned to make their way, hand in hand, toward the main gathering of guests. Doubtless Captain DuPonte would be found at the center.

The topic within the circle was not of love or dancing or gayety on any level. This circle embraced the only topic possible in a gathering of men in the heart of the confederacy and a retired veteran of a recent engagement. These men spoke of war.

"It's been a few years since your last command, Captain," spoke one of the elders. "Are you anxious to get back at it?"

"Why do you think he came back?" asked John Beaumont. "He could smell the approach of war. Am I right, Sir?"

Captain DuPonte was less enthusiastic. "I returned to my home and family because my duty had been done. While proudly serving my country a continent away, my sister's husband was executed by the very enemy I fought so successfully. Henry was a brilliant officer, a brave soldier, a fine man and a wonderful husband and father whose passing I eventually grieved. I was earning an insignificant decoration while my beloved sister Abigail died of pneumonia. I thank God her two children were grown and had the support of you good friends and neighbors as I was of no help. I deeply regret this and so much else sacrificed for answering the call of war. That war is over and the land settled. I am home now."

"So you aren't looking forward to this one?"

"I'm not so sure there will be a war," the captain said calmly. "As I said earlier, there are good wars and bad wars. The way a war is measured is by the potential loss versus the potential gain. While the negotiations are valid, the truth is that there is a great vastness of wealth and growth beyond the few confederate states. If we separate from the Union, we deny ourselves any of that bounty."

"We have trade with France and England," spoke one of the men. Trevor Parks was a strong proponent of seceding from the Union. "And Spain. They are not part of the Confederacy."

"But we did not expel them in an act of treason," DuPonte said.

"England might disagree." Trevor smiled vindictively. "Their forces were driven out, yet they remained willing to barter."

"That's because we had more to offer them than they us. That is not true in this case. No. The fact remains that there is more to be gained by both sides if the conflict is abated. I doubt this war will ever take place."

Absolon had been standing in the circle long enough to realize this was not the best time for their announcement. He was further taken by the current discussion. "I pray you are right, Sir."

"You would," John said with disdain.

"So would I," said Trevor Parks, sensing the hostility. "I don't wish to see any of my friends sent off to battle, but if it is deemed that war is the only way, I have no doubt the brave and loyal men here will give a loyal and admirable accounting of themselves. Am I right?" He raised his glass to toast.

John Beaumont raised his glass as well, but watched Absolon abstain. "Is this what we can expect of you, Wilkes?" he demanded. "When the call is given, will your loyalty be to your country?"

"Interesting question," Absolon responded. "My country has declared any attempt to secede an act of treason and illegal. If my loyalty is to my country..."

"Will you fight? It's a simple question. How compelling is your fear?"

"I fear any world where men ignore whatever laws that don't suit the moment. In such a world, there is no law. No order. There's only criminals and the doom of us all is assured if these men prosper. No I won't defend any act that would bring about such anarchy."

John stepped into the center of the circle and looked Absolon squarely in the eye. "Is that your answer then?"

Absolon returned his challenge with equal resolve. "I won't take arm against my own government. I won't fight against an army set out to enforce the laws that protect us all. I won't fight. My answer to you is no."

John took another firm step to put him within reach of Absolon. "Then I say you're a coward and a traitor, not that this comes as any great surprise to anyone here."

Absolon felt the cut of these words. He stood in the presence of his beloved Anne. He stood in the judgmental light of her closest elder relative, a man of great stature and prominence. The whole of the community awaited his response to this horrific accusation. His next step would surely decide the course of the future he had vowed to spend with her. He had always been confident and assured enough to walk away from any such assault. But it was only he who endured the consequences then. Now he spoke for her as well. Now he must think of her first

"I demand satisfaction," he said calmly to John. "How would you have it?"

John did not hesitate. "The neutral ground north of this hall. I'll be there at sunrise, though I expect I'll be alone."

DuPonte interjected. "Gentlemen. If what you're suggesting is a duel, I must remind you that dueling is illegal. You both know that. You need to settle this like civilized men."

"An odd comment," Absolon said. "All things considered."

"Relax, Captain DuPonte," John said with an arrogant sneer. "This pathetic farmer is no gentleman and there will be no duel."

Absolon looked him in the eye without a waiver. "At sunrise then." John returned his unwavering stare, adding a barely discernable smirk, as though he drew some satisfaction just from hearing Absolon accept the challenge. Absolon was sure John's subtle, confident smile was intended to instill a note of fear in him and it succeeded, though he struggled not to let it be seen. Forcing an equally confident expression long enough to turn away from him, Absolon's gaze fell immediately onto the terrified face of Anne. The fear he effectively concealed from Beaumont came to brutal evidence as he suddenly realized how completely and tragically their fortunes had twisted. They came to announce their betrothal and plans for their future and instead, may not see another day together. She turned and ran from the hall in tears.

He looked after her, stunned at the turn of events. Then he looked up to Royal. "My God, Royal. What have I done?"

"You spoke your heart, my friend. Now what do we do about it?"

The ballroom was buzzing with murmurs of the impending duel so Royal led his friend outside to talk in private.

"Surely she knew my position on such things," Absolon said, still reeling from his outburst. "On war, on seceding, on my loyalty to my country. Surely she knew, Royal."

"And you knew hers. I doubt she expected either to be challenged so prominently this night. You truly could have held your tongue just this once."

"I truly wish I had. So what do I do now?"

"Have you ever dueled before?"

Absolon subtly shook his lowered head.

Royal allowed a look of concern. "Ever seen one?" His friend's answer was the same. He grasped Absolon by the shoulders. "Go home and try to rest."

"No," Absolon said. "I need to talk to Anne."

"Let me," Royal said. "You rest. I'll see you later."

"Rest? How can I rest with the thought of never seeing her again? I have to explain..."

"Explain what? Why you may never see her again? How can you expect her to hear those words on this of all nights? Better that you rest. Clear your head of all but what you have to do tomorrow. If your head's in the same place as your heart with half the conviction, you may be able to spare Anne any explanations. Now you rest."

Absolon reluctantly agreed and went home, though he prepared for a very restless night.

Anne's coachman hurried her home to the stately Carmichael mansion west of the city. She left the coach as it slowed and ran up the front steps in tears. The servants knew better than to intervene despite their concern. The three of them stood silent as Anne ran upstairs and slammed the door. Rosemary, the house servant, waited nearly an hour before tapping gently on the bedroom door.

"I made you a cup o' tea, Miss Anne," she said in a cautious tone to the closed door. She waited a full thirty seconds for a reply but none came. "You all right, Miss?"

"No," came the response over a weeping voice. "No I'm not. Please leave me alone. Just for one night, please."

Rosemary descended the stairway slowly, still carrying the silver tea tray. The other two servants met her at the bottom but asked nothing. Her expression and the clean cup told all. Her life of servitude to this family compelled her to care, to want to do something to relieve her mistress' torment. But she had no idea what to do or say that would do other than worsen the mood. This was her initial fear when she heard the knock on the heavy front door. She was greatly relieved when Royal appeared in the doorway.

In her bedchambers, Anne sat at her vanity with head in hands. Through her own sobbing, she could not hear the soft rapping at the door. She looked up and into the mirror and saw the door opening.

"I told you to leave me alone!" she shouted over her own sobs.

"I must've missed that order." Royal stepped cautiously in.

She turned and ran to him, pressing her face against his chest and holding him tightly. He put his arms around her for support, but deliberately kept them a soft touch. He felt the warmth of her breath and the moist tears against his chest and struggled against his own emotions to remember why he was here in her chambers.

"Please forgive me, Anne. I had to come…"

"Oh Royal!" she sobbed. "How could he do this? How could it happen tonight of all nights?"

"He had little choice, Anne. You know how strongly he feels about these things."

Anne looked up at him. "But a duel! John Beaumont is a trained soldier and blueblood. You know Absolon is no match for him."

"There's so much tension in the air, what with so much talk of war. It was brewing. But I'll be there to insure no advantage is taken."

"The advantage is there already. Will you fight for him? Can you do that? John can't best you."

"Even if I could, you know Absolon wouldn't stand for it."

Anne held Royal as tightly as she ever had. She looked directly into his eyes and forced him to look back. Then she begged him. "Royal. You're like brothers, you and Absolon. You didn't just sell him a plot of land, you taught him to fit in, to be one of us. He told me in confidence that he couldn't even read until he met you. You made him a land owner and a gentleman."

"He's taught me a few things as well. I knew nothing of farming or rotating crops. Did you know there are different types of chicken?"

"You're his best friend. You're *our* best friend. I beg you not to let this happen. Please bring him back to me. Can you promise me that?"

He looked down into her tearing green eyes. He saw her quivering lips and was powerless to say other than, "You have my word, Anne. Tomorrow will see you two together. You'll yet announce your future plans. I swear it."

"Oh thank you," she wept. Her arms tightened around him in gratitude, though it pained him to feel only that.

He finally pulled her arms from him. "I have to go to him now. He'll see you tomorrow." With that, he left her room.

Royal's estate was less than a mile from the town center so he encouraged Absolon to stay there rather than trek the five miles across the countryside to his farm. It was also a logistical step as Absolon's farm was furnished with only the essentials of farm life. He needed to practice and a shotgun was inadequate for dueling. The Pollard estate was well appointed and pistols were there for them to use in private.

Throughout the long night, Royal sat with Absolon and lectured him on the rules of dueling and the right to withdraw. Absolon was fair with a pistol but had never held a sword or saber. As it was he that laid down the challenge, the right to choose weapons was John's and they could only hope it would be pistols. They practiced the turn and fire over and over. Royal praised Absolon's prowess to bolster his confidence but knew that it was only better than it had been a few hours before. It was still slow and far too clumsy for the likes of a skilled marksman.

Royal kept one detail of dueling to himself. The most difficult part of the duel was to remain poised with a loaded pistol being aimed at you. Such poise can only come with experience under fire and it was here that John held an advantage Royal could not help his friend to overcome. He had watched John in conflict more than once and this could be Absolon's undoing unless a hint of uncertainty could be shifted.

The first rays of sunlight cut through the Carolina morning mist blanketing the wooded clearing near the town hall. Absolon walked across the wet grass to find John Beaumont waiting calmly. With him were two men. Trevor was the neutral while Tom Harden acted as John's second. John was somewhat concerned to see Royal acting as Absolon's second. Their friendship was no secret but this was a different act. He had not considered this and wondered to what extent Royal would stand up for his friend.

"You look like you had a rough night," John said of Absolon.

Absolon smiled. "Uh huh. I tried to sleep but was kept up by the braying of a jack-ass."

John's smile vanished. He looked crossly to Trevor.

Trevor held a sword in one hand and a pistol in the other. "By the time honored rules of chivalry, you have challenged this man to a duel of satisfaction. It is therefore his right to choose the weapon to be used. Do you agree sir?"

Absolon nodded.

Trevor turned to John. "Choose your weapon, Mister Beaumont."

Absolon drew a silent breath and held it for the eternal ten seconds it took John to nonchalantly adjust his waistcoat, exhale feigned boredom and finally place his hand on the pistol. They were only slightly relieved as Trevor nodded and turned away. John kept a calm look about him.

"Pistols, John?" Royal asked.

"Last man I killed with a sword was so inept I felt like a butcher," John said softly.

"I remember. William Hunter, wasn't it?"

John looked away as if in pain. "No. Hunter was killed with a pistol."

Trevor returned with an ornate wooden case and opened it before the men. Inside, four loaded flintlock pistols lay waiting. The two men simultaneously selected a pistol from the case and held it to their chest aimed upward.

Trevor announced the mandatory understandings. "You sir," gesturing to Tom, "and you sir," to Royal, "shall act as seconds only and are not excused to behave as belligerents in this dispute. This is a gentleman's duel and, barring any deliberate infraction of the rules of chivalry, shall end here and between these two. Is that agreeable to all parties?"

Tom agreed in a loud, clear voice. John was instantly aware of Royal's less vocal acceptance of the terms. He looked to see Royal staring down upon him as though it was he fighting the dual instead of Absolon.

"A pistol? Hunter was fairly proficient with a pistol as I recall," Royal said in the same low tone. "How did you manage to best him?"

John seemed uneasy for the first time. Absolon studied the pistol in his own hand as Royal awaited John's response.

"I didn't," John said in as calm a voice as he could muster. "That was you."

"Ah yes. Right you are."

John was under no allusion that Royal had forgotten who had out gunned an expert marksman in a duel. Royal spoke softly but his words carried enormous weight. "This ...ends here," John said to Royal in an almost inquisitive tone.

"Of that, you have my absolute assurance." With that word, Royal adjusted his waistcoat as though it concealed something, leaving John certain of his intent. Both he and John knew that chivalry existed to allow civilized men a controlled and final resolution to their differences believed otherwise impossible to settle. True devotion to a friend was a much older and sometimes greater hold on a man's actions and could not be measured with a glance nor governed by a rule. By his suggestion and the gesture of concealing a weapon under his waistcoat, Royal had assured John that his loyalty to Absolon was paramount.

John felt a smile of acceptance cross him as the facts were now clear. He looked up to Absolon. "I ask you again to renounce the Northern government and take an oath of allegiance to the Confederacy."

"I don't owe you no oath, John." Absolon's tone was steady enough to belie the uneasiness with which he nervously fingered the dueling pistol.

John spoke again. "You're clearly out matched, Wilkes. You have no chance. I ask you again to state you will fight or admit you are a coward."

Absolon pulled back the hammer of his pistol. "To that, I'll have satisfaction." He looked at Trevor. "Will you count us off sir?" He angrily turned his back to John to begin the paces.

John lowered his pistol. "Wilkes." Absolon ignored him. "*Wilkes!*" Now Absolon turned back to face him and saw the pistol hanging at his side.

"You know you will die this day if we continue, yet you proceed. This is not the act of a coward. Merely that of a man who strongly disagrees with me. When last I checked, you have that right should you dare to exercise it. In these perilous times, few men have the courage to speak their mind should it be different from the popular opinion. I withdraw my charge of cowardice."

Absolon was unsure of the protocol. He looked to his second for guidance. Royal nodded and Absolon slowly lowered his weapon. John placed his pistol back in the case and Absolon followed suit. Then Absolon extended his hand.

"Don't press your luck, Wilkes." John refused his hand and turned away with only a brief glance to Royal to insure that was acceptable.

Trevor closed the case and followed John and Tom from the clearing. Only then did Absolon realize he was trembling like a leaf. Only at that moment did it come to him how terrified he was of never seeing Anne again and what her reaction would be to his death. Only when he watched John leave did he know to what extent he was failing to hold these thoughts at bay in order to concentrate on the task at hand. Only now could he plan to live on.

Royal grasped him by the shoulder and slid his other hand inside his coat. He pulled from the pocket inside his waistcoat, a silver cigar case. Taking one for himself, he offered his friend a cigar.

"I didn't bring any brandy, but this might help."

2

"How old *is* that nigger?" Clifford Huxley asked in a taunting laugh. He sat in his buckboard watching Bill Schultz prod his aged slave to unload the contents of a broken wagon.

The rear wheel had collapsed under the excessive load of feed bags and the wagon had to be unloaded before a new wheel could be fitted. Bill shouted and ordered the slave faster but the old man seemed to have only one speed. He walked to the wagon, lifted one bag of grain, carried it to the street, dropped it and slowly repeated, seemingly oblivious to the shouts of his master.

Orangeburg was far from the largest city in South Carolina, but the railroad provided ample trade and foot traffic to populate a small gathering of spectators. Huxley and the gathering crowd enjoyed the spectacle of Bill's impotent shouting. Finally a wagon stopped and a man asked the neighborly thing.

"Need a hand?" Mason Corbel asked. He sat in the seat next to his foreman, Tom Bridger. Without waiting for a reply, Bridger turned and gestured to the slave in the back of their wagon and the young black man hopped out to pitch in. Mason stepped down and approached as well.

"Appreciate it, Mase," Huxley said. "If'n I don't get this wheel fixed before the smith goes home, I'll be here all night. I got hogs to feed."

Mason smiled. "Still might be after dark at the rate you're going."

"Well I tote a firearm for protection, but I'd sure prefer to be back home before night sets in. That's for damn sure."

Without further discussion, Mason stepped up and picked up a bag of grain. The older slave hesitated, surprised to see a white man doing slave work. Mason's slave seemed undaunted and continued. The gallery of onlookers was already curious, but some gasped aloud when Mason stopped and asked his slave for advice.

"Window," he said to the tall young slave. "You know a faster way of doing this?"

Window Graham thought briefly before nodding. "Yassah. Too much walking." He instructed Mason to get into the wagon and he positioned the old man on the tailgate. Window stood in the street and handed the first bag to Bill. Bill had reluctantly followed Window's instructions and laid the bag next to the pile already begun. The human chain moved much faster as Mason simply lifted the sacks and handed them off. The old man took them and dropped them to Window. He had taken this spot because he didn't think the old man could catch a fifty-pound sack.

As the spectators watched in relative silence, a young man stepped up to Mason's wagon. "Ain't that your boss over there working?"

Bridger nodded, recognizing Daniel Jacobs as a friend. "That's him all right, Danny. Over there doin' nigger work again. Though on his property it's kind of hard to tell what is and ain't nigger work." Then he turned to Daniel. "Almost makes me wonder what your sister ever saw in him."

Daniel merely shrugged. "Mason works hard and he takes good care of her. He hasn't got a mean bone in his body nor a harsh thought for anyone. You'd be hard pressed to find a better man."

"Well he'd be a lot richer if he'd learn to raise the whip to them slaves instead of doing things his damn self."

"He's doing well enough to keep you and me in grub stake, Tom. If I were you, I'd forget about that whip. Mason would sooner take it to you than those slaves. He says they got enough troubles."

The wagon was emptied just as the smith rolled a fresh wheel up. With the load off, the large wagon was more easily lifted and the new wheel slid on almost perfectly. The chain was reversed and the wagon was half loaded before the smith had tallied up the bill. The spectacle had lost its appeal for most and the crowd was disbursing when a boy came riding hard down the main street.

"Where's Ned Porter?" he called out excitedly.

No one responded until Tom called to him. "Why? What's wrong, Jake?"

The boy drew a winded breath. "His kids got themselves treed out by the sawmill. That big tree in the clearing."

"Treed by what?" Bill asked.

"Them Branson dogs. Looks like all of them. We didn't have no gun so me an' my brother lit out to get help."

Bill stopped loading. "Well I got a gun in the wagon but we'd need a few more. Them dogs are worse than wild." He stepped toward the front of the wagon where the gun lay under the seat.

A few started readying for the hunt. Tom remained in the wagon. "Long as they stay up in that tree, they'll be all right. Somebody needs to go find Ned. Where's your brother, Boy?"

Jake pointed to Mason. "He headed to your place, Mister Corbel. It was the closest and we didn't know who'd be here."

Mason froze. "My place?" He turned to see his brother-in-law sharing his concern. Daniel barely mouthed the name, "Vickie", but Mason had already realized how his wife would react to this news.

Her younger brother, Daniel knew this as well and darted for his horse. Mason grabbed the reins of Jake's horse.

"I need your mount, Jake." The boy slid off the horse's right side as Mason mounted on the left. "Your gun, Bill!"

Bill Schultz tossed the black powder revolver to him and Mason turned to gallop toward the mill with Daniel close behind.

The Branson pack was actually several separate packs of stray dogs. Old Newly Branson raised hunting dogs for years. When he died ten years earlier, his wife fell into a deep depression. Alone in the world, she refused to care for the dozens of hounds penned up around her ranch house. For weeks they were fed nothing more than her table scraps. One day she went out to find a chicken to kill for her dinner and found the large dog pen empty. The dogs had dug under the fence and escaped. Before she could think of the consequences, the pack came upon her. She was killed and mostly eaten.

The pack ran into the woods and eventually split into several packs, each many times more vicious than wolves. Wolves actually never attacked humans and only bit humans from a cage or trap. These wild dogs seemed to hate people and over the years had killed several children and a few men. Though mostly known for killing sheep and chickens, they had brought down cattle and horses and were capable of nearly anything.

Mason pressed the tired horse. Daniel kept up with his relatively fresh mount but they knew the horse's health was secondary to getting there in time. Mason was considered by most to be the best horseman in the territory. He knew of only one person who could out ride him. This thought plagued him the whole long way.

Riding where there were no trails, Victoria galloped at breakneck speed. She truly did ride as well as any man and better than most. But she was only a passive shot and had to get close. Her prize quarter horse, Big Willy, charged boldly over the hills and onto the flat clearing. Fifty yards away and alone in the center of the clearing, an old oak was surrounded by no less than twenty dogs. They circled and leapt toward the branches and barked threateningly. Their noise and focus on the close quarry blinded them from the rapid approach of the brown charger.

Victoria had the pistol ready and tucked into her belt. She leveled the shotgun at the pack and as she closed to within ten feet of the closest hound, she emptied the first barrel. The dog's ribcage exploded and a third of the other dogs scattered. At the same instant she heard one of the children scream. Startled by the gunfire, but still alive. She rode through the pack sweeping close to the tree and fired again. The second barrel took the head off another animal. From the corner of her eye, she saw the hem of a pale white cotton dress in the branches but she knew better than to stop in the center of this hunting pack. She swung the spent gun at a dog that lunged at Willy's legs. The heavy steel barrel laid open the dog's head just above his eye and he fell to the ground.

She rode through and beyond the snarling pack. She knew they could and surely would bring even a big horse down if she stopped. As she sprinted to a safe distance, she pulled the revolver out of her belt and turned for another assault. One of the dogs was on her heels and she dispatched it first. Then she held the big horse at a standstill and aimed into the pack.

"Steady Willy," she whispered, trying to steady her own, unskilled hand. Five dogs fell on successive shots. She could do no better but the remaining dozen mongrels now viewed her as both enemy and supper.

They separated to surround her in pack hunter fashion.

With no time to reload the black powder chamber of the pistol, she shoved it back into her belt and drew the shotgun again. She had no more shells for the "greener" but it might serve as a club until she was free to reload the pistol. At least the dogs were stalking her instead of the children.

Backing Willy slowly away from the tree and the pack, Victoria lured the wild dogs along with her. "Stay in the tree, Kids!" she shouted. She feared that they would drop to the ground as soon as the dogs were away and she was not ready to defend them. "Stay up there no matter what!" The dogs were still circling but drawing closer. Her plan was to wait until they were away from the tree and fully focused on her. Then her would charge through their perimeter and run off, hopefully with them in pursuit.

With the greener at the ready, she heeled Big Willy and the stallion sprang forth. Riding at an angle away from the tree, she broke through the circle of hounds. Some started to give chase but one of the dogs in her path leapt and caught her by the ankle. Her boot protected her but the dog had a good grasp and pulled her foot from the stirrup. Despite managing to kick herself out of the boot, she was nearly pulled from the saddle and needed both hands on the saddle horn to pull herself back up. The shot gun fell and the horse slowed again. The wild dog dropped the boot and looked up with a snarl just as Big Willy lashed back with his hind leg. The dog was sent backwards reeling from the powerful kick.

Victoria struggled back into the saddle and Willy set to run but the dogs were all around her and swarming. Just as she was convinced the pack would bring her and her mount down, four shots rang out in close succession from the bordering brush. Three of the hounds fell. Another volley took three more. The remaining dogs stopped, unsure what was happening to their numbers. That was long enough for the next round to kill four more. The last two dogs ran hard for the cover of the woods.

Victoria looked to the origin of the shots. A grizzled, gaunt old man stepped out. He held a Henry repeating rifle under his arm. Three boys of varying age were behind him. He merely nodded reassuringly and said nothing. She turned and rode to the tree.

From Big Willy's back, she could reach the lower limbs and help the children down. The boy was nine and had done his best to protect his sister of only six. He slid from the horse to the ground. The girl clung to Victoria as though the dogs would return. "Ain't them Ned Porter's kids?" asked the old man as they stepped up.

Victoria held the small girl in her arms. "Yes. Thank God you came. I couldn't reload and I think they had me."

"My nephew will be the one thankin' God. As for me, I'll thank you."

Victoria let the calmed girl slide to the ground. "I'm Victoria Corbel. My husband and I have the plantation off that way about..."

"Virgil Porter," he interrupted sternly. "I know your place. Up close to Knotts Hill. I heard Corbel took him a wife. 'Pears he done well by it."

"We've been married a few months, now," she said as one of the boys handed her the lost boot. "Thank you. We should have you and your family over for..."

"Well I'm pleased to meet you but I don't cotton to town folk much. Me 'n' the boys tend keep to ourselves 'cept for kin. Them young 'uns is kin and for that, I owe you. I won't forget it."

From the other side of the broad meadow, Mason and Daniel rode hard into the clearing. Virgil saw them and clearly wanted no more to do with them. He nodded to Victoria and turned away. Two of the boys turned with him but the middle-aged boy, looking to be sixteen or more, stood and stared at her with his mouth agape, as if hypnotized.

Virgil turned back and called him by name. "Jeb!" he said sternly. The boy broke his stare and followed his brothers. Virgil looked at Victoria. "Forgive his manners, Ma'am. He don't see many people at all. To him, you're a sight o' wonderment"

"Am I?" she said in curious tone. Mason rode up to her and quietly listened, hoping for a glimpse of what he missed.

"You sit that big horse like a man," Virgil continued. "But you're as pretty as a picture book lady. Musta confused the pants off him. Forgive my language, Ma'am."

She smiled sincerely. Mason placed a hand on hers, not wanting to interrupt, but still grateful she was all right.

Virgil looked at Mason. "You be Corbel, then?"

Mason Nodded. "I'm Mason Corbel."

"I knew your ma. Sorry for your loss. That's some woman you got there, Corbel. Mind her well." With that, he turned and ushered the boys back into the brush.

The Corbel home was something less than a mansion. It was a large ranch house and quite comfortable for two of them with room for more. Mason had inherited the plantation when his father passed away eight years ago. A boy then, he didn't hesitate to set aside the games and boyhood things most consider part of growing up. Sterling Corbel was a stern man but he kept his affairs private. When he died, there was no time to casually find the records and procedures he ran his business by. Mason was dealt a poor hand by fate and accepted his tasks with greater maturity and conviction than many grown men might have. His mother and the families that lived and worked here relied totally on his ability to run a ranch and he seemed to be born to the task.

Mason's mother survived long enough to meet the young girl that had moved to Orangeburg with her family. Myron Jacobs, a prosperous Philadelphia lawyer had two children and wife, Davila, who was bound and determined to be an aristocrat at any cost. The children were well schooled and polished but the influences of the laid back southern lifestyles quickly sought to undermine the solid upbringing Davila demanded shine from her children. Her plan to be the biggest fish in this small pond was in grave danger and after only two years of defiance, she convinced Myron to move to Charleston. She insisted the move was in the best interests of her impressionable teen-age children as they would be better challenged by the money and opulence of the capital city, and best removed from the underachieving trends surrounding them in Orangeburg.

To her chagrin, young Victoria refused to be uprooted again. Davila attempted to discuss the matter like reasonable adults but her mother ended the debate by throwing her nose in the air and telling Victoria she had no idea what she wanted and was far too young to make such decisions on her own. Victoria was ordered to cease her pointless objections and obey. That was the final mistake.

Victoria was every bit as headstrong and determined as her mother though her intent was in a different direction. She told her mother on that fateful day that she would go where she pleased. This day it pleased her to remain in Orangeburg and in the company of her beloved. She had been courted for some time but the matriarch did not view the Corbel estate to be of suitable worth and dismissed the relationship, truly believing that would end it. The love was, in fact, fueled and came to a point where she was considering the matter of Mason's proposal.

What may have been a bitter and heartbreaking separation of the Jacobs family turned to an affirmation of love and faith. Myron stifled his wife and told her he knew something of this estate and more of the young man. He handled some of the legal matters for Mason when his mother passed away. In doing so, he saw a young man with the maturity and heart to put his welfare behind that of his family without hesitation. His worth in gold may not be lordly but he could surely care for Victoria and she was given his wholehearted blessing.

Her mother was more reluctant, especially when young Daniel chose to stay as well. Mason had offered him a position on the farm before and now that job seemed measurably more attractive. She wanted to put an impotent foot down but only too recently she had denied him a position with his uncle in Tennessee. They had a relative who published a newspaper there and was quite influential in that county. Daniel asked to go off and be a newspaper man but the notion was shot down when his mother suggested with her usual inflexibility that he would be better suited in a management roll on a plantation or farm. That showed a promise of prosperity that the seedy publishing of political views did not. As her own mandate loomed, she found herself without a reasonable defense and in one fell swoop her children were gone from her life.

Victoria married Mason in the autumn earlier and immediately took an active role in the business. The winter was a romantic fantasy for her and they were the picture perfect newlywed couple. It was only in the past month that Victoria seemed irritable and distracted. She worked harder, spoke louder and laughed less than Mason had ever seen and he was less than satisfied with the one word answers he had been receiving.

They entered the house this night in silence. Mason wanted to slam doors and scream and demand. But it simply wasn't his way. As Victoria set about preparing for bed, the house servant waited with a warmed over dinner and an anxious heart. She knew Victoria had left to help the children. Now she returned with her head held low.

"How's the children?" Bella chanced to ask.

"They're fine," Victoria replied in a tone drained of emotion. "We got there in time and some family showed up. No one was hurt."

"Well that's a relief. When I heard dat pack o' killers set on dem babies I was truly fearful." Bella hoped the sound of voices would diffuse the tension. It did not. She tried again. "You two should eat somethin'. I got supper on the table and I been…"

"We're not hungry now, Bella," Victoria replied in the same tone.

Bella looked to Mason. He quietly nodded to reassure her and gestured for her to leave. She quietly obeyed.

"What were you thinking?" he asked in a soft voice.

"I was thinking some children were in danger."

"So how does getting yourself killed change that?"

"I didn't."

"You were lucky. Why, Vickie? What is it with you lately?"

Victoria sat at the table and rested on her elbows. "When I heard it was children… I don't know. Something happened. I couldn't wait. I couldn't think. I just had to help."

"Even if it got you killed?" He moved next to her, his arrested tone gaining in strength.

"What if it were our children? What would you do then?"

"It wasn't. That may sound cruel, but it wasn't our children."

"Maybe that's the problem."

"What? The children? Ours?"

Victoria turned to look Mason in the eye for the first time this evening. "I saw Doctor Whitney again last week. He says it's very likely I can't have children." She held a rigid posture, clearly staving the tears to get his reaction.

Now he knew. As if the words were a dagger thrust into his heart, he knew why she had been so distraught. Nothing meant more to them than raising their family here and watching the plantation grow along with them. All things of their future seemed to be tied to their children. She spoke continually throughout the winter of the grandiose plans.

"Why, Vickie? Why didn't you tell me?"

Victoria fought back the tears. "I don't know. I had to accept it myself first, I guess. We had so many plans. Everything we wanted for them. All the things they were going to have." She gazed without focus as she spoke, unable to look Mason in the eye. "God I'd even named them. Our first born would be Mason Junior. I knew it would be a boy. The second would be Myron, after my father. The third would be a girl and we'd call her Angelina. She'd have reddish blonde hair and she'd be so spoiled rotten she'd drive her brothers crazy. But they wouldn't mind. Not really. Little Mase would protect her and Myron is so quiet he..."

Mason only now sensed a fraction of the anguish his wife had been carrying these past weeks. It was less a feeling that the dream was dead but more as if the children were dead. In her dreams, she was a mother and a good one. Now those dreams were a bitter and painful memory. Now it was his job to find the words that would spare her this agony. Now, for the first time in his life, Mason felt like a failure. He had no words that could take the pain from her. He could only lay his hand on hers to let her know that he knew. With that touch, she broke down. The weeks of pain came pouring out in a bath of tears as Victoria fell against him. Her head buried in his shoulder, she wept for the death of her children, never born.

Mason held her more tightly than he ever had.

3

April 12, 1861

Major Robert Anderson stood near the main gate at Fort Sumter with his senior officer. He stood casual and reserved, starkly contrasting the apprehensive, nervously fidgeting lieutenant at his side.

As they watched the gate being pulled open, Lieutenant Saxon turned to him. "Think this is Beauregard's reply?"

General Beauregard commanded the Confederate forces amassed outside Fort Sumter and had demanded the surrender of the fort.

"I pray God it's not," Major Anderson replied soberly. "I'd hoped a counterproposal would give them something to chew on. Maybe buy us some time."

Their supplies were dwindling nearly as fast as their hopes of replenishments. Without a few days grace, they would fall and Anderson had been sleeping with the consequences for some time. His orders were clear. Hold this fort. No allowances were made for hardships. The courier entered and came before him. After a brief salute, the soldier handed Major Anderson a message.

Lieutenant Saxon's curiosity overcame him as Anderson quietly read. "What is it, Sir? How much time do we have?"

Anderson did not respond to him. Instead, he smiled and shook the courier's hand.

"If we do not meet again in this world, I hope we may meet again in a better one."

Within hours, the cannons opened fire on Fort Sumter and the Civil War had begun.

The concussion was felt everywhere, including Durham, North Carolina. The tension over the past several months had finally been broken and the jubilation poured from every avenue. It was as if a party had begun instead of a war. As passersby shouted and fired guns into the air, men lined up in the street to enlist.

From the comfortable lounge above the bank building, John Beaumont sat passively with his friends, discussing their commissions and watching the jubilance in the streets below from relative displacement. John was of one of the oldest families in North Carolina and a true blue-blood who, like the men and women in his circle, took pleasure in looking down on those he considered less fortunate.

Mark Fowler, a local aristocrat, seemed totally disinterested in the goings on outside. "I wonder how many of them will be in my command. Most, I expect."

"Think so, do you?" Tom Harden challenged. "You think all of these men will serve here? Not likely."

"Where will they go then?"

"Where ever they're sent," John said. "As will you."

Mark didn't like this assault on the authority he had yet to assume. "Why would I be sent anywhere? There's need of a garrison here."

Trevor sat and poured himself a drink. "A small need. The real fight will be west of here and hopefully kept there. Unless your pull is second to none, you'll go where the action is and take orders like the rest of us. Right John?"

"Most likely. But I will choose my staff officers. That much I know."

"Who have you got in mind?" Trevor asked.

John was distracted, hesitating to answer. His eyes were drawn outside, down to the other side of the street below. Absolon stood with Anne as they watched appalled at the anarchy all around them.

"Fools," Absolon muttered to Anne. "Idiots."

"They're just happy they finally have a war to fight. Sometimes I think that's the only thing that makes men happy."

"For some, it is. But most don't give a hoot about the war or the cause. They just want to kill someone. It won't be until the Yankees shoot back that they realize there's a fellow across the battlefield thinking the same thing."

"Waiting for the line to shorten, Wilkes?" John asked smugly as he approached.

Anne responded. "Waiting for a breath of reason, perhaps."

"That line can't get short enough to suit me," Absolon said. "But good luck to you, John. I hear they made you a Captain straight away."

"I'll pick my staff as well. It would be not only civilized but strategically sound to have a staff that considers all options. I could use your views, Absolon. Would you accept a junior officer's commission to aid the cause?" His tone was sincere and almost friendly, but Absolon maintained his distance.

"Don't tell me you'd dare turn your back on me in battle."

"My opinion of your political views is common knowledge. But you've proven, to me at least, that you're no coward. I believe you'd be an asset." Absolon looked at Anne, then looked John straight in the eye. "I don't think so, John."

Beaumont stepped closer to Absolon, speaking in near a whisper. "If it's your background, I assure you you'll be treated as a true aristocrat. Your bloodline won't be an issue."

Absolon refused to back away, but kept his tone loud and impersonal. "I appreciate your overlooking my shortcomings. I'll give your offer all the consideration it deserves."

Despite Absolon's irreverence, John kept his low tone. "Don't think about it too long, Wilkes. You need to make a show of support for her sake."

"For Anne? What's she got to do with it?"

"I tell you as a friend there's been talk. If you're not for them, you're against them. If they think you a Unionist and a traitor, you are in peril. They would take the next step and brand Anne a Union sympathizer. You see, we none of us are alone in this. We must consider all aspects of our loyalty."

Absolon moved still closer to whisper. "Then consider this. I'll kill the first ten men, ANY ten men who come near her. I have to assume you're equally prepared to defend this lady's honor." He leaned back and spoke loud and clear. "Warn your friends, John."

John stared at Absolon, waiting for a smile or elaboration, but found only Absolon's determined stare in return. John finally smiled and turned away.

4

The starry spring night lent to calm spirits as the slaves sat around the open fire. Some of them had cook stoves inside their quarters, but they chose not to heat the tiny cabins when the night air was so inviting. Two men and two women sat and watched the flickering flames and inhaled the aroma of the seasonings as their dinner neared readiness.

Bella and Hermione hummed a soft tune in rehearsed harmony as they turned the hog parts in the big iron pan. Old Herman puffed his pipe and listened intently. Only Window seemed uneasy. He sat still, but slightly annoyed.

"Wonder what it's like to eat the meat part of that hog," he finally said between hummed verses.

"Don't know why you care," Bella replied. "You get plenty of gizzards and you ain't never complained about them."

Window continued to sulk. "Gizzards. That's what they give us. Guts and ears and snouts and anything else they too good to eat."

Herman took the pipe from his lips and spoke calmly. "You're missing the point again, Window. We always got plenty to eat here. Some places they get starved half to death; den beat if they speak up on it."

"That's right" Hermione added. "You be thankful for what you got."

"Oh yeah," Window said in a sarcastic tone. "I'm thanking the white folk for letting me eat their garbage.

Hermione took a firm, motherly tone. "No. You be thanking the lord for providing when so many is doing without."

Window stood and walked away. "You thank him. I'll wait until I got something to be thankful for."

"Don't you be blasphemin' round here, Boy," Hermione cautioned him. "I done told you about that."

The others silently returned their attention to the pending meal. They were accustomed to Windows discontented opinions. He rarely voiced them around white people or strangers and was usually of good spirits so they knew that this too would pass and he would eat with them as always.

Inside the big house, Mason and Victoria sat before the fireplace. Mason tried to read but his attention was drawn to her. Victoria sat emotionless and stared at the crackling fire. Mason finally closed his book and spoke softly to her.

"He'll be fine."

At first she gave no indication she heard him. No turn or shift of her lips or brow. She just stared. Then she spoke as if speaking to the fire. "It's a war. No one is safe."

"He's a smart man. He knows the enemy can shoot back. He'll be careful."

"He's all the family I have left. If mother knew I let him."

Mason set his book down and leaned toward her. "He was going. I'm sure they know he'd do it. They should thank you for talking him into enlisting under your uncle. Felix is a newspaperman. Not a General. He has no one there to fight and likes it that way. Danny couldn't be in better hands."

She finally turned to look him in the eye. "I know. I just worry. We need something to go our way and I just don't see that being it."

Mason slid from the armchair to grasp her reassuringly by the shoulders. "I see plenty going our way. The rest will come in time. You hungry yet?"

Victoria allowed the closest thing to a smile Mason had seen all evening. She squeezed his hand. "No. I couldn't eat. I told Bella to go off."

"All right. You rest. I'm going for a walk."

"Want me to fix you something?"

"No thanks, Sweetheart. I'll be back in a bit. Maybe we'll have a cup of tea then."

Outside, near the slave quarters, a young boy stood holding a tin pan as Bella and Hermione forked savory bits and pieces of sizzling meat onto the pan. Bella looked up and saw Mason approaching. Herman followed her stare to see his master and stood to greet him, more of courtesy than fear.

"Evening, Mister Corbel."

"Evening Herman," Mason replied pleasantly. "Hermione."

"Miss Victoria feeling better, Mister Mason?" Bella asked.

"A bit. Still not eating though."

"How 'bout you? You need to eat."

"I'm starting to agree," he said, sniffing the air. "What *is* that I smell cooking?"

"Ain't nothing but some gizzards and jowls," Hermione said proudly.

"Smells really good. You wouldn't have an extra portion there. Would you?"

Bella picked up a tin plate. "Sho' do. Mister Mason." She spooned a portion onto the plate and handed it to the boy, taking the bigger plate from his hands. "Tui. Run give this to Mister Corbel."

Accepting the plate from the silent boy with a grateful nod, Mason's face lit with delight as he tasted a bit of the seasoned meat.

"That is delicious. How do you do this?"

"Just cook it with some spices and pepper and a little bit of patience to loosen it up," Bella answered. "That make anything taste good."

Hermione took umbrage. "Speak for yourself, woman. That's my own recipe and I takes pride in it. You enjoy, Mister Corbel Sir."

Bella scoffed. "Special recipe my Aunt Sadie. You cook it the same way everybody else do."

"Same way you wish you could," Hermione said.

Mason just smiled and sat with them to enjoy the savory meal. A few shacks away, Window stood near the corner and peered around, watching with disdain as Mason invaded their personal time.

Window had no real love for these slave quarters. He never once in his life called them home. Mason had not interrupted anything. Even the casual dinner proceeded with an air of pleasantry. Still Window hated his presence here. This was not his place. This was the only place left them at the end of a day spent kowtowing and working for the whites. As he studied them, he remembered a time, years ago when he was barely old enough to know that others had things he did not. They huddled in the dark. Window remembered the men around him, all fully grown and half of them afraid of something, the other half angry at it. He wasn't afraid yet because they hadn't told him to be. Most of them were already in the wagon when Window and a few others were led out of the quarters and loaded into the back. The small boy stared into the faces around him. One man stared back.

"What you lookin' at, Boy?"

"Where's my Daddy?"

"He ain't coming."

"Be grateful of that, Little Winston," said another. Window strained his eyes against the dim lighting in the closed wagon to see the vaguely familiar face of another slave from the plantation where he was born. This was a field slave and had spent little time around the house or livestock so Window barely knew him. "That's what they call you, ain't it? Winston?"

Window nodded silently, unwilling to explain the origin of 'Window' to this man.

"Grateful?" challenged the first man. "He should be grateful they likely beating..."

"You don't need to be telling this boy that."

"Tell me what?" Window asked.

"Your daddy didn't want you in this wagon. He made the mistake of telling the white folk that. Now they's giving him what for."

Window was not sure what that meant, but he knew his father was in a bad way. Turning, he tried to peek between the poorly fitted side boards of the covered wagon they had been piled into. Packed in like cattle, it was difficult to move at all, let alone turn. But the agile boy made a valiant effort to spot his father. Until this moment, he had ignored the sounds outside the dark enclosure. He felt relatively safe inside though he was not sure why. Despite the inane security of the enclosure, the boy was suddenly more concerned with what was going on outside.

Through the slats, he could see white people milling about. They were still at the plantation. Then the wagon gate creaked loudly and daylight filled the dark space. The blast of sunlight forced Window to squint and shield his unadjusted eyes. Peering through his fingers, he saw the unfriendly faces of two white men. They pushed and prodded the already cramped occupants of the closed compartment, forcing them back away from the opening with blunt poles.

When the slaves had scooted back as far as they could, the white men backed their heads out. Another slave was thrown in, face first, on top of the human pile. This man was barely conscious and bleeding profusely from the freshly opened gashes across his back and shoulders.

The gate was closed and locked again. Window heard one of the men speak to the other as they walked away. "That was a waste. That nigger weren't worth nothing before you beat him to death. How the hell am I supposed to sell him off looking like that?"

"Stand him up and put a shirt on him," came the familiar voice of Window's owner. "Maybe you can get someone to buy him for picking. Hell he ain't even worth feeding. Never was."

Inside, the beaten man stirred and tried to move. Those around him did what they could to give him room, but there was little sympathy expressed. They stared coldly at the man as though they would share his fate for acknowledging him further.

Window pushed his tiny head between the huddled bodies to see the man struggling to roll over. His wounds would never allow him to lie on his back or side but he continued to writhe in agony. Window stared mostly out of curiosity. To his horror, Window saw the agonized face of his father on the beaten man as he rolled over.

"Daddy!" the child cried as he fought to get to his father. The onlookers gave him no more creed than they had his father. Squeezing between the huddled occupants, he pulled himself to the beaten man's side and grabbed him, causing the man to wince in pain.

"Window?" the man whispered, lacking the strength to open his eyes or reach for his son. "That you, Boy?"

Window stood and started pounding on the top of the wagon and calling out, "Open up! Open up! Help us!"

One of the slaves pulled him back by his arm. "Don't be callin' them white folks in here, Boy," he sternly ordered.

Window was in tears. "But he's bleedin'. I got to get him a doctor or something. I need to ask them for some bandages and…"

"You don't ask them for nothing. If we don't got it, we do without. That's all there is to it."

"But he needs help."

"And what makes you think he going to get it from them?"

"You think they want to make this easy for him?" asked another man.

"No sir," added a third from the back. "They want him to hurt until he learn. They want us all to learn. That's why he's in here bleedin' on us."

His father mustered the strength to reach out and grab Window. With a bloodied hand he pulled the boy close to him. "You listen to that man, Window. You listen *good*. Never ask them for nothing. Never ask *anybody*. Hear me? If you didn't earn it, it ain't yours."

"But we needs it, Daddy," he sobbed.

"If they give it, they's just as likely to take it back. The only thing you take is what you earned. Don't go begging them for what ain't yours. And don't you thank them for what is."

Window was weeping openly, no longer wiping away the free-flowing tears that coursed his face. He saw the blood seeping from his father's wounds. He felt his pain. "Let me ask them, Daddy. Just this once. Can I ask?"

"Ask them what? Who do you think did this? You give them cause to come back in here they might do this to someone else. Maybe you. That what you want?"

The child wiped his running nose and reluctantly shook his tiny head. Amid the muttering of agreement throughout the wagon, his father waited for the boy to accept the blood-written rule before he continued.

"We don't need them in here. Listen to me, Window. We don't *want* them in here. This ain't nothin' but a box and it's their box. But at least they ain't in here with us. That makes this box a good place to be. You see? Where ever they ain't is where we want to be. Don't ever go inviting the white folk in. They got the whole damn world. They don't need to be in the only place we don't have to be looking at their ugly faces. Whatever it takes to get by without them is what we do. You don't call the white folk for nothin'. You don't ask them for nothing. Not ever."

Window looked around the dark wagon. The stares were vacant, the eyes without hope. The first man to have spoken to him spoke again.

"You mind your Pappy, Son. They ain't your friend and they ain't here to help you do nothin'. They is nothin' but the one's what done this to him. That's all."

Window looked at the open wounds on his father's back. He wondered what kind of man could do that to another man. It sunk in then that he did not want such people near him. He would not forget the pain they inflicted on his father and the sense of hatred that welled within him that day. This dark box they were crowded into was actually a sanctuary from the oppressors. Even though they could open the gate at any time, for now the gate was closed. For now, they were safe. Everyone in this dismal place from the dark stranger in the corner to the naïve child to the bleeding soul lain between them was, for the moment, equal and safe. The fear and the rage that blanketed every waking moment of their existence could be ignored here. This was a special time. The greater the atrocities they endured and witnessed, the more they relished these moments of relative tranquility. The child had risen to a new level of awareness within the ranks of human bondage.

Window had, in the past, overheard adults talking about passing out as being a good thing or a special achievement. This was because they would no longer feel the bite of the taskmaster's whip. Once they were unconscious, the master generally stopped beating them and put them back into their safe place. Now he knew what was meant by this. He saw what his father endured for not passing out. This is the world they lived in. Passing out to avoid being beaten to death was among the good things in their life. It was a reward the whites could not deny them. So little else belonged to them in the precious moments and private places where they dared speak their mind and act as they chose without first asking permission. Such moments and places were all the whites left them.

For the whites, with all that they had, to intrude on the sanctity of this box or sit at their fire was the ultimate insult. For a white man to dare eat the scraps left them and sit and smile at them as if they were all family or friends or equals was an insult Window would never stomach.

As Mason sat and shared the meal with the others, Window watched from a distance seeing nothing in it but intolerable intrusion. He would not eat with this man. He would not smile at this man. And he would never, ever thank this man.

5

July 21, 1861

The battlefield was already littered with the dead and dying in both uniforms. From his strategic vantage point, General Thomas Jackson commanded his Union forces toward what was intended to be a decisive victory against the encroaching Confederate forces of General P.G.T. Beauregard. While the men afoot battled ferociously, the generals were tentative as neither sent more than half their forces into the midst of the contest.

"What would happen," Jackson posed to Commander McDowell, "if we gave him our best punch and he came back for more?" Respectful of the rebel tenacity, General Jackson had requested an additional five thousand men to drive them back, but his request was denied. Congress believed the Confederates to be farmers and plow hands, easily bested by the better trained and equipped Union soldier in a one-to-one contest.

Members of this very body of Congress had come out this afternoon to observe the victory. With childlike naivety they stood on the hills amidst picnicking families and watched what they truly believed would be a day's entertainment and demonstration of the might of their righteous army. Among the flippant spectators, a trio of civilian men stood and viewed the goings on analytically. One of the men, Joe Hooker, had heard that the viewing public might include some of the more influential bodies in Washington. Ambitious and opportunistic, he took advantage of any chance to rub elbows with success. It was he who had persuaded his friends to come out for the battle. He had experience as a commissioned junior officer in the Mexican war and felt bitterness at having been denied rank in this engagement. Like most of the Union, he was confident the war would be over before it started and there would be few opportunities to prosper from the spoils.

"This worth coming all the way from California, Joe?" asked Peter

Kincaid, seated comfortably in the grass in front of them.

"It will be," Hooker responded. He had deliberately positioned them so that the nearby politicians might be impressed his commentary on the current engagement. Gaining a conversation with these established leaders could do no harm to his career. As interested in the battle and impressing congressmen as he was, he had trouble keeping his eyes off the young ladies nearby. They had come out in their finest spring dresses to witness the rout of the Confederate upstarts.

"Do they have weather like this in Los Angeles?" asked the other young man. Horace Taggart stood next to Joe and helped him assess the nearby lovelies.

"Better," Joe casually responded, shielding his eyes with his right hand. "Year round weather that can't be beat. But I must admit I like the view here right now." His gaze alternated between the distant fighting and the giggling girls who appeared aware of and comfortable with the attention they were drawing.

"Who's winning, Joe?" Peter asked.

"I think I am," Hooker responded.

Peter looked up at him and followed his line of sight to the girls. "I mean down there."

Hooker returned his attention to the battle in the valley below. "Hard to say. It should've been done and dusted by now. It doesn't look like Jackson's using his reserve. He might be holding back to flank him. Good move if properly executed. But if he waits too much longer..."

"What would you do?"

"Fight," he said with a resounding tone. "Plain and simple. Never take a step backward in a fight. Never hold a card and not play it. I never retreated in Mexico. Just go at them with anything you have and they always turn." He turned just enough to check his peripheral vision. None of the bureaucrats seemed to notice his bravado.

The battle would surely belong to those fated as neither side gained decisive advantage. Beauregard was concerned, unsure why Jackson hadn't come full force yet. Jackson thought the same of his adversary. As he gave the order to extend his flank, hoping to spread the rebels beyond their experience, he saw what appeared to be a column of infantry marching toward the battlefield. His reinforcements, he dared think. Someone in Washington was of a military mindset and the day was his.

Beauregard saw the same column approaching and could not make them out through the smoke of battle and the distance. He watched them through his field glasses, struggling to shield the lenses from the afternoon sun. There, he thought, comes the balance of this battle. He watched, as did his opponent, as the wind shifted to cross the column. His heart lifted as the new gust unfurled the Confederate flag at the head of the advancing force. "Yes!" he gasped with delight. "We got them!"

The new column hit the Union on the right flank, forcing them back into rank. The Union soldiers were stepping over themselves to get to safer footing. Then Beauregard's six and a half thousand Confederates came at them en masse, charging with a blood curdling scream as they sprinted fearlessly against the Union ranks. Running as if they were bulletproof, or wanting to die, the rebels took the Union by surprise, shocking them into panic. The Union army had their first taste of a rebel yell and did as they would in countless charges over the next two years. They turned and ran.

The girls had crossed the short distance to the young men to ask what they were supposed to be seeing. Horace was trying to explain the strategy to them as if he understood it when one of the girls noticed the gunfire growing louder.

"Doesn't that sound like it's getting closer?" she asked.

"It's just the acoustics," Horace explained. "It seems louder when the wind shifts."

"So we're not in any danger?" another girl queried.

Joe watched the goings on much more closely than did his suiting mates. While the bulk of their attention was drawn to the fair maidens, Hooker's military experience kept him focused on what was now clearly an approaching battlefront.

"I think we need to find higher ground, Gentlemen," he said in as calm a voice as he could muster.

Peter scoffed. "What's this? Joe Hooker taking a step back?"

The gunfire was now clearly within their range and Joe looked down the hill into the terrified faces of the Federal troops. They came at him with nothing about them resembling military structure.

"Run!" Hooker shouted and turned, grabbing one of the girls by the hand. "Now, Miss! We need to move!" He and his band did their best to stay ahead of the soldiers, the other spectators and the general panic that had set in.

Terrified by the sheer numbers and the unorthodox attack, the Federals ran back without course or reason with the Rebel forces gaining adrenalin and determination with each stride. Commander McDowell later reported that, "The retreat became a rout and this soon degenerated into a panic."

The Yankees ran in disarray toward Washington, outrunning their superiors and denying any chance of regrouping. The shocked congressmen on the hill were trampled and carried as the retreat into chaos overtook them. One of them was knocked to the ground by an apologetic Hooker who managed to conceal the majority of his face as he ran on. The soldiers gathered picnickers and spectators as they ran. Soon the victorious rebels felt they were chasing all of the northern population across Bull Run. This Confederate victory was not the first, but was the most demoralizing to date for the Union.

Word of the victory at Bull Run had yet to reach Durham in any great detail. They knew only that there was a battle and men had been killed. A small crowd of people gathered in the street near the post office as Sheriff Burrell Wilson came out and tacked a paper onto the wall outside. As soon as he pressed the document flat, people began to gather apprehensively around him. A man gently pushed his wife back and ran his finger down the printed list of names, reading aloud.

"Maddox. Miller. Morgan. Morgan...." He suddenly paused and took a breath before reading the next name. "Murphy, Peter."

He turned to his wife as she collapsed into tears. Embracing her, he helped her out of the way as others fearfully gathered to read the rest of the dead list.

Across the street, Anne had stopped her buggy. She listened to the names and watched the emotions pour from the concerned family members. Two men walking away from the list slowed as they passed the front of her buggy.

"Don't worry," the first man said to her. "Your man ain't likely to be on that list."

The second man snickered. "Naw. He made another one though." They both laughed.

Anne tried to ignore them, keeping her attention focused on the calling of names across the street.

The first man spoke loudly to his friend. "I asked Wilkes if he knew he was on the cowards list. Know what he said?"

"What?"

"He said he was too scared to look!" Both men laughed and walked away. Anne refused to acknowledge them, as she refused to stay out of town. She knew the taunts and jeers were coming and prayed they would simply tire of it and stop. So far, they hadn't.

That evening, Absolon sat in his modest ranch house writing by the light of a lantern. He hired help during harvest or planting but mostly ran the small property alone so his evening hours were generally spent alone with his thoughts and dreams.

He had dreamed of a real ranch since his childhood. His father was a farmer, simple and uneducated in anything other than farming. That he knew well and imparted his amassed knowledge onto his only son. Two seasons of drought in Huntsville, Alabama left the Wilkes farm struggling when, on Absolon's sixteenth birthday, his mother passed away from tuberculosis. The young man had little time to mourn the loss as he immediately fell to the task of keeping his father of a clear mind.

Joseph Wilkes was more than devastated by the loss of his wife and partner. He could not recall a day when he didn't come in from the fields and assure her the next crop would be a good one, that he would be able to buy her all the things she wanted but never asked for, that he was taking care of her. Absolon should have been his greatest concern but he could not take his mind off of his wife. Nothing else mattered, not the drying fields, not the empty cupboards, not the young man that now spent his every waking hour trying to draw a living from the withering farm.

Eighteen months after the passing of his beloved wife, his heart gave out and Joseph Wilkes died in his bed. Barely qualified for adulthood, Absolon was left alone with a badly depleted plot of land as barren as his store cupboard. On his best day, his father might have been able to coax another season of crops from the overplanted soil, but Absolon was beaten.

Alone in the world, the young man walked from his empty farmhouse and looked up to the stars. He was not a religious man, as learning to read was always in the plans for next year so the Bible was only what his mother had told him. But when men have nothing left to hope for, that last thing left them is often prayer. He could see nothing in the stars that appeared to care about him, yet he looked up and softly asked God to give him a chance. He wanted nothing for free, but he just needed a chance to survive.

His farm was dry and worthless, as farms go. But the railroad was moving across the country and his dirt was worth far more to them than the crops it once produced. Absolon, at sixteen, was a man of worth. With no home or family to tie him, he bought a train ticket and headed east. Along the way, he had a conversation with a man who told him about a friend who had more property than he needed. The man rode with him to Durham where Absolon was introduced to Royal Pollard.

Royal sold a small piece of his vast estate to the ambitious young man, confident he would be forced to abandon the homestead after the first winter. But after an unusually harsh season, he rode out to check on him to find that the young man had not only survived, he had built a small house and three pens, stocked chickens, pigs and a mule and had already plowed four acres. Royal was beyond impressed with the feat. He began spending more time with Absolon, aiding with supplies and advice and learning about farming.

The two became fast friends and Royal invited Absolon to join him at the spring festival, then a barn raising, then a county social, but Absolon declined each time. He finally confided in Royal that he felt out of place with the blue-blooded aristocrats in Royal's social circle for a number of reasons, including his attire, his manner of speech and the fact that he was completely illiterate.

Royal committed himself to grooming the enterprising young man for society. The effort included reading and writing and elocution. He also tried and failed to provide Absolon with slave help but each time he sent slaves to the house, Absolon sent them back with a good meal in them and a few coins in their pocket. He had no stomach for slavery and refused to conform.

Still under the light of the lantern, Absolon struggled to keep his mind on his studies but his mind continually wandered to Anne, how he never would have met her without Royal's help, without meeting a stranger on the train, without the railroad buying his land. Funny, he thought, how he and Anne seemed fated to meet.

Suddenly he heard a single shot ring out and he jumped to his feet. Absolon ran out of the house with a lantern in one hand and a shotgun in the other. The oil lantern generally gave a man enough light to see his own arm but Absolon strained his eyes to peer into the darkness. As he neared the stable, he saw his mule lying dead inside the fence. Then he turned to the sound of horses galloping away. Leaving the lantern, he mounted his horse bareback and rode off after the sound. He rode into the woods surrounding his ranch, struggling to follow the trails in the darkness. Absolon finally realized that he wouldn't be able to track anyone in this darkness and turned back. Coming to a hillside that overlooked his ranch from a short distance, he saw a blaze in the direction of his house.

He rode dangerously fast through the woods, the scent of smoke in his nostrils, to find his barn engulfed in flames. Dismounting, he ran to the well to grab a bucket and saw the flickering inside his house. At first, it seemed like a reflection in the window from the barn. Then black smoke began to billow from the open window. Looking back, he figured his barn was lost and ran toward the house with the bucket.

It was a short time later when Royal rode up to Absolon's ranch. The barn was smoldering and the house still blazed out of control. Absolon was exhausted from battling the blaze. Royal jumped from his mount and ran to his friend.

"Are you all right?"

"It's gone," Absolon breathed in defeat. "It's all gone."

"Did you see them? Do you know who it was?"

Absolon lethargically shook his head. "They shot my plow mule and rode off. I heard them and tried to follow."

"They were luring you out."

"I can't believe it! How far will these jackals go?"

"For what it's worth, it doesn't look like they meant to hurt you."

"Just run me off."

"They won't get away with it."

"They already have, Royal. They destroyed everything I have. Everything I care about is…"

Royal gasped with a sudden realization. "Not everything."

Absolon stared back at him and immediately caught his meaning. "How far will they go?"

A few miles away, a band of hooded riders sat in the cover of a wooded clearing within eyesight of the stately Carmichael mansion. The leader studied the mansion long enough to be sure no one was stirring inside. Then he looked to his right.

"You two torch the stables," he said in a calm voice. "Then get back here." Two men left the group without a word and rode toward the house. The vigilante leader then turned to the rest of his raiding party. "We'll wait here until they come out of the house. We don't burn the house until we see the girl. Got it?"

The others nodded and waited silently for a signal. After a few minutes of silence, they began to show concern.

One of the men to the left of the leader could sit silently no longer. "What's keeping them?"

"Don't know," replied the leader in a now whispering voice. Then he spotted the riders slowly returning. "I… Here they come."

The two hooded riders came up to the band and separated. One went to the left and one to the right of the group where they stopped to sit silently at the rear of the party.

The leader looked back at them curiously. "About time. Anybody see you?"

The man on the right just shook his hooded head in response.

"Well soon as we hear someone, we'll torch the house."

The retuning vigilante on the left spoke as he raised his rifle. "Change of plans. We're going to surrender."

The leader and others turned to see the man remove his hood. Absolon stared back at them from behind his rifle. The leader turned to the other man sent to torch the stables and Royal was already unmasked and smiling back at him. Before they could react, Josh stepped out of the bushes in front of them with a pistol in each hand. With Royal and Absolon flanking them from behind they were surrounded.

"Those flour sacks should be feeling a bit silly about now," Absolon said. "How about you boys shedding them?"

One by one, the vigilantes reluctantly removed their masks. The leader was the last and he slowly pulled the hood off to reveal John Beaumont staring defiantly back at Absolon. His gaze was as though he was the one who had caught Absolon, as though he was the one in the right.

Absolon returned his stare as Royal ordered the group to drop any weapons to the ground. "Whatever you've got, boys. Rifles, pistols, knives, pea shooters. Don't let me find you still armed."

As the diverse array of weaponry fell to the ground, Absolon took particular notice of a double-barrel shotgun that landed under the rider closest to him. He looked up at the man who had dropped it.

"That wouldn't be the scatter gun I heard kill my mule, would it, Fred?"

The man attempted a brave stance. "Weren't nothing personal, Wilkes. I was just following orders."

"Following orders? So he gives all the orders? Suppose I ordered you to get down and reach for that greener? Would he order you to leave it?"

Puzzled by the challenge, Fred turned and looked to John Beaumont for the proper response, for a clarification he could only get from the man giving orders, a condemnation that that Beaumont could no longer deny.

Absolon again locked eyes with Beaumont. "Don't take it too hard, John. Fred was just confirming what we already knew."

"You knew nothing."

"Sure we did, Beaumont," Royal said. "This kind of attack required a certain kind of man, a true leader, a devious bastard with a habit of taking the credit for the achievements of others and letting them take the blame for his mistakes."

Absolon added to the list. "A spineless coward who makes a habit of hiding behind tradition. In short, you."

"You brought this on yourself, Wilkes," John said. "And on her. I warned you what might happen."

"Did you, John?" came the woman's voice from the darkness. "Did you tell him that you'd burn my home?"

They turned to see Anne stepping out from the shadows. Only when John was confronted with the innocent woman he nearly murdered did John begin to appear uncomfortable. "You weren't to be hurt, Anne. They had strict orders."

"This is what's in your heart?" she said, stepping closer to him. "This is the nobility you hold in such high esteem? What Absolon lacks? You're a coward and a criminal and everything about you sickens me."

John forced an unwavering stare that failed to conceal his pain at her biting words. "The shame here is not on a man who believes in laws and his country, or of those who stand behind him as loyal friends. The true shame is with those who simply want to be on the winning side, whatever that side may be. You are without honor and if this is the comprisal of our forces, we are all shamed and thus doomed."

None among them had response. They looked silently at one another but daren't move nor speak in defense of their act.

Absolon broke the contemplative silence. "Go on home. All of you. There'll be no lynching here tonight."

Without contest, they turned to a man to leave. And they all would have without hesitation had Royal not cut John off to look him squarely in the eye. Holding the flat of his rifle barrel against John's chest, he spoke in a clear and deliberate tone.

"You know, John. You just put your mark on this. If anyone... *ANYONE* raises a hand to her or this property, you'll be the first man suspected. I suggest you take your division off to play soldier and establish your alibi for the laws already broken tonight. The sooner, the better."

John looked away, dead ahead as firmly as the situation permitted. "Our orders are in. We leave tomorrow. Will that suffice?"

Royal pulled his rifle back and gave John passage to leave. As the dejected marauders disappeared into the night, Absolon dismounted to go to Anne. She fell into his arms.

"Will they try again?"

"They might. Not the same ones and not straight away. But the cause is still there."

Josh still held his six-guns cocked and ready. "We should have killed them. Every last one of the murdering bastards. We had every right."

Absolon held Anne tightly as he spoke. "They were your neighbors, Josh. And they will be again. This war has brought out the worst in them."

Anne pulled away from him. "So as long as there's a war, they have an excuse? I can't live like this."

"No. I'm the one who brought this on you. It's my beliefs they hate and you only for our love."

Royal watched from his saddle. He holstered his rifle as he spoke. "I'd better go check my place. Absolon. You'll need to stay at my house now."

Absolon nodded and said to Josh, "Stay alert." Josh nodded and holstered his weapons. Then Absolon grasped Anne reassuringly by her delicate shoulders. "You'll be safe enough tonight, Anne. I'll see you tomorrow."

As he gently kissed her check and she returned the affectionate touch, none saw Royal divert his eyes as if slapped. Absolon left her to mount and follow Royal.

Royal Pollard's estate was pristine and comfortable, devoid of family but warm with comfortable furniture and servants in good spirit always meandering about. This morning, Absolon stood on the veranda and sipped his coffee. His mind laden with the events of the night past, he stared out across the rolling hills as if his resolution would come across the countryside to him at any moment. He never heard his friend approach from behind.

"Seems so peaceful now, doesn't it?" Royal said coming up next to him. "You know, I wanted to plant a vineyard. Grapes don't grow well here. I was that close to selling out and moving to California."

"California? All that way for grapes?"

"Farming. Ranching. A new prosperity. But I just couldn't bring myself to leave...," he hesitated, stopping just short of speaking her name. He diverted his eyes. "...To leave all of this."

"Hard to envision all this a battlefield."

"It may well be, and soon. What will you do then? When the war comes here? When it comes to you?"

"I'd do what I have to do. Fight. But there it is. Last night was only the beginning. I'm endangering her just by being here."

"I wish I could argue with you. The battles lines were drawn before she had a chance to pick sides."

"There are places where those lines aren't drawn."

"Such as?"

"California. You said it yourself. It's settled now. If we went there until..."

"Until the dissention is settled? Either way, one of you'll be returning a traitor. And what will you live on until then?"

"I don't need much to get by."

"I was thinking of her. Would you really take her away from her home? Her family? Can you really see Anne squatting in a river panning for enough gold dust to scratch out a living?" He stopped himself at a sound argument and just short of begging Absolon not to take her away.

"No. I guess not. But it's just too dangerous for us here."

"True. But to take her away..." Royal was sure to be out of Absolon's view as he spoke of her, fearful of the detection of a contradictory tone or mannerism.

"Then there's only one thing to do," Absolon said, content to return his gaze out across the hills. "Last night was bound to happen and will again unless... I have to go. I have to leave until this conflict is over. She'll be safe then. I mean if I'm not here. We'll get married when it won't be a life and death choice for her."

"Where will you go? This fight is pretty much everywhere now."

"I'll go where my beliefs are more popular. All the more reason I'm relying on you. It's the only way, but if word gets out, she could be in even greater danger." With that he turned to look Royal in the eye. "Promise me you'll stay close, Royal."

Royal struggled to maintain eye contact. "Are you sure this is what you want?"

"No. I want this all to go away. But until it does, she's all that matters. Give me your word that you'll stay close and keep her safe until I come back. I got no one else to turn to. Even if I did, I'd come to you."

"You know you can count on me. But promise you'll write, to her and to me, and keep us posted on your state."

"I will, as best I can. I only pray she'll wait."

"Of course she will. We all have to wait for happiness until this blasted war is over. When will you leave?"

"Today. This morning."

Royal raised an eyebrow at the turn. "So soon?"

"The sooner they know I'm gone, the safer she'll be. Besides, if I wait, I might change my mind."

Royal smiled. "I can think of greater tragedies. Just stay alive. Come back in one piece. I'll keep your life as you left it, for what that's worth."

"It's worth everything. Thank you, Royal. I knew I could count on you."

He shook Royal's hand, then embraced him like a brother, tight, emotional and brief, before rushing off. Royal stayed on the veranda, watching Absolon ride across the fields and off to his destiny. Only when his dear friend was well out of sight did Royal come back into the opulent den to stand near the fireplace. He took a piece of paper from the pocket of his waistcoat and read. At that moment, his house servant came into the den.

"Is your guest gone, Mister Pollard?"

"Yes. He had to leave."

"Is he coming back?"

Royal sighed but did not look up from the document. "Not for a very long time, I'm afraid."

"Then I'll make lunch just for you. Can I get you some more coffee?"

Royal finally looked up to her. His face was that of resolve, though a hint of pain shown through. "Why not? Looks like I'll be here a while."

With a sigh, Royal dropped the paper into the fireplace. As the flames consumed it, the seal of the Confederate States was engulfed, along with his order of commission as Captain of the Artillery.

6

Cairo, Illinois Union Volunteer Headquarters
September 1861

The vast gridiron was covered with scores of Union soldiers. Each company of raw recruits stood proudly in their new blue uniforms. The rows were as straight as the occasional sergeants and corporals could maintain. By the thousands they stood, all facing north, all waiting for the address that would ensure their fate, all ready to a man.

In the center of the thousands of soldiers armed and ready to face the Confederate forces, Absolon stood at attention. The man next to him was from Missouri. The next was from Ohio. They were no more Union that he was, nor any less. Like them, he awaited the address of his commander. This event was the first to move Absolon to take pen to paper and begin to honor his promise to Royal.

Dearest Anne,

I pray this finds you well. For my part, I am fine and in good spirits. As I could neither join the Confederate Army nor take arm against my old friends, I have come a good way away to enlist with the Union. There is little chance of meeting anyone known to me on the battlefield. This general seems to be a sharp one. If he is any indication, I expect this ware won't be long fought.

I pray you can forgive me for doing this. If you don't know now, you will someday realize it was the only way. It was hard for me to ride away from you while we had so much planned. But it was hard to know I was hurting you by being there. Write to me and tell me if you understand.

Yours faithfully,

Absolon

With thousands standing at attention, General Ulysses S. Grant stepped up to the podium. The hush across the gridiron made his words heard to all.

"Men. Many of you will follow your commanders against the enemies of this country. I will lead some of you personally into combat. But be assured of one thing. You have come to fight and fight you will. This is a war and you are in a fighting outfit."

The volunteers at the Midland Tennessee Confederate Headquarters milled around or sat in the grass on the field outside the town. Most of them were in uniform, or at least wearing a gray jacket. Less than half carried weapons and no one seemed in charge.

A few men in complete uniforms came from the main road and disbursed throughout the ragtag militia shouting orders that few knew how to obey.

"Fall in!" a sergeant shouted.

"In what?" a man replied in earnest.

"It means get in line," he said. "Start here. You men stand behind him. Start another line right here!"

As he and his corporals herded the recruits and volunteers into a semblance of military order, a gold braided officer stood in the bed of a buckboard at the front of the ranks. When he thought they were ready, General Felix Zollicoffer cleared his throat and addressed his command. He was plump and pleasant looking but forced an official poise.

"Men. We may indeed be called upon to defend some hill or boundary or something. I hope not as we're clearly not ready, but let's try to get our heads around that, shall we? Stay together and be ready. If I get orders, I need to know where to find you. Now I'd like to see the officers in my office. The rest of you should probably practice."

With that, General Zollicoffer adjusted his glasses and stepped down from the wagon. As he made his way back to the main street, his men stared in casual disbelief at the lack of leadership. Amidst the unformed, disbursing ranks of yet to be trained infantrymen, Daniel Jacobs stood with rifle at the ready and a look of bewilderment and disappointment.

Daniel had agreed to enlist under his uncle Felix Zollicoffer to placate his family. While he lost so much of his aspirations for glory in combat with the disheartening speech, hundreds of miles eastward, his parents were able to put worries of his welfare aside long enough to deal with the hardships new to them.

Myron Jacobs received word of his mother's illness back in Philadelphia. The letter from their family physician told of rapid deterioration in her condition. She was not expected to survive the next moon and his attention was requested.

As Myron packed his suitcase, Davila sat and watched in silent, reserved dignity. It was her way when she disagreed. As was the bond between them, he felt her concern with each item packed but forced himself to continue until the final items were neatly arranged and the case was buckled securely. Only then did he turn to face her.

"Well that's everything, my dear."

"Is it?" she responded dryly.

"The train leaves at seven so I expect I'd best be off."

Davila looked soberly at him. "How long can I expect to be alone?"

Myron smiled and sat next to her on the upholstered bench and wrapped his arms around her. She remained rigid and tried to look away to hide the fear in her eyes.

"I'll be back as soon as I can. I promise. The paperwork and the execution of her will, distribution of assets, funeral arrangements all together should take no more than a day or two. Then I'm back on the next train."

"These are perilous times to be gallivanting about. I just wish you could have one of your colleagues handle it."

"Two things. First, I need to be with her right now. I'm handling her estate because I'm going to be there anyway. She needs me." He paused to let his point sink in before continuing. As Davila stared silently at the floor without retort, he spoke again in a softer tone. "And second. You're never alone. We may be scattered all over the country, but we're all joined at the heart. Victoria is safe and with a fine man. Daniel is under Felix's watchful eye and doing well. And I'm simply taking a train ride. If times were better, you'd be going with me but I can't risk that."

"So you admit it's dangerous."

"I can't risk it because if you ever got back to Philadelphia, I'd never get you out again."

She finally allowed a hint of a smile. "Well that much is true."
She turned and put her arms around him in an outpouring of pent up
emotion. "I just hate being alone. You know that. Come back just as
quickly as you can."

7

October, 1861

The tavern in the heart of Durham was the busiest place in town this day. It was a popular gathering point, but rarely packed to this extreme in the early afternoon.

Amid the drinking and simultaneous banter, Royal sat on the bar waiting for the opportune moment. Sensing it was as good a time as would present itself, he pounded a bottle repeatedly on the bar top to get their attention.

"ALL RIGHT! We're here for a reason!"

"Yeah. 'Cause we didn't join the army!" said one of the men. The others joined him in laughter.

"We've all got property and families that need protecting if the Yankees get here."

Sam Gottwick stood nearest to Royal. "I had a plan in mind. Why don't we hide everything of value until the war is over? Guns, tools, chickens. Then they'd have no reason to bother us."

"They'll burn us out just for being Confederates," Josh replied.

"Can't blame them. It's a war and we can't just hide and hope it passes us by."

Parnell sat to the side with a glass of whiskey. "We could do like your friend and join 'em."

Royal gave him a long, stern look but said nothing. Turley tapped Parnell on the shoulder to distract him.

"It's a safe bet they're coming. Not today or next week. But mark my word they'll be here if this war lasts through the spring. So do we want to bury all our valuables, including our food and our women, or do we want to get ready to defend ourselves?"

"I'm for both," Josh said. "We shouldn't look too attractive a target or they'll be here all the sooner. But a militia is important."

"But wouldn't troops draw the enemy?" Sam challenged. "Shouldn't we look peaceful? Non-military?"

"There's some logic in that, Sam," Royal said. "But the first groups we'll see will likely be smaller bands of advance scouts. They'll be less likely to come in close if they see us ready for them. That will buy us time. Weeks or even months before the main body arrives. Hopefully we can protect ourselves until our own boys get in on it."

"You seem to know the Yankees pretty well, Royal," Parnell shouted. "Been talking to your turncoat friend? Or did you squeeze it out of his girlfriend?" He was laughing and looking to his friends to join in so he failed to notice Royal hopping off the bar and charging toward him. "Maybe I aught to go out there and squeeze some information out of her my..."

Royal grabbed him by the collar and lifted him from his chair. Holding him close enough to smell the whiskey on his strangled breath, he spoke in a clear, arrested tone. "Maybe you just crossed a line, Parnell."

He shoved Parnell back. Standing to face him, Royal pushed the tail of his coat back clear of his pistol.

"You're carrying a gun in your belt. If you truly belief what you were about to say, finish it and be ready to back it up."

Parnell slowly fingered the handle of the gun in his belt, glancing around in hopes of spotting an ally in the crowd. No one moved or spoke in his defense. He stared at Royal who was surely angry, but calm and ready. A deadly combination for such a skilled gunman. Parnell slowly lowered his hand and his eyes.

Royal allowed Parnell to back away safely but retained his defiant stance as he addressed the room. "The braying of this jackass or any other won't hurt my feelings. I know why I'm here. And as for my good friend Absolon, he isn't made of glass and is none the worse for your petty insults. I dare say he has more strength of conviction and more courage than any man in this room and has nothing to prove to any of you. But when you publicly cast doubt on the integrity and honor of a true lady I will take exception."

No one among the attentive audience dared draw his attention at this time. Royal returned his attention to Parnell, still standing but with his hand clearly away from his pistol.

"For your comment, you are now my enemy and I'll have satisfaction."

Parnell already knew where he stood. With a subtle, forced smile he spoke in a clear and sincere tone. "To tell truth of it, I'd sooner shave a bobcat's ass in an outhouse than tangle with you, Royal. It's plain to see Miss Carmichael is popular here so my comment ain't. I'll take it back if it ain't too late."

Royal didn't accept his apology just yet. They were waiting for it, so they were listening and there was more to be said. He again addressed the room collectively. "There were plenty of you laughing when he said it. I don't hear any now. If anyone among you feels so about her, say it now."

No one dared speak. Few dared look up for fear of incriminating eye contact.

"I thought as much. I wonder who among you would have the courage to stand by your beliefs as Absolon does. He puts his life on the line for peace and for law and for that, you cowards burn his house. You cast doubt on the good name of a fine woman for nothing more than her association with him? By what measure of arrogance do any of you presume to be above Absolon, or *anyone* for that matter? I dare say he's the best man among us. If anyone wants to challenge his honor, do it through me. I'll proudly stand up for him until he returns home to do it himself."

Again no one spoke up. Royal sipped his beer and took a more relaxed poise.

"Then I assume that's a dead issue. Let's leave it that way. So as long as I have your attention, there is a calling here, Gentlemen. Let's get a list of names for our militia."

After a few seconds of group murmurs to be sure it was safe to speak aloud, Sam Gottwick tested the air. "I still don't see what chance a bunch of farmers have against a regular army."

"That's a good point," Turley added. "Maybe we should leave the fighting to the army."

"Then we might as well hang up the welcome sign," Royal said with conviction. "Like I said, they'll come. They may expect some moderate resistance from a few farmers with squirrel guns, but a well-drilled battalion will take them unawares. By the time they rank for battle in earnest, the battle will be ours. It will take some work. drilling and practicing every day. But work we will. If you fail me, you fail us all."

Less than a week later, Anne looked out her bedroom window toward the town, to the field a short distance off. She could see columns of men marching in military formation, slightly better than they had looked the day before. They were too far off to make out faces, but she knew which one was Royal.

They marched in four straight columns. At Royal's command, they turned to the right. The first row dropped to their knees and aimed, clicking unloaded rifles. The second column fired over their heads, then dropped to their knees to reload as the third and fourth columns aimed and clicked in turn.

As the fourth column clicked in synchronized unison, the first column stood again and aimed.

"Almost perfect!" Royal shouted. "Buck and Davie! Did you have time to reload?"

Two men looked at him and shook their heads.

Buck, the elder by a good measure, lowered his rifle. "I can't get my arms up fast enough, Royal. I mean *Captain* Royal."

Royal spoke in a calm, but assertive tone. "We'll practice, Buck. We don't have enough repeaters to go around. You'll just have to get quicker or get your head blown off by the man behind you."

"Well if it's going to happen, might as well be by a friend," Buck quipped.

Royal looked past Buck to the window in the distance. He could just make out the image there. In barely a whisper he said to her, "I won't fail you, Anne."

Then he returned his attention to Buck. "We'll get you a shorter gun. How's that?"

November 4, 1861
Dear Absolon,
I pray this finds you well. I was advised not to give a great deal of information the

Yankees might find useful should they intercept this so I will be brief. Let me assure you your precious Anne is well and watched carefully. She can see the militia drilling near her home and it is my hope that this gives her a sense of well-being and gives anyone watching a reason to steer clear of these parts. Should they not, we are ready. I continue to honor my promise and keep the matter of her welfare close to my heart, though I wonder how long it will be before you are back again to marry her. Until we write again or, in God's mercy set eyes on one another, God keep and protect you, my good friend.

Yours faithfully,
Royal J. Pollard

8

At the Tennessee volunteer headquarters which previously and still served as the local newspaper printer and office, Daniel Jacobs swept the floor enthusiastically. Two other soldiers stretched out in the corner trying to sleep. In the middle of the floor, Daniel stopped sweeping and shouldered the broom like a rifle. Coming to attention, he commanded himself through the manual of arms.

"Right shoulder *arm*! Left shoulder *arm*. PA-rade REST!"

His soldiering roused Gus, the senior and presumably in charge of the trio, from his midday nap. Gus lifted the cap from his brow.

"At ease, General Cowpie."

Daniel dropped the broom in disgust. "I'm tired of being at ease. I thought we were supposed to be an army unit."

The other soldier sat up. "Well your uncle knows what he's doing. Ain't no need to go off pickin' fights. They'll come to us soon enough."

"And if they don't?"

Gus leaned back comfortably. "Then we don't get our asses shot off.

Suits me just fine."

Andy stretched the stiffness from his muscles. "Let them Carolina boys fight. They're the ones what started it."

The door opened and General Zollicoffer entered. He wore his general's jacket over street clothes and asked for no acknowledgement from his men. He went straight to his desk.

"Drilling eh?" he said after a quick glance. "Good, good, Lieutenant. Carry on."

Daniel set the broom at parade rest and tugged the single stripe on his sleeve. "It's me, Uncle Felix. I mean Sir."

Zollicoffer turned and stepped closer to Daniel, adjusting his glasses. "Oh so it is. Well good show, nonetheless. Practice makes perfect, Corporal. Keep it up. After I get this edition of the paper out, I'll join you."

He did not see the other men in the room and they remained quiet, enjoying the invisibility. Zollicoffer returned to his desk and started working. As he shuffled the pile of papers and notes on the cluttered surface, he came upon a telegram and read. Studying the note, he became concerned.

"What's this? When did this come in?"

"About an hour ago, General," Gus said, finally standing.

Zollicoffer was slightly startled by the new person in the room. "An hour you say? Did you see the word "Urgent" at the top here?"

"Didn't look at it at all, Sir. Ain't none o' my business, I figure."

"Hmmmm Well I suppose you have a point there, Lieutenant. Protocol and all. Gather the men and assemble with full gear in the field north of town. It appears we've been called out to defend the Cumberland."

Daniel started to get excited with the news of deployment. "We're going into battle?"

"Afraid not. There's no one there to fight. Hopefully our presence there will ensure that continues. Now then. Fall out."

It took the rest of the day and the following morning to assemble the undisciplined division. They marched and walked through the brisk morning air toward what they all believed to be an overnight camp out.

They remained in fair spirits all the way to the banks of the Cumberland River. Finding a shallow crossing, Zollicoffer led his troops across to a wide, flat embankment on the northwest side.

"Corporal!" he shouted from horseback. "Have them pitch my tent here. We should have a cup of tea before nightfall."

His Lieutenant was next to him. "General. I have to remind you we're not supposed to be here."

"You think the tent should be pitched up there?"

"I mean here! Our orders were to camp on the south side of the Cumberland and not cross until ordered."

"Well we're actually sort of on the north*west* bank so the orders don't technically apply. Besides. There was no suitable place to camp over there. This is a much nicer place. Don't you think?"

"Nice place for an ambush," the lieutenant said under his breath.

"Eh? What was that?" Zollicoffer asked.

"I said there's a nice place up by that *bush*. We'll pitch your tent there."

November 22, 1861

My darling daughter,

Thank you so much for the update on your brother's condition. I try not to worry as that only seems to bother your father more. I have a great deal of faith in your great Uncle Felix to send Daniel home safely but a mother must fret it would appear.

I have not heard from your father since his arrival in Philadelphia last month. I am to assume your grandmother has passed away as it was anticipated some time ago. Once her affairs are in order your father will rejoin me. I must confess I have never felt so alone. In truth, I have never been alone before. I married your father and left my family home only then. It now occurs to me that throughout our twenty-five years of marriage your father has never left my side. This feeling of dependency is something of a surprise and I now wish so very badly that he returns to me. I long to refer to this experience as that silly time long ago when I was frightened over nothing. It is silly of me, isn't it?

The war effort is strong in Charleston. Everyone here speaks of it and of the encroachment of conflict. I pray level heads arrive at a diplomatic solution soon. Please write me straight away, Victoria, and tell me of what eases your mind. I so want to hear of it now. Until then I remain,

Mrs. Myron S. Jacobs
Your Mother

December 26, 1861
My dearest Absolon,
I am well and pray the same of you. I write in hopes you had a joyous and peaceful Christmas, God willing. I received your letter and am waiting as patiently as I can for the next. I hear such dreadful tales of the war and I have some doubt as to the validity of the stories told here. The men seem to only tell of Confederate victories and I know the Union must be better ready for battle. Each tale brings such mixed emotions as I am happy for our friends and neighbors but worry so about the most important man in my life.
You were wise to leave Royal to watch over me. My brother spends so much time in town and out scouting for Yankees that I am all but alone save my servants. But please don't worry. Royal is never far. He cares so much and gives without thought of reward. I wish you would write him and tell him it is all right to accept a glass of sherry or a brotherly embrace in gratitude. Well I hope this gets through to you soon and I pray every hour for your safe return. I cannot begin to make wedding plans until you are back at my side. Until then, I remain faithfully yours.
Anne Carmichael

Just a few hundred yards from her window, a lone rider sat on a hilltop and stared at the light from her lamp. Royal sat as if on guard duty, forbidden by chivalry to come closer. He wanted to come closer. He craved it every waking moment of his pained life. Absolon's absence was at the heart of every wicked, selfish dream and the anguish of the closeness of his passions burned within him like a fever. The pain of wanting to approach her was the very ache in his desperate heart that forbade him. He stared hard that a silhouette may pass across the window or a glimpse of her may come to his wanton eyes. The guilt of his desires, however painful to bear, was less a burden on his thoughts than to ride away with the thought of a moment missed. So he sat without hope or expectation and pined until the lamp was blown out.

9

January 18, 1862

General George Crittenden rode into a lazy, poorly manned Confederate camp on the north bank of the Cumberland River. No guard met him. As he rode through the camp, he observed filthy uniforms and antiquated weapons. The men slept or sat idle around haphazard fires. They played cards or just sat. Even when they saw him, no one bothered to come to attention, though he heard a few acknowledge his presence to each other.

"Hey. Ain't that a general?" asked one soldier without rising.

"Might be," said the other. "Look at all that gold."

"Tell him we already got one."

General Crittenden held his tongue and temper until he found the command tent of Zollicoffer. Dismounting, he entered to find Felix busily writing an article for his newspaper.

"Felix?" he said to announce his presence.

Startled, Zollicoffer stood and turned. Stepping closer to be sure who it was he was addressing, he smiled pleasantly. "Ahhhh. George. Come in. You should read this. It's for the paper, you know."

Crittenden was not interested. "Never mind the paper. What the hell are you doing here? Do you have any concept whatsoever of where you are?"

"On the Cumberland, General. As ordered."

"You were ordered not to cross. Do you realize the river has risen? There's no ford for miles. You can't get back across if you need to."

Zollicoffer was calm and confident. "Now if Napoleon had thought that way, he'd never have..."

"And you're surrounded by high ridges. Good God, Man. This camp is completely indefensible. You've left yourself totally vulnerable to attack. Are you comprehending any of this?"

"Not that we have anyone to defend ourselves against. Eh George? Would you like a cup of tea?"

Now Crittenden began to let his outrage be heard. "With the enemy bearing down upon you, you dare to sip tea and write gibberish for a newspaper? I'll have you court-martialed, Felix."

The outburst brought his lieutenant into the tent. He immediately saluted the general who was beyond anything but gaining Zollicoffer's attention.

Felix still failed to grasp the severity of his offense. "Calm down, George. If that were a factor, we wouldn't be in this relaxed state."

"If you read your orders, you'd know that General Thomas has his full force at Logan's Cross Roads."

"Uh huh. So that would be...," Felix said, pointing to his right.

His lieutenant, still holding the unreturned salute, used his left hand to move Zollicoffer's arm to straight ahead. "That way sir."

"Just *ten miles* that way," Crittenden growled. "My God, Man. Are you drunk or what? They're coming here for you and you've left yourself a sitting duck. What do you intend to do?"

Zollicoffer calmly replied, "Not to worry. When Alexander the Great was..."

"Move out, Felix," Crittenden interrupted sternly. His patience exhausted, he could stand no more of Zollicoffer's flippant negligence. "You have no choice but to advance. Hit them as they're breaking camp. You may catch them unawares and you'll surely have a better footing for battle than this."

He spun and exited the tent, leaving the lieutenant to cautiously lower his salute.

The Union encampment of General George Thomas stirred with activity. Now ten thirty in the morning, the men were awake and fed. Rows of stacked rifles and smoldering campfires ran along the center of the large camp. These soldiers, however relaxed, were trained and of a military disposition. From the brush around them, gray uniforms moved stealthily into position behind any tree or mound available.

Daniel lay in prone position next to Gus and took aim. He was suddenly incredibly aware of his own breathing as he drew a bead on a seated Union private. Gus touched his trembling arm gently to calm him, then raised his own weapon.

At the soldier's command, the first volley was fired and the Union camp fell into immediate turmoil. The Union soldiers scrambled for their rifles and pulled the fallen to cover as officer's shouted commands. The Confederates fired at will and the air was soon filled with dense smoke. For a few fleeting moments, Daniel felt like a true soldier. He was fighting and winning.

But the Union quickly regained their composure. Their soldiers returned fire, forming ranks and flanking expertly. Feeling the change, the Confederate forces started to fall back. Each new volley seemed to turn the rebels back until the tide had completely turned. The Union, better drilled and commanded, soon had the Confederates on their heels.

A Corporal ran to General Zollicoffer, who was well behind the lines at a small table studying notes.

"The Union is turning on us, General. Thomas has the upper hand. They're attacking hard against our left flank."

"Right, right. Just as the Bengal Lancers did at Waterloo. We need to counter with a volley from the right to protect that front."

"There's no cover on the right, Sir. They'd be wiped out."

Zollicoffer was still reading from his notes, as if the battle was taking place on paper. "No, no. It's all right here. We'll follow this and vanquish them by our superior intellect. History is on our side Colonel."

"Corporal, Sir. Corporal Murphy."

Zollicoffer suddenly came away from his notes and mounted his horse. "Whatever. As Napoleon conquered, so shall we."

Corporal Murphy watched him ride off toward the battle. "Didn't Napoleon lose?"

General Zollicoffer rode with reckless abandon through the heavy gun smoke. Stopping amid the fighting men, he drew his saber and began shouting orders to the men.

"They mean to break our left! You men! Flank them on the right and fire at will. You there! Affix bayonets. Hold that line and repel them at all peril!"

The men stared at him but did not move. Realizing the ineffectiveness of his commands, Zollicoffer leaned forward and adjusted his glasses. Through the smoke, he now saw blue uniforms all around him. A Union colonel looked at him in bewilderment. Then, as the Confederates looked on from a short distance away, the colonel drew a pistol and shot General Zollicoffer off his horse.

The rebels were devastated by the humiliating loss of their commander. Then they heard the laughing and taunting from the Union ranks. One by one, the demoralized rebels tried to slip away. Daniel was stunned as he watched the lifeless body of his uncle laying amid the enemy ranks. His trance was broken when Gus got up and ran, leaving him alone against the encroaching Yankees. Without guidance, he did as he had done all along and followed Gus. It was merely seconds before the Yankees came over his spot and emptied their rifles.

10

March 1862

Absolon had followed Grant's forces into battle three times and never the same outcome. Win, lose or draw, General Grant came away looking like a hero in the eyes of President Lincoln and his men, though the record of losses would hinder his career. His leadership led to the first change in the ebb tide of the war and the Confederate army was being handed regular losses. The reports and dead lists grew with each passing week.

A crowd gathered outside the post office in Orangeburg, South Carolina. Joe Mallory came out and tacked the list onto the wall in plain sight of everyone, then turned stone-faced to them. His unspoken message was that he didn't create the list so don't blame him for the contents. It was the most painful aspect of his job as postmaster.

The crowd looked at the list before some of the men crept slowly up to it, fearful of the outcome. One man finally ran his finger down the list and started reading aloud.

"Gibson. Gleason. Hobbs."

"Would you mind starting at the beginning?" asked an elderly woman. She was already shrouded in mourning clothes. He looked at her and reluctantly started over.

"Anders. Brewster..." A woman in the back fell faint at the calling of the name. Biting his lip and taking a breath of strength, he continued to read.

"Davis."

"First name...?" asked a man in front. The reader stood aside and pointed for him.

"I don't know letters," said the man in front.

"There's two of them. Davis, Aaron and Davis, Fred."

The man in front lowered his head. "Thank you." He walked away solemnly. As the names were called out, cries of grief and elation mixed throughout the crowd.

The reader continued, his finger trembling as he approached the fateful section. "Hobbs. Horace. Jacobs. Jones. Jones. Keller..." He stopped and glanced up and down without moving his finger. Then his face cracked into the most subtle, sacredly discernable smile as a tear formed in his eyes.

"Larson. Lembeck." He continued reading for his neighbors, but with a renewed strength. Now he did it for them. He still felt their anguish each time he called out a name and heard a scream or swoon behind him, as it could be him next reading. But not this time. Not him. His son was still alive and he could go on.

Across the street, Mason sat in his wagon, holding Victoria as tightly as he could. She wept upon hearing the name Jacobs. Daniel was dead.

That evening was a quiet one at the Corbel house. Victoria sat solemnly and stared at the fireplace. Bella brought her a cup of tea and cautiously set it on the table next to her. Victoria did not react. Mason nodded to Bella and moved closer to Victoria.

"Try to drink a little, Vickie. Try to think of something else."

"I am," she said in a cold tone. "I'm thinking of what will happen when the Yankees come here. How are we supposed to protect ourselves?"

"They won't come here. There's nothing for them here."

"There's food and supplies. There's Confederates to murder. What more reason do they need?"

"Our boys might have something to say about that."

"Our boys got butchered at Mill Springs."

"We've got more."

"My mother doesn't have any more brothers. Neither do I."

Mason held her tighter. "God, I know, Vickie. But that was one outfit. We have more divisions to keep them far away from here."

"More to kill. More to lose. More reason to... Oh, Mason. Take me away from here! Let's just pack up and go someplace far away from this madness." Her tears started again as she pressed her face into his chest.

"You know we can't do that. We'll be safe here. Trust me."

"I want to. I wish I could."

"Why can't you? It's not like you to take it like this."

She turned away from him and spoke in a whisper. "I wanted us to celebrate our good news tonight. Now it's the worst news I could get."

"About Daniel? We knew there was a chance..."

"Not just Daniel. Little Mason junior."

Mason gasped. "What? Are you sure?"

She nodded into her handkerchief. "I only found out this morning. I was going to break the news to you over dinner. But then we saw that ghastly list and I..."

Mason grabbed her and held her more tightly than ever. "Oh Vickie. We still have something to celebrate. We have to rejoice in this."

"I can't. Not as long as I know how frail our existence is. As long as they can take him from us, I can't risk enjoying a minute of it. I fear them and I hate them and..."

"Stop it. I'll be damned if anyone in any uniform will harm a hair on our son's head. I'll make sure of it."

She looked up at him in a new fear with the realization of his intent. "Mason no."

"I have to, Vickie. I can't sit this dance out any more. We've got so much at stake. So much to lose. How could I face myself if I didn't even try to fight back?"

"But not now. Now of all times."

"Especially now. More than ever. You have to see that."

"I can't do this alone, Mason. Please don't leave me now."

"I won't. I'll join the local militia. I'll be here to protect you and we'll have an army that'll fight like tigers. Think about it. We won't be fighting because some officer told us to. We'll be defending our families and homes. They can't beat that."

She forced the first smile he'd seen from her since well before the list was posted. "So you'll be here when Little Mason is born? He'll be safe?"

"Of course he will. But I think we should call him Daniel. Let life renew itself."

Victoria dropped her head into his chest, relieved for the moment. "Yes. We will and no Yankees will get anywhere near him."

"I swear it."

The next morning a line of men stood waiting to go into the Army recruitment office in Orangeburg. The outcome was slightly larger than usual, the surge typical after a list of fallen was posted. Mason stepped up behind the last man.

"Is this the army, or the local militia?" he asked the portly man in front of him.

"What's the difference?" the man replied over his shoulder. "We're all fighting the Yankees, ain't we?"

"I was looking to sign up for the militia. The local garrison."

A gruff, unshaven man in front of the portly fellow turned back to reply. "You're in the right place, Fella. If you can see around Ambrose, here, just follow me and do what I do."

Mason smiled at him. "Much obliged, friend."

The unshaven man turned to face the front of the line again. Neither Mason nor Ambrose could see his crooked grin, but when Ambrose gave him a subtle shove, he knew his prank was noticed.

One by one, the men were called in and ordered to put their name or mark to a piece of paper. Little else was said and few men chose to speak. As they filed through the office, they were assembled outside in the street. An Army officer came out and stood before them on the sidewalk. Looking over the recruits, he stood with such authority that his presence alone hushed what little murmuring was taking place and within a matter of seconds, held everyone's attention.

"All you men raise your right hand!" he said in a loud, clear voice. Hands went up throughout the crowd. He waited impatiently until all were right hands.

"Do you renounce the government of the United States and swear your allegiance and loyalty to the Sovereign Confederate States of America, and swear to defend the boundaries of the Confederacy with your life? Everybody say 'I do'."

The group mumbled a collective "I do" and he gestured to the soldiers near the large wagons waiting nearby as he continued.

"Congratulations, men. You are now soldiers in the Army of the Confederate States of America. From this point on, you will take orders from your superior, who is just about everybody, and you will learn to be soldiers. Now follow those men into the wagons and you'll be taken to the training camp. Save your questions until you get there."

As the group began milling toward the wagons, Mason tried to gain the officer's attention. Pushing his way to the edge of the group, he waved at the watchful soldier.

"Excuse me, Captain. When will we be back?"

"Soon as you win the war," the officer answered without looking down.

Mason was concerned as he watched the men being loaded into wagons. "I think there's been a mistake. I enlisted in the local militia. I need to stay here, you see."

The officer stepped down from the sidewalk and looked Mason in the eye. "Son. You just enlisted in the Army. I watched you sign up and I didn't see any gun at your head. If you go home tonight or anywhere other than the command of General Beauregard, you'll be guilty of desertion. Know what happens to deserters, Son?"

The man who told Mason to follow him grabbed him by the arm.

"Sorry, friend. We musta been in the wrong line after all." He and Ambrose let out a loud laugh.

Mason turned angrily and grabbed the man by his collar, but a soldier with a rifle at the ready stepped between them. The soldier looked at Mason and gestured with his head toward the wagon. Mason looked at him, then the captain, then finally and reluctantly climbed into the wagon with the others.

As the tailgate was closed, Mason looked back toward home. The wagons pulled away.

11

April 1862

Dearest Anne,

I'm not sure how or when this will reach you and I fear you may have already heard about the battle fought at Shiloh. The Rebs caught us off guard and just about took General Grant. Another General named Don Carlos Buel showed up and saved our bacon. At least that s how I saw it. So did this other fellow. General Halleck. He relieved Grant and told us to forget what happened before. We're in a fighting unit now. Seemed funny to me because Grant said that same thing right before he got a butt kicking. We're in a ware. I thought everybody fought but these generals seem to think they re the only ones. But those Rebs fight like banshees, every last one of them. They do a scream that puts the fear of God in you and makes you want to look off. If you do, like a lot of my friends, they got you. Best to try not to hear them.

I saw a lot of men die, both sides, at Shiloh. Makes me wonder if those negras know what we're all out here doing. I know they say it's not about slaves but to them out here it is. Talking to these fellas, they don't care a lick about the negras but they don't cotton to owning people and wish the negras weren't brought over here like they were. It isn't right and we aim to fix that part of it.

That other general, name of Beauregard, is more than fearless. He's smart. He seems to make a hundred men look and fight like a thousand. He turned, but not before we were all but wiped out. Me and a few others got separated and wound up in a little hospital. It's a tent where we can lay and get well. I'm all right. Just got knocked down. A big fellow named Sven fell on top of me and we both got taken to this hospital. Grant has moved on and I hear Halleck is going after Beauregard as soon as the rest of the troops get in. I'll likely be with his outfit for a spell. I'll write and tell you which one so you don't worry.

Faithfully yours,

Absolon

The battle of Shiloh was nearly a rout as General Grant was caught unawares and nearly overrun by Confederate forces led by General

Beauregard. The main body of Union infantry escaped with a claimed victory with some luck and help but Grant was embarrassed to say the least.

In the heat of battle, it was difficult throughout to know which way any division was falling. A wounded Confederate fell during the retreat and Mason Corbel bent to help him to his feet. Thinking they were advancing instead of retreating, he accidentally told his friends to go on without them.

"We're falling back!" the soldier told him. "Don't stop."

Mason looked every direction, realizing his error. Wrapping the wounded man's arm around his shoulder, he tried to stand. A cannonball ripped the man from his grasp. A clean shot on the wounded man burned Mason's ribs and broke his arm, throwing him ten feet back. The soldier who had told him not to stop grabbed him and lifted him to his shoulder to carry him along. They managed to escape Shiloh with a few holes, a few broken bones and a memory of war that stayed with them a lifetime.

May 28, 1862

Victoria Corbel's screams pierced the night at the Corbel house. Bella leaned on her, struggling to control her flailing arms.

"Miss Victoria! You got to control yourself. Settle down or you'll bleed to death!"

Victoria thrashed about with all her strength. "My baby! What's happening to my baby?"

Bella pinned her arms down and looked her sternly in the eye. "You done lost that baby. I'm sorry, Miss Victoria. But if you don't calm down, you won't be here to try again. Hear me?"

"Oh my God," she gasped, falling back into the pillows with the realization. "My God, let me die then."

"No Ma'am. I ain't about to do that. You stay alive. Hear me? You stay alive for him, if not for yourself."

Victoria stopped fighting and glazed over at the mention of Mason. Her arms fell limp and she came to barely a breath.

Bella eased her grip on Victoria's wrists. "That's right, Ma'am. You relax and get well. The master be back soon and better times are ahead."

It was the dire emotion that had thrown Victoria into early labor. Already weak but guarding her condition, she had for weeks remained bedridden, sending Tom to town for news of her husband and the war. As he lay drained of the strength to weep, her reddened eyes fell on the letter open and crumpled on her nightstand.

My Darling Victoria,

My news is not good so be so prepared. I received word from a colleague that your father was taken prisoner for suspicion of espionage. His Charleston address and the unfortunate timing of his trip led the army to fear him a traitor. He was imprisoned and held there until recently. I was told by this same friend that your father was among several Confederate spies killed whilst attempting to escape. I'm told the matter is being looked into but the outcome will not be changed. I'm sorry to bring such news. I've been told by many that I am fortunate to be of such a strong constitution. In truth, I don't feel strong at all. I am weakened and lack the strength to make the next decision. I'm told also that this will pass in time. I pray you fair this news better. Pray for me, my darling Victoria.

Your Mother

June 1862

Durham was far from the smallest town in North Carolina. But in this time of war, strangers were duly noted. As the townsmen look on, seven strangers rode slowly through town this afternoon. One of them wore the striped blue trousers of a Union soldier. Another wore a dark blue shirt under the long gray duster. The auspiciously armed band made their way along the main street without a comment to anyone, aware they were attracting attention but clearly comfortable with it.

Billy and Parnell stood on the wooden sidewalk outside the mercantile watching as the intruders passed.

"Yankee scouts," Parnell said quietly. "We gotta do something."

"Should we wait for Royal?" Billy asked.

"We can take 'em. You go find Royal if you want. I'll get the men. We'll meet these blue bellies at the livery stable."

Outside of town, Anne stood in the breeze and sunshine, hanging laundry and humming a light tune. From behind her, Royal quietly approached. Rude as it was, he could not resist pausing in secrecy to take in the vision of her bathed in sunlight and beauty.

"Now there's a true vision," he finally said aloud, thus announcing his presence. She turned, not at all startled and clearly pleased to see him. "Shame to have to ask you to stop it."

"You shush now. Why aren't you playing soldier with the other boys?" she replied with a slight blush.

Royal moved the rest of the way up the yard. He came to her side and handed her the next garment. "Day of rest. We'll be ready if any Yankees do come around, though I'd rather not invite them."

"Nor would I. I don't really want your soldiers this close, to tell the truth. Getting so as a girl can't have a lick of privacy."

"They drill close by to let anyone watching know they're close by. But you're defeating the purpose with this."

"What? Laundry? You expect us to walk around in filthy clothes?"

"In the first place, I'd rather your servants are seen out here doing this so you don't look on your own. In the second place, the items hanging here are a bit too enticing," he said, handing her a pair of bloomers. "All women's clothes. What do you think a passing division of soldiers, theirs or ours, would make of this?"

"And what do you suggest? Josh stays in town now."

"That's just it. It's bad enough you insist on trying to run this place alone. If you don't have any of your brother's clothes around, I'll lend you some of mine. But you should keep some men's clothes out on the line, just for show."

Anne smiled as she hung the underwear on the line. "Thanks for the tip, Captain. I'll remember that."

"Then remember this. The best show in the whole county is the vision of you out here in the sunlight. That alone is enough to draw men like moths to a flame. Until this thing is over, I wish you'd keep that in mind."

"Why Royal. I can't tell if you're trying to protect me or flatter me."

"In another world, I'd say both. But until our Absolon returns, please try to keep a low profile. Just in case."

"Maybe I will. Then again, maybe I could give you men something to think about other than violence." She batted her lashes at him with a coy smile.

"You know I'd rather be doing anything other than fighting. I hate violence nearly as much as Absolon. But you suggesting such enticing alternatives... to anyone but me... can lead to no good."

"You are truly amazing, Royal. You practice war, but hate violence. You come and flirt with me, but can't be enticed. I swear you're a paradox. I almost wish you'd do something horrid just to help me clear my thoughts."

Royal stood deliberately tall and erect, firm in his resolve. "Noted. I intend to stomp on one of your baby chicks on my way out. Is that horrid enough for M'lady?" He bowed elegantly.

Anne started to share a laugh with him but they were distracted by the sound of an approaching rider. Billy rode hard with a sense of urgency. Royal took note and stepped toward him as Billy pulled the horse to stop.

"Captain Pollard! Captain Pollard! You need to come to town quick!"

His suspicion of trouble confirmed, Royal turned back to Anne. "Anne. Please go inside. I'll deal with this." She nodded with concern and went into the house as Royal stepped off the porch.

"Gotta come quick!"

"Stop your shouting, Billy. What is it?"

"Yankees. Bunch of them rode in. The men took them prisoner or something."

"Or something? How many?"

"About half a dozen. Nothing they can't handle, so Parnell said."

Anne had been standing just inside with the door ajar. She came back out at the word of trouble. "Royal. What will they do?"

"Nothing if I get there in time. You stay here." He avoided direct eye contact with her so as to keep her from seeing the alarm in his expression. With a reassuring touch of her arm, Royal left her on the porch. He ran to his mount and raced back to town.

Billy led Royal to where Parnell said he'd meet them. As Royal rolled open the door of the livery stable, he gasped at the horror he found inside. Stepping inside, he found several of his men standing around proudly as five men hung by their necks from the rafters.

"Oh my God," Royal muttered, more stunned by the atrocity than fearful of the consequence. "What have you done?"

"We lynched a bunch of Yankees," Parnell said with pride.

"How do you know they're Yankees?"

Charlie pointed to one of the swaying corpses. "One of them's wearing blue pants."

Royal looked at Charlie with disgust. "So are you."

Charlie looked at his own pants and noticed, as did the others, that Royal was quite right. "Well, we know I ain't no Yankee."

"And we didn't want to take any risks with these riders," Parnell added. "Better safe than sorry."

Royal paced slowly through the grisly scene as he spoke in anger. "Is that what you'd say to their families? To their wives and children? And what if Charlie rode through Mount Pilot in those pants? What would they say to your family that would matter? Sorry? He was wearing blue britches?"

Most of the men looked at each other, feeling the shame of Royal's words. Only Parnell stood firm. "We couldn't take the chance, Royal. When we find them other two, we'll do the same."

Outside the stable, Anne approached quietly. Her curiosity had the better of her and she came in to town just moments behind Royal, keeping back just far enough to avoid detection. It was not difficult as Royal was so focused on what lie ahead in the stable. She could hear voices inside and tiptoed closer to the door.

"Other two?" Royal demanded. "There's more of them? Where are they?"

"Not sure, exactly," Charlie said with reluctance. "We thought they'd all come in here together. When they didn't, we took care of these ones."

Royal rubbed his face in frustration. "That means two of them are off to tell their friends…" He was cut off as one of the hanged men kicked.

Parnell was standing nearest the still thrashing man. "Don't pay this one no mind. He'll be dead soon enough. Neck's broke but he just wouldn't die."

"My God Man!" Royal gasped, genuinely appalled. "You just let him hang there and suffer?"

"I hung him. What more you want me to do?"

Royal looked at the twitching man at the end of the rope. His neck was surely broken and stretched hideously. His face was purple and his tongue was extended and pulsing, adding to the grotesque sight. Denied the luxury of retching, Royal forced himself to extend mercy to the tortured soul and drew his pistol. It was at that moment that Anne looked through the door of the makeshift gallows. She saw the dead men hanging and gasped, clutching her mouth with her hand to keep silent. Then she saw Royal aim at one of them and fire, hitting the hanged man squarely in the temple. She screamed, terrified by the atrocity.

Royal turned just in time to see the horror on her face as she ran away. The split second glimpse turned his blood cold as he instantly saw the act through her eyes. He looked back, stunned at what she saw and what she must surely think of it.

"Cut these men down and get them buried," he ordered. "Some of you scour the town. Find the other two before they get out. Billy. Go tell Josh to keep an eye out for them on the north road."

He turned and ran out of the stable, leaving the stunned vigilantes to ponder on what they had done, half of them with no idea what they had done wrong.

Anne ran down a back alley behind the stable and store to a corner of the building, weeping heavily. Royal caught up to her and grabbed her by the arms.

"Anne! You shouldn't have come. You shouldn't have seen that. I'm sorry..."

In tears and nearly hysterical, she pushed him away and pulled from his grasp. "You murderer! How could you do that? How could I think you were any better?"

"Anne... I had to. He was..."

"What? A Yankee? A stranger? Is that what you intend to do to anyone who gets near?"

"No. Please. You don't understand." He was stunned beyond words. He wanted to tell her everything in a single word, to undo it, but instead found the words jammed in him.

"You understand this!" she scowled. "You stay away from me! Stay away from my house. Do you hear me? Don't come near me you murdering monster! Stay away from me forever!"

Anne returned home, drained from hours of sobbing. As she steered her buggy nearer the high arch at the end of the front walk leading to her house, she noticed a dark figure hanging from the archway. Her eyes became locked on the slowly swinging object. In the darkness, she was twenty feet away before it was evident to her the figure was a man hung by the neck. She could just make out that his hands were bound behind his back and a white sack covered his head. Terror welled within her as she approached. So dark and shadowed was the fearful thing that she came to within a few feet before she noticed the twisted right leg and oddly worn boot of the man. Anne screamed with the realization that this was her brother, Josh.

Overcome and terrified, she made her way inside. No servants greeted her and the house was ominously dark and quiet. She staggered upstairs and into her bed chambers. Quickly as her trembling hands would allow, she locked the bedroom door and placed both her hands on it, suddenly terrified of what may lie just outside. Fear forced her to back away from the door, farther from the fear. It was then she heard the sinister, sneering voice of the stranger just behind her

"Well, well, well. Looky what we got here."

She reeled, her heart in her throat, to find two of them grinning at her from the shadowed recesses of the elegant room.

One of them, an unshaven, heavy man wearing the blue jersey and wide brimmed hat of a Union Cavalry soldier, stepped toward her. "You're gonna need to hire you a new guard, Miss. Afraid yours got himself hanged."

"Who are you? What do you want? Get out."

The second man, smaller, older, dirtier, counted on his fingers as he leaned against the door. "American soldiers. To have our way with you. And we'll be going just as soon as we're done."

Terrified, Anne lowered her eyes, fearful of looking the intruder in the eye, struggling desperately to find the strength to control her emotions. It could not end for her. Not like this. Her eyes lowered, she saw the pistol in the large man's belt. But as the weapon drew closer to her, so did it's bearer. She fought to control her breathing, her trembling hands, her clarity of thought, all threatened by the welling panic in her heart as the man stepped slowly closer.

Royal sat on his horse a short distance from the house and stared longingly at the flickering light in the upstairs window. Though the rest of the house and yard was dark, he spotted something strange outside. He had spent many hours here and had come to know every tree and shadow so the new object, though nothing more than a shade, came to view even at this distance. He strained his eyes and suddenly made out the corpse hanging in front. Then he saw a brief flash in the upstairs window and heard the distinct crack of gunfire.

Riding toward the house, he pulled his knife and cut the rope as he passed, bringing Josh to the ground with a single swipe. He entered the dark foyer slowly and cautiously, his pistol cocked and ready. The only sound was a muffled thud from upstairs. As much as he wanted to retain the element of surprise, he found himself bounding up the broad staircase.

In her bedchambers, the smaller man lay slumped on the floor just inside her door. The other man wrestled the smoking revolver away from Anne and knocked her to the bed. Unarmed and drained of strength, she lay helpless as he began to unfasten his belt.

Just as the belt fell from his waist, a shot rang out and the heavy man fell lifeless over Anne. Royal stepped over the first fallen man and put the weapon to the second man's head. The stunned and mortally wounded man slid off the bed to his knees. He died without the second shot being called for. Anne jumped up and into Royal's arms.

Royal clutched the weeping girl, pressing her tightly against his chest. Everything he feared about the war had come to him in the past few minutes. The one thing he most treasured was so nearly lost to him that, as he held her tightly, he absorbed the overwhelming euphoria of feeling her arms around him, safely and, for the moment, affectionately.

"I'm sorry, Anne," he finally dared speak. "I should have been here."

As if awakened from a nightmare, she suddenly pushed away from him. "They murdered Josh. Because of your butchering, my brother was murdered!"

"No. It wasn't what you saw. Let me explain."

At that moment they heard a horse riding off. Royal turned to see that only one of the bodies was still on the floor. The smaller man, the one she shot, had slipped away.

"Where did you shoot him?"

Anne pointed to the floor. "Right there."

"I mean where on him. His chest? His arm? Was it a fatal wound?

"I don't know. You're the expert on fatal wounds. Not I. It was all I could do to close my eyes and fire."

Royal looked out the window. It was too dark to chase the man. He was gone. "He'll be back. And this time he'll bring plenty of help."

"And I'm sure you and your soldiers will look forward to meeting them, but it will be anywhere but here. I want you as far from my home as possible."

Royal turned to face her. "Anne. This is where he was shot. He'll most likely come straight..."

"I don't care. I don't want you or your murdering friends anywhere near here. You are not welcome here. Ever again."

Royal looked at the fallen man, then at her. Hers was a stare of such cold conviction that he knew not to challenge it. No words would be heard clearly this night. The elation felt only moments earlier as he embraced her made the rejection so much more hurtful. His heart laden, he left her alone.

12

May 29, 1862

The entire town of Corinth, Mississippi had been converted into a giant Confederate hospital. Sick and wounded soldiers were everywhere. Some of the more seriously wounded were laid in tents or abandoned houses. Some on exposed cots and most lay on dirty blankets in the streets. Mud and filth are everywhere. General Beauregard walked through the horror with his colonel.

"We can't stay here much longer, General," said his officer. "More of them are dying from disease than wounds."

"How's our food and supply holding out?"

"Even with the rationing, it's not much better than the ammo."

The general shook his head in dismay. He had fought a brave battle and escaped with his division mostly intact but the true price was not assessed until the march south from Shiloh. His men carried each other, desperate to leave no one behind. Wounds festered and infections set in as they escaped.

General Grant did not pursue them as he had yet to explain his near defeat. His superior, General Henry Halleck had relieved him of this command and ordered reinforcements. As soon as the new troops arrived, the twelve thousand men and artillery were added to the ranks and they set off to finish the brash rebels.

For days they followed Beauregard's trail. Smaller bands of Confederates hit them several times in hopes of drawing them off the scent but Halleck would not be deterred. They were coming. Each night and every time they stopped, they dug trenches. Halleck would not be caught off guard as Grant was. He advanced with the assumption that the Confederate army was watching his every move, daring him to drop his guard.

In Corinth, General Beauregard viewed the apparent hopelessness of his plight. He watched his men die in filth and it turned his blood cold. He was delivered the fateful blow when his scout rode in with an update on the enemy's position.

The man came directly to him to dismount and salute.

Retuning his salute, Beauregard asked him the fearful question. "What have you got, Sergeant?"

"They've been hit four times at least, but they keep coming, General. They'll likely be in cannon range by nightfall."

The news, though anticipated, bit hard on Beauregard. He summoned the strength befitting a general. "Is it Grant?"

"No sir. It's bigger. I can't tell how big but they got a lot of reinforcements. Cannons, horses and the lot."

The colonel threw his newly lit smoke into the mud in defeat. "Well that's it. I say we arm any man that can pull a trigger and make a show of it."

"No," said the general. "I'd say that's exactly what they're preparing for. I'm not ready to give up yet."

Less than a hundred yards from them, a soldier knelt next to a cot where a wounded man lay. The kneeling man was the closest thing to a doctor they had. "If we had the time and a drop of clean water, I'd have had that arm off by now, private."

Mason forced his eyes open. "Don't take my arm. Please."

"It'll fester soon and kill you then. Either way, I'll need to add you to the list, Private. What's your name?"

Beneath the massive bandages and weakness, Mason could barely form words. Having spent what little energy he had to plead for his arm, he now struggled just to remain conscious.

"Mas... on," he whispered.

The doctor scribbled on a list he had pulled from his pocket. "Private Mase. Got a first name?"

"No... Cor... l," he faded away, exhausted.

The doctor wrote it as he heard it. "Private Cory Mase. I'll see your family is notified."

Beyond the strength to object, Mason closed his eyes. His wounded right arm was bound to his chest in blood-stained rags. His left fell limp and slid from the cot to splash into the mud.

The next morning, that very mud was parted by the boot of a Union soldier. The soldier walked through it and kept moving as mud was all that remained of Mason and the entire Confederate army of General Beauregard. The Union troops combed every inch of the town but found nothing of Beauregard's men, wounded or otherwise. Not a scrap of bacon or soiled bandage or cannonball was left. Even the dead had been packed away in the night.

From a hillside nearby, General Halleck stood with his officers and gazed angrily at the ghost town.

"Were our scouts wrong?"

"Absolutely not, General," said his captain. "They were here at sunset and in poor shape to boot. We had 'em dead to rights."

Halleck looked at him. "It would appear, Captain, that we didn't."

In the town, Absolon walked along with his friend, Sven Jorgensen. They strolled casually along the deserted street, their rifles no longer held ready as they were convinced all threat was long gone.

"They sure got out," Sven said. "It's like they just vanished."

Absolon looked around in amusement. "I'm starting to think this is what happens when you join a fighting unit."

13

July 1862

Deathly quiet mornings had become common at the Corbel plantation. Victoria rarely came from the house and few went in. No one seemed to want to draw attention to themselves so they walked on eggshells, going about their work as best they could.

Bella was in the henhouse gathering eggs. As she put a few in her basket and turned to leave, she bumped into Tom and nearly dropped the basket.

Tom's reaction was over forceful anger, as had become increasingly typical of him. He shoved Bella angrily and growled. "Watch yourself, damn it!"

Bella lowered her eyes and tried to pass him. "Sorry Mister Tom. I didn't see you there."

"I may not be allowed to take that whip to you yet. But don't think I won't shine my boot with your colored ass."

Bella had not yet given in to this type of abuse. It was never allowed when Mason was around and she prayed those days were soon to return. She turned and looked at him defiantly but did not answer. She started to turn and head toward the house but he extended an arm to block her way.

"Oh you don't like that? Maybe you'd like something else instead? Well just wait, little missy. Couple more letters of bad news like the one I gave her yesterday and you'll be getting plenty soon enough."

"You ain't got nothing I want, White man. Now let me be. I need to get Miss Victoria's breakfast out."

Tom put a warning finger in her face. "Don't you sass me, Nigger. You ain't nothin' but livestock around here and don't you forget it."

She pushed past him and hurried toward the relative safety of the house. Tom started after her until he saw old Herman staring angrily at him from across the yard. Tom stopped in his tracks.

"You just mind your business, Old Man. You hear me?"

Herman stared at him for a moment showing nothing but contempt before silently turning away.

Bella came back into the kitchen and put the eggs down. Despite the courageous front she presented to the overseer, her hands were trembling. She looked through the doorway to see Victoria sitting quietly in a rocking chair, staring out the window. Victoria's expression was empty.

"I'll have your breakfast in a few minutes, Miss Victoria."

Victoria did not move for more than a sigh. "I'm not hungry, Bella."

Bella looked out the kitchen window. Tom was walking confidently across the yard behind the house. She went into the room with Victoria and knelt next to her. She stroked Victoria's head and pushed the long, uncombed hair out of her face.

"We going through this again, Miss? You know you got to eat. You got to take better care of yourself. The master'll be wanting to come back to a lady. Not a willow branch. Don't nobody want a bone but a dog."

Victoria spoke without breaking her stare from the window. "I'll be fine. Run along."

"I can't do that, Miss. I know you got bad news and all but you got to look at the good of it. Himself is still out there. You got to get up and take charge of things around here for his sake. Besides, that no account overseer of yours is scaring me."

"Tom is just the foreman. Don't pay him any attention."

"That ain't what *he* say. He needs to be told, Ma'am. Told he ain't in charge. And you need to eat. Mister Corbel's out there worrying about you right now."

A glimmer of light came to Victoria's face for the first time. "He is, you know. He doesn't even know."

"He went off to protect his wife and baby. If you ask me, his place is right here. He needs to be home protecting his wife and... well let's just say we'd all feel a whole lot better if'n he was to come home."

"Home," she echoed in a whisper. "He shouldn't be out there."

She fell back into her trance at the thought of Mason out and away from home, as was her father. The last letter from her mother weighed heavily on her, calling upon what strength she had left to keep her head above the grief of her father's death. The new letter was beyond her to rise above. It lay open on the floor next to her chair. Bella had tried to remove it twice during the night but Victoria ordered her off. All through the night she wrestled to bring her mind back to a time when she was in some form of control, where she had some family out in the world. So much of her dream world had been devoured by the cruel reality of the letter at her feet.

"What? What did you say?"

"Forgive me, Miss Victoria. But if Mister Corbel knew the situation here, he'd be back in a heartbeat. He'd put things right."

Victoria suddenly spoke with conviction. "Yes. Yes you're right, Bella. He needs to know. Mason needs to come home to me. He needs to be here before…" She stood out of the chair. "Bella. I'm going into town. I need to get a message to Mister Corbel."

Bella stood and turned away with vigor. "Now you talking! Yes Ma'am!"

They both left the room on their missions, leaving the devastating letter at the foot of the chair.

To my daughter, Victoria,

I cannot begin to tell you of the pain in my heart. Never before have I felt so very alone. I have tried to take solace in the fact that you are out there and presumably well but I am afraid it has not been enough.

Since your father has left my life, I have found I have no life without him. He provided so much more than a roof over my head and food on the table. The security of his presence, the assurance of his touch, the confidence of his protection against life's harshness is all gone forever. Even his shortcomings I now miss dreadfully. His style of dress was a public humiliation and his voice had become quite high and irritating in recent years. But he was my partner in this life and I feel I must now break my vow to God. I swore to be his wife until death do us part, but I cannot honor that restriction.

I felt very weak at his loss. Though told my continuing in life was due to my strength, it was in fact the product of my weakness to do otherwise. Now I have found the true strength I needed. By the time you read this, I will be with your father and once again whole.

Please know that you have always been a source of pride and inspiration to me. Take from your man all that he has for you in love and be happy. My pain is at an end at long last and I am happy.

Finally and with love eternal,

Your mother, Davila Jacobs

May God have mercy on my soul

The town of Bentonville was in near chaos. It was like the aftermath of a huge celebration. Shots were fired into the air for no reason. Drunks staggered around the streets even at this early hour. With the young and strong mostly off to fight, only the worst element remained in town. Cowards and men of low or no morals.

Victoria wore Mason's coat and hat. Speaking softly to Big Willy, she rode slowly past the drunken rousers. Up ahead she saw the telegraph office. She saw the dreaded dead list hanging on the wall outside the door. As she approached, an older man stepped out and grabbed her reins.

"Why ain't you off fighting, Fella? You look fit enough to me."

Victoria stared at him for a second. There was no answer that would satisfy this vermin. Her hand moved subtly toward the shotgun on her saddle.

A second man stepped up on the other side and aimed a rifle at her head. "I wouldn't try that, Mister. We don't like spies around here." The man then took notice of Big Willy. "Especially a spy on a fine animal like this. You know, I think I lost me a horse just like this one. I'm thinking this horse just might be mine."

"I'm thinking you're wrong," Victoria said in a firm tone.

The man was surprised to hear a woman's voice. He looked at her, then at his friend with a smile. Then he looked up at her. "Well now. I guess I found me two treasures."

Before he could think of how best to exploit his power, it was lost as he was struck soundly in the back of his head with the butt of a rifle. As the first man started to turn, two more rifles were aimed at him from a few feet on either side. He froze and Virgil Porter stepped in front of him.

"Don't kill him, boys," Virgil said in his usual cold tone. "At least not unless he moves a whisker."

Victoria exhaled for the first time in what seemed like minutes. "Virgil. Thank God. I'm always so glad to see you and the boys."

"Seems like you been taken for a man again, Ma'am. Nowadays, I don't know which is worse. What brings you into town?"

"Sending a letter. Mason is off in the fighting and I wanted to send word."

"Good luck with that. They don't seem interested in anything but the list of dead. Lost my oldest."

"I'm so sorry, Virgil. Is there anything I can do?" Her tone was sincerely sorrowful.

"Not for him. That's been done. But I'm trying to find out about Moses, my next. He went off too and they don't know where he is or if he's alive."

"Well if he's not on the list, that's one good sign."

"T'ain't enough. If I was more of a man or twenty years younger I'd go find out for myself. As it is, I'll just have to wait." He turned and looked at the man still held hostage by his sons. Their barrels were close enough to touch him one either side of his sweating face. "Leave that coward go, boys."

The boys obeyed and the coward slowly and fearfully crept away. They watched as the one on the ground followed his partner. Jeb looked up at her and smiled. Victoria returned his smile and turned to Virgil.

"Good luck, Virgil. If you ever need anything, please come by the house. We'd love to have you."

Virgil's leathery face nearly cracked into a smile. "Reckon a civilized, sit-down dinner wouldn't be the worst thing for us. Maybe I'll take you up on that sometime. Good day to you, Ma'am." He left her with his loyal boys in tow.

Victoria entered the telegraph office. The room served as post office, telegraph office and Army headquarters as soldiers had manned the post since the onset of war. A young soldier sat behind his desk writing. He took note of her but did not react to any degree.

"Can I help you, Mister?" he asked without looking up from his work.

Victoria raised her head to look at him from under the wide brim of her husband's hat. "I need to get a message to a soldier."

The young soldier looked up, having heard the woman's voice, and realized his mistake. Standing, he addressed her more politely. "Oh. Sorry Ma'am. The look fooled me."

"It's all right. I'm getting used to it. Makes it easier to move around these days. About that post."

"Is this fella stationed close by, Ma'am?"

"I don't honestly know. I just know he enlisted a few months ago and I need to get word to him."

"Well you can leave it with us. Soon as we get a new courier, we'll try to get it to him. But I gotta warn you. We haven't had much luck getting through. The Yankees have cut off most of the main roads."

Victoria was visibly upset. "What do you mean by new courier?"

"The last one didn't quite make it. He's laid up over at the doctor's."

"I don't think you understand. This man needs to hear about his family. There's been a death. Don't you make allowances for that?"

The young soldier took the most mature tone yet. "Ma'am. I understand there's a war on and people are dying all over the place. Unless you can take it to him yourself, you'll just have to wait and hope like the rest of us. I'm truly sorry, Ma'am. That's just the way it is."

Victoria walked out of the office as if she'd been beaten. She held her head with a limp neck and dragged her feet across the sidewalk. The energy she had drawn from this quest was gone and more, leaving her emotionally and physically drained.

"No," she muttered, fending off tears. "No more. No more without you. I need you, Mason."

She made her way to the side of her horse. Before mounting, she gazed across the street. Hanging alongside the general store, she spotted the shingle of the doctor's office.

Inside the doctor's small office, a wounded man had been laid on a makeshift bed with a sheet spread over most of him. He was alive but unconscious. Victoria stepped quietly into the side door and looked at the man. She could hear voices from the next room.

"I've done all I can do," she heard the doctor tell someone. "It's in God's hands now and I expect this boy will be as well come dawn. I just wish they'd found him sooner."

Victoria looked at the young man on the table. Then she saw the gray uniform draped over the chair in the corner. Next to it was the leather saddlebags.

Late that evening as Bella busied herself straightening up in the house, the front door opened without a knock and Tom strutted in arrogantly.

"Miss Victoria ain't here," she said.

"Did I ask you?" He sauntered over to a big leather chair and drops into it, testing the comfort.

Bella was nervous, but did her best to put on a stern face. "You got no business in here. Go on now."

Tom boldly took a cigar from the ornate wooden box on the table and smelled it. "Word in town is she lit out. Probably after her man. Know what that means, Nigger? It means I'm in charge."

This news put a fear in her. Bella started backing nervously toward the back door. "You ain't in charge of nothing but them fields. Miss Victoria said so. Now you go on out of here."

Tom got out of the chair and turned abruptly toward her. "I'm in charge of whatever I choose to be in charge of until someone named Corbel returns... if ever. And I'm about dogged tired of listening to your sass." He stepped to within inches of her. "I think it's time you started listening to me."

Bella responded quietly. "What you want then?"

He truly enjoyed the feeling of power. Examining her like a show horse and tugging at the front of her dress, "Well for starters... I think I'm hungry. Go fix me a boss-man meal. Something his lordship would eat."

Bella stepped away from him. "Like what?"

"I don't know. Whatever he had last time he ate here. You fixed it for him. Didn't you?"

"I fixed it." She allowed a note of contempt to show.

Tom caught it and cocked his head a bit. "How 'bout a yessir?"

"Yes sir. I fixed it."

"Then do it again."

"I don't think you'd like it much. It was…"

"What? Rich man food?" he snapped angrily. "Get in there and make it just like you did for him!" With that, he pushed her through the doorway and returned to his comfy chair.

The last bit of daylight was just fading as two Confederate soldiers walked along a road toward town. One of them spotted a rider approaching and waved his arms. The mounted soldier stopped next to them.

"Where you headed?" asked one of the foot soldiers.

The mounted soldier barely looked up from under the bill of the gray hat. Victoria covered her chin and jaw with a scarf and kept the hat pulled low.

"Carrying post to any camps I can get to," she replied in as gruff a voice as she could muster.

"If you go through Appleton, can you deliver one to my Ma? It ain't military. Just a letter."

She wanted to make an excuse and get away from them, but she looked down. The soldier was just a boy. Sixteen at the most. His pleading eyes told her he needed to send the letter nearly as much as his mother needed to get it. As it was her overwhelming need to get a message to Mason that led her to this bizarre situation, she could more than sympathize with the hope of this lad spotting a courier. She wanted to make an excuse, but she heard herself saying, "I'll take it. But I can't promise when I'll get there."

"It's all right. I just have to try. You know how mothers worry."

"I suppose I do."

It was a short time later when Bella came into the dining room with two steaming, covered dishes. Tom saw her and popped out of his chair. With an arrogant swagger ridiculously exaggerated, he came to the dining room table and sat at the head chair.

With knife and fork in hand, he grinned hungrily. "This is the pay off. What have we tonight?"

Bella lifted the lids and he looked down at a bowl of steamed greens topped with gizzards and a platter of pig's ears and snouts resting on a bed of tripe.

Tom stared in disbelief at what he could only define as garbage. Then his expression turned angry.

"What the hell is this slop? You think this is funny, Nigger?"

"It's what the master ate his last night here. He likes the seasonings."

"You lying bitch!" Angrily swiping the dishes from the table onto the floor, he stood and slapped her across the face. "You serve me this slave food and think I'm not going to know?"

She tried to turn away but he grabbed the front of her dress and slapped her again. Pulling away from him, she fell to the floor covering her face and whimpering. Looking down on her with contempt, he saw that he had torn the front of her cotton dress. He calmed himself to a sedated grin as he gazed upon her exposed bosom.

"I think I know what the master liked. I think I'm having me some of that right now."

Bella saw the focus of his gaze pulled her dress closed. Getting up at a crawl away from him, she made her way out the back door.

Outside the house, she turned the corner and tried to run toward the slave quarters but Tom cut her off and again shoved her to the ground.

Standing ominously over her, he began to unfasten his trousers. "You want an audience? That's okay with me."

As his pants fell, Tom was grabbed from behind and thrown face first into the dirt. He rolled over to see old Herman standing over him.

"You keep your hands off my daughter," he said defiantly.

Tom looked up at him with an evil grin. "Nice grip for an old man."

There could be only one result of such an act of violence against a white man. Tom summoned two ranch hands and they dragged Herman across the yard to a big tree. Berg and Ethan were hired as seasonal help but had been more of a regular fitting lately. Tom had promised them a higher station once things worked out as he thought they might. At his instruction, they tied Herman's arms around the thick trunk while Tom went into the house. As they checked to be sure he was secure, Tom returned from the house holding the coiled bullwhip in his hand.

"I been looking forward to this for a long time. Tie him tight. Don't be afraid of hurting him."

"He ain't going nowhere," Ethan said as he and Berg stepped back to watch. Several of the slaves had also come out and stood a safe distance away, watching quietly.

Tom unfurled the long black whip and looked at the old man's back. With a sinister grin, he tossed the whip behind him without taking his eyes off his target. Then he threw his arm forward to strike but the whip stopped him. Before he could turn to see what caught it, Window rushed up behind him and looped the whip around his neck. Berg and Ethan started to step forward but Window pulled the noose threateningly tight around their boss' neck.

"I wouldn't try that, White Man," Window said in a believable tone. Tom struggled but the hold was firm.

"Let him go, Nigger," Berg warned.

Window gestured toward Herman. "Let *him* go first."

"Don't go giving me orders, Boy. You know what happens to a nigger that puts his hands on a white man?"

"Sure do. You grab the oldest and weakest man and beat him."

Ethan started to argue, pointing at Herman. "Now that one..."

"Didn't do a damn thing," Window said. "I'm the one what throwed this man off that girl. The man didn't see me 'cause he was too busy rolling around all scared."

Berg looked at Tom curiously. "That true Tom?"

Tom gasped for air. "Get... this... nig..."

Window tightened the noose and lifted until Tom's feet left the ground. "Turn him loose or I'll kill this white man. He don't matter to me no how."

Berg turned and started to untie Herman. As he did, Window let Tom's feet touch the ground. Seeing him start to relax, Ethan took a cautious step toward them and Window immediately yanked Tom up again.

"You think I'm joking?" he shouted. "You want his neck broke?"

"Now easy there, Boy," Ethan said, backing down. "'Pears you're right and this old man ain't done nothing. So what do you say we just forget the whole thing? How's that?"

Window watched as Herman was freed to step away from the tree and into the waiting arms of Bella and the other slaves. Then he returned his attention to Ethan and Berg.

"Well I'd do that. But somehow I don't see y'all just forgetting I just about hung this here little dung heap of a man. Lord knows he got it coming. But I'm thinking you white folk are fixing to hang me instead."

"So what do you figure on doing with him?"

Window looked at the struggling man in his grip. "Seeing as I'm out of a job at the moment, I think me and this little man gonna take us a walk. We're going that way and we're going alone. Y'all hear me?"

"How far you think you're gonna get?" Berg asked snidely. "Nigger dragging a white man."

"Depends on you folk," Window said as he started to pull Tom toward the woods. "You want to see this man again, just wait here and he'll be around soon enough. You want him dead, just follow me until I get nervous. Your choice."

"You hurt him, Boy, and they won't be no place for you to hide," Ethan warned.

"Just hang on, Tom," Berg said.

Window tightened his grip and smiled. "I like your attitude, boys."

He dragged Tom into the brush and started moving faster. Once out of sight of the white men, he threw Tom face first to the ground. Holding him down with his knee, Window tied Tom's hands behind his back with the whip and slipped the rest around his neck like a leash. Pulled back to his feet, Tom was dragged along at a jogging pace through the dark woods. They stopped when Window found an empty wooden keg in the brush.

"Well looky here, Boss man. Somebody done drank all that rum and didn't leave us nothing but the rotted old barrel."

He rolled the chest-sized barrel up to a tree and dragged Tom to it. Lifting the cooperative captive onto the top of the barrel, Window balanced him precariously there.

"Don't fall now," he warned.

"Looks like you gave this some thought, Nigger," Tom said with what little breath he could draw.

"No more thought than you put to taking that whip to someone."

Then he reached up over Tom's head to anchor the handle of the whip in the limbs. The noose was taught enough to keep Tom on his toes. Window ripped Tom's sleeve off of his shirt and used it for a gag. With that, Tom was effectively trapped.

"I don't know what happened to your boss and his missus and I truly don't care. Ain't nobody ever gonna whip me like a dog. Now if you stand real still and wait, I'm sure those friends of yours will be along. If you go getting fidgety and slip off'n this here barrel you gonna hang yourself. Like everything else about you, I don't give a damn. Good luck, Boss man."

As Tom struggled to keep his balance on the rotted wooden keg, his hands bound, his mouth gagged, his footing precarious and the noose already tight around his neck, he could do nothing more than watch as Window disappeared into the night.

14

August 1862

A Union infantry division led by Major Jeffery Aubuschon marched slowly along the road near Durham. The officers rode at the front of the column leading the cannons and foot soldiers. As they approached a fork in the road, Major Aubuschon waved behind him and his lead scout rode up to his side.

Major Aubuschon barely glanced away from the path. "Which way?"

The scout pointed first to his left, then right as he laid out the choices. "That road leads into Durham but this one takes you right up to that big house."

"And the militia?"

"Ain't been seen for a while. We think they broke up and ran. No Reb forces neither."

Aubuschon smiled ever so slightly at this. "Indeed. Then we have a small debt to repay." He signaled at the fork and the column followed him and his staff to the right and directly toward the Carmichael Plantation. He led with confidence, trusting the scouting reports of a disbanded militia and no enemy forces nearby. Though tested in a few engagements, Aubuschon had earned a reputation for being unwilling to take chances in the field. He was no coward, but neither was he a gambler. With his path clear, he led his forces into the valley.

From a wooded hilltop nearby, Royal and Billy lay prone as they watched the advancement through field glasses.

"I was afraid they'd do that first," Royal said of their course.

"There's too many of them, Captain Royal. What are we supposed to do?"

Royal lowered the glasses and smiled confidently. "Surround them."

The Union column advanced toward the mansion, marching through a broad meadow with wooded hills on both sides. Aubuschon didn't care for the strategic advantage given up as it threatened his unblemished record in combat. This was a dangerous position for them but he chose to trust his scouts on the absence of rebel forces. He and his staff watched the hills on either side carefully as they moved further into the gap. His captain thought he saw movement on the ridge and squinted to see it. Aubuschon clearly heard movement in the trees but saw no one. They had seen and heard just enough to put them on guard. Though no horses or men were visible, they heard hoof beats on the top of the ridge. Major Aubuschon called the column to halt. They sat quietly and listened as the sounds grew louder, clearer. The soldiers held their weapons at the ready and awaited a command, but the Major continued to listen.

They soon heard the clear sounds of several horses and saw the dust just over both ridges. Then they heard orders called out, directing troops and ordering cannons into position. The voices and billowing clouds of dust and sounds of horses seemed to be the length of the hills on both sides and Major Aubuschon, for all his caution, realized he had marched into an ambush. They were surrounded by a force close enough to fire but too concealed to return fire upon.

Livid, but restrained, he growled at his scout. "Exactly where did this division come from?"

The grizzled scout seemed more impressed than afraid. "Beats me, Major. They sure as hell got the drop on us."

"So it would appear."

As they studied the ridges looking for any target or sign, a uniformed officer rode out into the clearing just over a hundred yards ahead of them. The officer was flanked by two adjutants on either side. Coming to a halt directly in the path of the union division, Royal, dressed in the uniform of a Confederate officer, raised his saber and nearly the entire disturbance on the hills hushed to a whisper. Major Aubuschon stared, knowing the advantage and the right to first move belonged to the Rebels. Royal returned his stare long enough to let the Federals know he considered communicating with them, then deliberately elected not to. He dropped his saber and a cannon fired from a concealed position on his left. The round landed a short distance away from the column but close enough to startle the major into ordering retreat.

"Bugler! Sound retreat!" Aubuschon shouted as he turned and spurred his mount.

The fearful bugler obeyed as more explosions were heard behind them and a volley of gunfire emanated from the surrounding hills. With no visible targets at which to shoot, the only recourse left them was to run. Unranked and praying aloud, they saw their major and his staff pass them as the enemy was heard in pursuit from the hills.

Atop the hills and just out of the line of sight of the Union infantry, a few riders dragged large branches and logs behind their horses to raise dust and clatter. They fired weapons into the air and shouted orders and names as they rode, creating the illusion of greater numbers of riders. On the hill behind Royal, two men threw another stick of dynamite, pretending to be the second cannon.

As the Union division vanished into the hills, the militia started to cheer. Their first defense of the home front proved a brilliant, bloodless victory.

Royal was drained but managed to keep a stern front for the elated troops. He looked to Billy, looking all too at ease and natural in his Confederate blouse and cap.

"They'll send a few scouts back to assess our numbers. Have a few men flank them at the river. Let them know they were watched all the way out of the county. Sam? You get the cannon back into your barn. If they see it, they might figure out it's the only one we've got."

Sam, having served as the officer on his right, nodded and he and the others rode off. Royal had yet to fully relax. For him, there remained one thing more to dread. The threat gone and everyone off, he turned and rode toward her.

Anne stood on the porch and smiled as he approached her apprehensively. He did not dismount just yet.

"They're gone for now," he reported coldly.

"I know. Thank you."

"Just thank you? Not 'Thank you now get out'?"

"No. Come inside. Please."

She turned into the house. Royal watched for a second, weighing his emotions. Then he did as he had in a thousand dreams since his exile.

He dismounted and followed her inside the house.

Anne strolled casually across the foyer, her back to him as Royal entered the house. He stood just inside, hat in hand, and said nothing.

"So it actually worked?" she said, looking back over her shoulder. "You fooled them?"

"As far as they know, they barely escaped a full division of Confederate troops. They think they're lucky to be alive so I'd say you're safe for now."

She had two glasses on a silver tray. She poured sherry from a crystal carafe as she spoke. "I've always felt safe. You've seen to that. But lately… it doesn't seem to be enough." She turned to face him, a glass in each hand. "There are so many other reasons to want the company of a man."

Royal stepped closer to her and took his sherry. He could have interpreted her statement two ways, but he forced himself to act on the chivalrous intent. "You mean Absolon? I know. I miss him too. And I do worry about you out here alone. How are you managing without Josh?"

She stood close enough to him to insure he could smell her cologne. "I still have the servants. I don't try to get rich. Until this war is over, I'm just trying to get by, to keep food on the table. I do worry that occasional passersby might be enticed to stop in."

"Enticed?"

She tilted her head coyly and seductively fingered her glass. "Yes. Enticed, by the garden and the livestock. Why? Don't you think a man might find that sort of, you know, alluring?"

Royal felt the attraction play on his desires. He had a commitment to Absolon, to chivalry, to Anne and he called upon his memory of Absolon for strength. "They might, and they might not be gentlemen. Keep the men's britches on the line and we'll keep drilling nearby. I think that would be best, while you're alone."

"So how long do I have to remain alone, Royal? What is the rule on that?"

Somehow, her bringing the game to an end and showing her cards strengthened his resolve. He swallowed his drink and smiled at her.

"Until Absolon returns."

"Am I to wait that long to feel the comfort of a man's arms around me?" She stepped closer and ran her empty hand up along the brass buttons of his uniform. "I deserve to be protected and fought for, but not comforted? That's hardly fair."

"Fair is a word I've all but stricken from my vocabulary, Anne." As though out of his control, his arms closed around her as she leaned against him. "I've learned to simply do what I must and watch fairness pass me by."

"It doesn't have to. You deserve better. You deserve so much more. We both do."

Royal suddenly grasped the seriousness of his situation and released her to step back. "Anne. You have to wait for him. We both do. Nothing else matters." Anne became angry, wounded by the rejection. "Nothing? I don't matter? You don't care how long I sit out here and wither away?"

"Of course I do but..."

"Am I a widow already? Why do you think I remain alone? Who do you think I'm waiting for?"

"You're waiting for Absolon," he said sternly.

"I'm waiting for you to speak your mind. Say what's in your heart for once. *Your* heart, instead of what your stupid conscience tells you to say!"

Royal ended the five second stare, setting his glass down and turning. "I should go."

Anne lashed out, dejected and insulted. "You can't do it, can you? You know it. The whole county knows it. But you won't say it. How can I expect you to ever act on it?"

"You can't." He didn't turn back to look at her, protecting the uncertainty in his own eyes, hiding the pain. He walked out of the house and made to his horse, hoping to mount and leave without the rest coming. But she came out onto the porch.

"Go on then. But don't expect me to wait until you find your manhood."

Royal saw the pain and anger in her eyes. With no response to give, he turned the horse and rode off.

15

October 1862

A column of Union cavalry soldiers rode single file along the treacherous road. The trail had been cut into a steep hillside of the densely wooded mountain. They moved slowly and seemed mostly concerned with looking down the wooded mountainside. Despite the surefootedness of their mounts, they knew a fall here would likely be fatal. As they crept along, none among them noticed the horse and rider standing quietly in the trees just above them. Big Willy stood deathly still as Victoria lay against his back to watch the enemy pass by.

Grant needed a victory and Vicksburg was to be it. He called men and artillery from everywhere to the campaign against the walled fortress. Only the injured and a skeleton crew of caretakers were allowed in the vicinity without being called to the fight.

Such a camp of nonbelligerent wounded and medical staff sat eighty miles north of Vicksburg. Other than the blacks who were not yet considered a fighting force and the medical staff, a minimum compliment of able soldiers manned the camp. Their purpose was mainly to guard the ammunition and food supplies stored there.

Window walked alongside a loaded wagon as they entered the large encampment. On the other side of the mules, an older black man, Tope Frawley walked along humming pleasantly.

Window looked around at the tents and soldiers strewn about with no apparent order. "What are we supposed to do here?"

"Wait," Tope said in a calm, pleasant tone. "The fight is off south. We supposed to wait here and go when they wants us."

"You mean want us to tote something for them."

"Well it ain't going to get their by itself."

"Don't that bother you? All we do is tote for the white men. Don't you want to fight?"

"Well if the white men need me to tote stuff for them to kill each other, I reckon I'm okay with it. Least they're killing each other."

Window smiled at that. "You got a point there, Old man."

"What would you rather be doing, Young Buck?"

"Fighting. I don't know why they care who helps them kill Rebs." They stopped the wagon near a tent where Absolon, Sven and Dooley stood with tin coffee cups. Sven had heard the end of the conversation.

"It's not that they care. They just aren't anxious to put a gun in the hands of a man they'd held in slavery for two hundred years and then turn their backs."

"Scared once we start killing white folk we won't know where to stop?" Window said with a smile, ensuring they knew he meant no real insult.

Sven took no offense. "Something like that."

"Ain't like we any good with a firearm anyway," Tope said as he pulled the team into position to unhitch.

"Speak for yourself, old man," Window challenged. "I can shoot just fine. And I can load a gun as fast as most can aim and shoot."

Absolon took notice of that brag. "You can load as fast as a man can shoot?"

"That's a God damned lie," Dooley said.

"*Aim* and shoot," Window clarified. "Sergeant I was with showed me. Learned me a few shortcuts."

"You gonna tell me a white soldier taught you to shoot knowing you would never get to fight?" Dooley challenged. "That ain't nothin' but a waste of lead."

Window spoke with a righteous calm. "Wasn't like that. He was always telling fetch this and fetch that. One day we got jumped by a band of Rebs. Surrounded we was. Me and Sergeant Marx got ourselves pinned down behind a stump. He fired and reached out and I put a loaded gun in his hand. He got him another and soon as that I handed him that other rifle." He gave Absolon a cocky nod of reassurance. "It was loaded. He didn't have time to think and just shot him another. Well I didn't have no time to be scared nor wait to be told so I kept shoving powder and balls in them guns and he kept shooting. I figured I was keeping me alive but it didn't matter. Time it was done Sergeant Marx had shot hisself a dozen Rebs and the rest run off. They thought there was more of us under that stump than one sergeant and a scared nigger so we let 'em think that while they ran. That was us for the summer. Him shooting and me loadin'. Killed us a mess of Rebs, we did."

Sven smiled broadly. "That's one I'd like to see."

"So would I," said Absolon.

"Line 'em up," Window said with confidence. "I'll load and you fire. But you got to hit the target. Not just pull the trigger."

They leaned three rifles against the wagon. Absolon's still had the brightly polished bayonet attached. Window stood with a powder horn strung around his neck and a handful of wads and balls in one hand.

"Pick you a fair target."

"That tree out there," Absolon said. "The dead one broke in half. See it?"

Window looked out to the dead tree across an uneven clearing. "Good shot. Ready?"

"Ready. I shoot and you start."

"Go, White man."

Absolon aimed and fired and put the first gun down. As he lifted the second rifle, Window poured paper and powder into the third gun. Absolon aimed and fired again. He put the second rifle down and reached for the third just as Window pulled the ramrod out. With Dooley, Sven and Tope shouting encouragement they continued to load and fire. Absolon raised and aimed as Window rammed the wad and ball into the next gun. Absolon suddenly stopped and cocked his head to listen. Window let the ramrod slide into the barrel and stopped as well. Something was coming.

Suddenly the thunder of nearby artillery filled their eyes and cannonballs rained down upon the encampment. The men throughout the scarcely populated encampment dove for cover, hiding in or under the flimsy tents and wagons. Each object hit claimed at least two victims. Explosions were everywhere. A blast destroyed the wagon they were leaning against, hurling the tongue and axel half into the air. The encampment was pummeled for several minutes, then as quickly as it began, all went quiet.

Absolon lay pinned under a thrown wagon wheel. Breathless and shocked, he made no attempt to free himself. The only stirring throughout the encampment was the smoldering of the horrific attack. Finally, Absolon started to move an arm. Just as he attempted to push the heavy wheel from his chest, he froze. Only his eyes followed the sound of approaching voices.

From the west side of camp, near where Window and Tope had entered, three Rebel soldiers walked into the clearing. Looking around with rifles ready, they initially saw no sign of life. Nothing threatening. They relaxed slightly as they walked further into the encampment, poking bodies and muttering to each other. One of them came upon the remains of the overturned wagon. From the near side, he saw Tope's lifeless legs pinned face-down under the frame. The blast had knocked him out of his tattered boots. Then they saw Window's upper torso extending from the other side. He lay on his back with his right hand inches from Absolon's rifle, ramrod still plunged into it and bayonet still attached.

"Looky there," quipped one of the soldiers. "We done blew that nigger in half."

The second man came over to see. "Look at him. Reaching for a gun that ain't even loaded."

The third man glanced, but maintained a more serious attitude. "Just keep looking. Could still be some live Yanks around."

Twenty paces further, they came upon Absolon pinned under the wheel of the wagon. He tried to lay still but his shallow breathing drew the attention of the first Reb.

"Hey. This one's alive," he stated matter-of-factly, pointing to the trapped Yankee.

"Kill him," said the second.

"Shouldn't we take him prisoner?"

"Sure," scowled the third man. "Let's take all the yanks we find. Take 'em right down to Vicksburg. Maybe we should take the Yankees some food and ammo, too. Shoot him, God damn it."

The soldier raised his rifle and aimed at the forehead of trapped Absolon. Just as his finger neared the trigger, a shot rang out from behind him and a ramrod burst out of his chest from the back. Stopped when the blunt end hit his ribs, the metal rod had pierced his heart. Gasping, he fell forward, landing to Absolon's right as the other two turned to the sound of the gunfire. They saw Window sitting up, still trapped under the wagon. He held the smoking rifle with the bayonet.

They stared but a second, stunned at what appeared to be a man severed in half sitting up and shooting at them. Then the second soldier raised his gun to kill Window again. He never got to aim before he was shot in the back of his head. Absolon, too, still had his rifle.

The third man turned, rifle ready, to Absolon. Absolon couldn't get up from under the wheel and his rifle was spent. His only recourse was to swing the spent weapon, knocking the Reb's rifle away. The Confederate aimed again and Absolon knocked it away in time. He finally stepped back out of reach and took aim.

"Damn it, Yank!"

Window had but one chance and hurled the rifle like a spear. The bayonet struck the man in the small of his back just as he fired. The shot went wide and he fell forward into the desperate hands of Absolon. There it was finished as Absolon strangled him to death.

His strength regained, spent and again drawn, Absolon wriggled free of the heavy wooden wheel and went over to Window.

"You all right?" he asked, looking for a means to safely free him.

Window winced as he tried to pull out. "I think so. This thing is heavy."

Absolon looked at the lifeless set of legs protruding from the other side as Sven and Dooly walked up. Dooley's head was split open and bleeding but they seemed well enough.

"I think they thought he was you," he said, pointing to Tope's remains.

Sven looked at the dead man. "I was about to say we were lucky to be at the edge of the camp instead of the center. Everyone there looks like they got blown up."

The three lifted the wagon off of Window and he pulled himself free.

The camp was almost totally devastated by the shelling. They all agreed they were indeed fortunate to be at the outer edge and behind a cluster of trees. Gathering what food and supplies they could, the quartet made off before the main body of the confederate troops came through. They were still soldiers, but with a new mission. Absolon knew who to thank and felt justification for his stance in the courage and strength of their new comrade in arms.

The battle of Vicksburg went on without them and the best thing to come of the bloodbath there was the lesson learned that the negroes could fight. The sound accounting of courage and devotion humbled the main body. Window was fortunate to have missed out of participation in this milestone battle. Had he been there, his addition to the number of dead would have been insignificant.

The winter taught them survival and combat lessons the infantry and cavalry forces in larger numbers could not. They picked up stragglers as they followed the fighting. Their numbers grew to as many as eighteen when they joined another band of guerillas and dwindled back to six when the larger group drew the attention of a Union scout. Absolon and Window, though lacking official rank, became the leaders of the band by experience.

Window enjoyed the relative animosity of the secluded style of warfare. Here and in the arm-locked embrace of tried and true soldiers bonded in blood, the colored soldier was treated as a man and an equal and he found himself going days without even thinking about the "affliction" of his heritage. Any time new men joined them and started on him, Absolon quickly addressed it by establishing himself as in authority, then asking Window how or what to do next. They built a small company of trusted soldiers and made it clear to new arrivals that the race issue would be their undoing. Anyone who felt they could not treat Window as an equal needed to move on.

They moved wherever fighting and fortune led them over the next few months. The fighting was hit and miss for the first few weeks. Then winter set in and took the fight out of any division not commanded by a general with luxury accommodations. In the warmth of a heated tent with decent food, warm feet and dry clothes, a leader could see worth in a long offensive. But the men trying to make a bed of frozen mud and dead leaves wanted only to survive. Looking for a fight when your fingers were too cold to pull a trigger was not the way of the guerilla bands roaming the Tennessee hills.

Absolon and his rag-tag band of stragglers found life more tolerable without the restrictions of high command. They weren't deserters by any means. They picked up any lost or separated men they could. They spent most of the days scavenging and the nights around the fire. Fighting happened when they couldn't duck an enemy patrol. It was many a time they lay in the snow while a column of Confederates rode past them unmolested. None among this band objected to living another day.

But confrontations were inevitable, though sometimes weeks between, and in those desperate times they fought like soldiers and comrades. They watched out for each other and followed the leader of the day. This tended to be Absolon the majority of the time and he found himself giving orders to men who technically outranked him.

Window got better with each fight. The rage and reckless abandon that drove him through the first fights cooled with time to reflect. He realized that he was fortunate to have thrown himself in harm's way and walked away while so many others were left dead and dying on the battlefields. He was also increasingly aware of Absolon's watchful eye. If he went into dangerous territory, his friend was sure to be close behind. Even so far from anything he ever called home and anyone he knew even a season ago, Window was not an island and had to consider the consequences of his carelessness. He could not be responsible for the death of this man. Some, perhaps. But not this one. He learned to balance his caution with courage and found in that delicate balance a fighting style the Rebels were defenseless against and the Yankees, once exposed to it, were forced to accept as something special in this war.

The cold and inhospitable climate seemed to be little more than an aggravation to Window. He took these seasonal hardships in stride and the others spent many a frigid night listening to his tales of life in the slave quarters. He knew his was far from the worst so he embellished a bit to hold their attention. He didn't want their pity, but he greatly appreciated any small gesture of respect.

One early February evening, they made camp in a suitable site. They had picked up five stragglers from an infantry division out of Illinois. The men seemed all right, but not at all anxious to fight and so far had said nearly nothing to Window. As they all settled in, one of the most seasoned of the new men stopped another from building the fire.

"What do you think we got a nigger for, Lou?"

His man stopped and looked at him, noticeably puzzled. They were both oblivious to the immediate stares from all around them. The heavy jawed corporal then turned to Window and snapped his fingers. "Let's go, Boy. The white folk is getting hungry."

After a full three seconds of tense silence, the bunch erupted into deep felt laughter. The new men stood dumbfounded, unsure what they had done to warrant the laughs.

Window was laughing as well. He stumbled to an iron pot and waved it toward the corporal. "Yassah Massaah!" he laughed. "Ahs a fixin' yo vittles directly, Sah."

The laughter rose in intensity with Window's stereotypical portrayal. Some of the new men were starting to smile, seemingly getting it. But the veteran corporal was less than amused.

"Somebody tell you a joke, Boy?"

Absolon stepped in between them, still smiling broadly, and looked him in the eye at close range. "You did, Corporal. At least you better have because we don't talk that way in this outfit."

Another of them lost part of his smile. "Is they serious, Burl? We got to eat with niggers?" The man was tall and ridiculously lean with an oddly pronounced Adam's apple. He stood with his corporal and eyed the others.

Sven spoke with no trace of humor in his tone. "No. We eat wit' each other. Any man who can't stop at the uniform and can't look inside need to move along. You onnerstan dat, Private? You and your Corporal der?"

Three of the five new men were in close formation in the center of the group. They looked as if they were about to be attacked. But still they waited.

Dooley added his two cents worth. "The fella you just told to fetch your beans has saved the lives of half of us nearly a dozen times. We stand with him. If you can't, well head off and no hard feelings."

The new men looked at each other, then at their senior for a decision. The grizzled corporal looked at Window a long time, then at the faces of those men defending him like a brother. Finally he spoke.

"Nope. I just can't stomach it. We'll be heading off." He started gathering his gear. The others slowly fell in behind him.

One of the new men looked at Absolon and pointed to his corporal. "You see how it is. No offense intended."

"None taken," Absolon replied.

"None taken, my Aunt Nellie," Window interjected.

There was no real harm done and they found going easier when they were all of the same mindset. The weather turned warmer and they found sleeping a bit easier for the next few days. Then came the rain like none they had ever seen. For a solid week it fell day and night. Then it stopped just long enough to let them think they might get dry and it started again. Moving was difficult and dangerous. They couldn't see more than a few dozen feet ahead and could hear next to nothing. The experience gained in the woods up to now had taught them that they generally heard their enemy before they saw them. As the driving rain pounded the ground, sloshed the puddles and rustled the trees, any sound other than rain was literally drowned out.

George Pascenal, one of the newer men, was raised in the Louisiana bayou and was no stranger to rain. He talked of times when you couldn't tell where the sky stopped and the swamp started. His mother called it flying gator weather. But even George had trouble remembering seeing this much water falling in so short a time.

The band had dug into the side of a wooded ridge one evening and just missed the passing of a large division of Confederate cavalry. They watched the Rebels push slowly into the woods but couldn't be sure how far they went before nightfall. Unable to hear or see them, Absolon's band clung to that ridge well into the night. Their guns were at the ready but they could find no target in the deluge.

"What say we slip out the back and get out of here?" Dooley whispered to Absolon.

"What do you think, Window?" he asked as he had become prone to do.

Window did not rise from the mud. As he peered over the soggy ridge toward the spot where the Rebels were last seen, he spoke cautiously. "I don't like it. We know that trail wraps around this here ridge all the way down. For all we know, them Rebs is behind us right now. Better not to move until daylight."

"Makes sense," Absolon agreed.

Sven, normally on Window's side, was tired of lying in the cold mud. He adjusted his saturated hat and craned his neck to look out. "I don't tink they're out there, you guys. I tink they done moved on like we'd do if we didn't see them. You tink?"

Of the eight men currently in their band, these four made the bulk of the decisions. George and the others were all fairly new to them and to the army in general and were glad to let someone else lead them out of trouble.

Absolon shook his head. "I gotta agree with Window. We shouldn't be moving until we can see where we're going."

"And get your head down," Window warned Sven.

Sven chose not to heed the warning and slowly stood to look out into the night. "Naaaa. Nobody out there unless they got a boat. I tink we..."

At that moment his rain drenched hat flew straight up off his head. The big Swede wobbled back and forth rubbery before slumping face first into the mud ridge.

Dooley grabbed him to pull him over and found a hole in the center of his forehead. Sven was dead before he hit the mud. It was difficult to tell through the thick, wet locks of blonde hair that the Rebel ball had opened an apple-sized hole in the back of his skull. The bone fell open and back into place as they rolled him away.

Dooley snarled angrily as his eyes turned toward the ridge. They were out there. The murdering Rebs were right there. He pulled his rifle to his side and started up after them but Absolon and George grabbed him.

"Let me go," he growled. "They killed him! Don't you care?"

"I care. Course I do. But you getting killed won't bring him back."

"I mean to get a couple of them at least."

"How?" George asked. "You can't even see me. Them buggers can see well enough to pick us off for looking. I say we don't look."

"I think Sven's plan is sounding better," Window added to their surprise.

"What? Now that he's dead you want to listen to him?" George challenged.

"Nope. Now that we know where they are. If they's over that-a-way. We needs to be slipping out that-a-way," he said, pointing down the hill. "The man died to show us the way. I say we take it. Who's in?"

"How do we know they didn't just surround us?" asked Ludlow, the eldest of the group though still a private for enlisting at forty. They could be down there waiting for us."

"Nobody sees that good," Window asserted. "Not in this. Not no way."

"Okay," Absolon said calmly to the group. "Window's hasn't steered us wrong yet. I'm for risking it. What do you say?"

Ludlow scratched his bristly chin. "Well it's for damned sure we ain't safe here."

"Okay. I'm with you, too," George chimed in. "But we don't leave Sven for the Rebs."

"You want to carry him, you go right ahead," Window said.

Absolon was again the voice of reason. "We'll bury him here. Then move on. Agreed?" He looked mostly to George for approval. George was out of objections and Absolon had won the moment.

But burying the big man proved an unexpected challenge. Shovels or tools were unnecessary in the saturated muck. They clawed the mud away with their bare hands only to watch the hole fill up with newer, wetter mud. Again and again they tried to make and hold a hole big enough to cover Sven but nature seemed to be rejecting their offer. Finally they did the only thing left them. Four of them lay on the ground face to face in pairs. At Window's command they pushed away from their partner, opening a shallow grave by holding back the mud with their bodies. Two more, Window at the head and George at the foot, clawed what they could from the bottom and held it while Absolon laid Sven in the opening. The men held back as much as they could while Sven's body was covered with rocks to hold him down. Then they sat away from the mud and watched it close around the body. It looked to them as if the ground was slowly swallowing their fallen comrade. After a few moments and a little assistance, Sven was gone and they slinked away on their bellies.

It was thirty yards down the sloppy embankment before they had the nerve to stand and flee from the owl-eyed Rebel sharpshooters.   It was one of the longest nights Absolon could remember. Soldiers come and go, fight and die. But the big Swede was sorely missed by them. To a man, they respected him and honored his memory.

February 14, 1863

My Friend Royal,

I hope this finds you well. As for me, I have been uprooted yet again. This last time we got shot up but some really good soldiers came away. We have been fighting small fights. Gorilla fighting, they call it. Maybe because we always seem to be hiding in the trees. There are only seven of us and we pick up and lose fellas now and then. You surely hear tell of the big battles like Vicksburg. Me and these boys have been fighting the kind you don't hear about. Little fights here and there. We just fought twenty Rebs hold up in a farm house. We had them pinned down but they just won't give up. We're glad the weather turned warmer because we almost froze a few times. Now it won't stop raining. It's been steady for more than a week and we can't move. Sven stood up to move to a dry spot and a Reb shot him in the head and killed him.

It was pitch dark and raining hard. Either that Reb could see in the dark or he was close enough to slap. We tried to dig a hole for Sven but the mud filled it up as fast as we dug. Finally we laid side-by-side and held the mud open. Me and George set Sven in and weighted him down with rocks so he wouldn t float. Then we stood away and let the muck take him. It didn't seem altogether Christian but it was the best we could do. After that we crawled away on our bellies like cowards so that Reb wouldn't kill us too. Don't tell Anne that part. Just tell her we stayed alive.

The rest of the men are great friends and good soldiers. Even Window. He's a negra smart as a whip and fights like two men and an ornery dog. Any one of us is proud to fight with him. I think he knows how many white men have died for this cause. I just *hope the white men know what kind of men they're helping. I'll write more when I can. Until then, please keep my memory alive with Anne. As I write this, I can see your face clear as day. But I can't seem to remember her at all. I must have worn out the memory of her for thinking about her so much. I'll see her soon, I pray.*

Yours with hope,

Absolon Wilkes

February 1863

The field outside the Carmichael mansion remained the drilling site for the Durham militia, though Royal kept them a good distance farther from the house than he did at the onset. Some of the older men were having trouble with the uneven terrain. Merrill Burns had just about fallen into step with the rest when he stepped into a hole large and deep enough to swallow his foot up to the ankle. The wet bottom made the experience all the worse.

"Why can't we march up there no more, Captain?" he asked as he kicked the mud off his boot. "It's flatter and drier."

"That's exactly why," Royal sternly replied. "We don't pick our battlefields. We have to be able to drill or fight anywhere. Now get back in line."

The men came to attention, loyally awaiting their next command. Royal looked past them to the mansion. Despite the increased distance, he could see Anne out in the garden.

As he watched, Anne walked slowly across the grass in front of the house carrying a bundle of wash. Knowing she was being watched, she deliberately moved slowly and seductively as she began hanging the laundry on the line. She bent at the waist to pick up a white undergarment and stretched far more than necessary to hang it on the line.

Royal watched her every move. Even from this distance he could tell she was not wearing the dense petticoat normally worn under her dress. The flimsy material clung to her figure and the sunlight shone through the skirt. As he stared, hypnotically drawn to the vision she gave so willingly, he seemed to be pulled closer. He saw her as if he was standing within a few yards of her. He looked at her as if she were all there was.

Burns cleared his throat. "Whenever you're ready, Captain."

Royal composed himself. "All right. Attention."

"We *been* at attention."

"Forward... *MARCH!*"

At his command, the column stepped out smartly and marched like a true and well drilled military unit. As he marched along beside them, he saw the men glancing to the side now and again. They couldn't seem to keep their eyes off of Anne's flaunting any more than he could. He began to wonder who was truly the intended target of her display.

They drilled until it was too dark to be effective. Some of the family men were just glad to go home to their loved ones. A good deal of the others sought to unwind at the saloon before turning in. Despite the common day spent, the crowd once in the tavern broke into diverse groups. Parnell sat with three of his friends at a table with their beers.

"I swear I can't stand to watch her much longer, he said in just greater than a whisper. "I'm just about to go up there and get me some."

Merrill Burns sat across from him. "I hear you wouldn't be the first."

"Oh really? You mean besides Pollard?"

Burns leaned over the table. "Let's just say she's been *very* loyal to the Confederacy."

Sam Gottwick was at the table, though less comfortable with the talk. "My wife told me if we keep drilling near her windows, I may have to drop out. She won't stand for it."

Billy didn't care for it at all, but he was only recently taken as an adult and wasn't sure if men were supposed to talk like this when in a saloon. He knew some always did and some rarely did. He mostly wanted to be included. "It's just talk though. Ain't it?"

"Talk comes from somewhere," Parnell replied.

Two tables away, Royal sat with his back to them pretending he couldn't hear the demise of Anne's reputation. He raised his head only enough to swallow another mouthful of whiskey.

16

February 1863

Victoria rode slowly through the tents and campfires. It was barely dawn and the troops were just rising though she had ridden all night to get here. Between the scratching and stretching and rubbing of sleepy eyes, few paid any attention to the rider. She did as always, scanning for a face, a tuft of hair, a voice calling, anything of Mason.

A sergeant finally stopped her. "You looking for something, Corporal?"

She pointed to her laden saddlebags. "Got mail for the men and a message for your commanding officer. That would be General Braxton Bragg?"

The sergeant nodded with close to a smile. "Officer's tent is over there. I'll take that mail off your hands if it's all right."

She tossed the saddlebags to him. "Sure. I'll pick those up on the way back."

"Mind if we fill them up again? We got families to write to."

"Put whatever you got ready in. I'll drop them off where I can."

"Much obliged." He watched with admiration as the courier helped them feel they had a life to return to. With a single letter or hope of a word reaching outside their division, she allowed them to touch the life they had left behind, possibly for the last time.

At the top of the hill, a broad tent with open sides covered a table and several chairs. Some of the officers were gathering here for their morning coffee. Among them, General Bragg quietly sipped coffee from a china cup. Victoria approached and dismounted.

As he casually returned her salute, she handed him a sealed envelope. "Dispatch from Major Partee, Sir."

General Bragg handed the unopened dispatch to his next in command. "We didn't expect anyone to get through for a while. My scouts told me the Yankees had all the roads blocked."

"They do, mostly. I stayed off the main roads, Sir. Moved at night and stayed in the woods. Due east isn't hard to find."

Bragg smiled. "Well done, then. These orders are sensitive. You did well to slip through."

Victoria did as always when she felt she'd stood long enough to be studied. She lowered her eyes beneath the brim of her hat, tucking her chin into the scarf around her neck, and saluted. "Thank you. I'll be heading back now, sir."

The captain that read the orders spoke to her. "Well have some coffee and see to your mount. You can swap him for a fresh horse if you like."

"No thanks Sir, respectfully. He's the main reason your post got through."

"Well at all costs, please wait while I prepare a response," Bragg insisted. "Do you think you could get through to Beauregard's camp?"

"I came from there. I can make it back."

"Excellent. Have some breakfast and then come see me. We'll have another mission for you and your big horse."

After as fine a breakfast as one could get at a camp site and a well earned rest and feed for Big Willy, she left again. With her she took the praise and admiration of all who knew what it took to get to them. The one thing she left without, again, was her husband. This was not his camp.

As the officers watched the courier disappear into the countryside, the captain wondered aloud.

"Think he'll make it, General?"

"We need supplies and reinforcements and Thomas knows it," Bragg replied with a note of sorrow. "Beauregard needs to know we can't cover his flank. I had no choice but to send him but they're waiting for him sure as rain. He'd have to be some sort of magician to slip through."

March 1863

With each passing week the discipline was strained as Royal pushed them harder. It was as if keeping them drilling would quiet their tongues and clear their minds off else but the war. But Anne became more blatantly defiant, allowing herself seen anytime they were out there and within sight. He kept them as far away as possible and suggested alternate sites, but he found himself migrating back to the field outside her house as it was his only chance to be close to her. Despite the conjectures, he continued to stay close and keep the men walking away. He led himself to constant torment but was trapped in the cycle.

One day, as they marched and changed direction again and again, he saw no sign of her anywhere. Was she away, he wondered, allowing the militia to zigzag closer to the house with each turn?

He was a mere fifty yards to the side of the house when he saw her. She sat in the upstairs window brushing her hair. She seemed to be unaware of the audience as she stroked her long hair and looked into the hand mirror. The dressing gown fell off her shoulder and Royal heard a muffled snicker behind him. Turning, half the division was focused on the beauty in the window.

"Eyes front!" he shouted with force.

"Yes sir," Parnell said over a laugh. "After you, Captain."

The bulk of the men laughed at his retort, challenging the discipline and Royal's integrity. They more walked than marched.

"To the right... March!" he shouted. The leaders turned sharply away from the house and the whole of the division followed, turning their heads away from the spectacle.

Parnell still snickered as he marched along. "Guess we should've seen that coming."

Despite the incident, Royal could not resist turning back for another glimpse. She saw him and lithely stood from the vanity seat. Walking away from the large window, she remained in his sight just long enough to let him see the gown fall from her shoulders and arms.

He saw just a glimpse of her figure as she vanished from the window. The vision stirred the desires in him that chivalry and friendship had held at bay for so long that he was weakened by the constant fight. Knowing how badly he wanted to see more of her wrought his guilt to a boil, leaving him with only a foul taste and a laden heart.

As every evening, Royal sat alone and drank quietly, despite the rousing party around him. Parnell had had a few too many and could not resist provoking Royal for the sport of it.

"What's the matter, Royal? All alone tonight?" His words slurred with the drink. Royal sipped his whiskey, deliberately ignoring him.

"Don't tell me she turned you down. Naa can't be. She hasn't said no to any man since that coward took off and left her. 'Specially the Blue-bellies. Maybe you need you a Yankee uniform, Royal. Bet then she'd come around and..."

Already seething with rage and anguish, the liquor lessened his restraint to the point where Parnell's sneering was more than he could stand. Royal leapt to his feet and grabbed Parnell by the throat. His bare hands closed around the man's neck and he felt himself squeeze.

"You sniveling drunken coward. You'll never talk about her like that again! D'ya hear me? Never!"

Royal was not intent upon truly hurting Parnell. In his rage and determination to stop the assault on Anne, to protect her, to end the pain he suffered with each uttering of her name, he wanted only to stop Parnell from talking. Just stop him. Now, with his grip tight around the man's throat, he feared if he let go, Parnell would start again. He couldn't let him start again. No more, he thought. No more!

Several of the men jumped to pull Royal off the struggling man but his grip was tempered with such rage and passion that it took the lot of them to finally pry his hands loose. As they pulled him away, Parnell fell to the floor in a heap.

Royal stared at the dead man in disbelief. The silenced onlookers stared at him. Slowly he backed away and out of the bar. Stunned, he felt his way along the wall and out into the street.

Overcome with emotion, Royal staggered past his horse and down the dark street, sobbing and covering his face with his hands. At the end of the street, he looked out into the night. He stared toward the stars and breathed deeply. How had his life abscome such a nightmare? He could endure no more. He could not even face what he had done this night. As he struggled to compose himself, praying he would awake from this horrible dream to a sane world, a hand fell onto his shoulder.

Sheriff Burrell Wilson stood behind him. His gun remained holstered and his grip was that of a friend rather than of an arresting officer.

"You need to come with me, Royal."

Royal started to mouth words, but none came out. Finally he nodded and turned to accept the sheriff's escort. As they walked slowly down the dark street toward the jailhouse, Royal was silent and staring blankly at the ground before him.

"I know what happened, Royal. I seen it coming, to be honest. It don't seem right but I have to uphold what law there is around here. I hope you understand."

Royal nodded, but did not reply.

Sheriff Wilson looked away from him and spoke in a soft, sympathetic tone. "You know, I keep looking down these back alleys. If you were to hit me and run off down any one of them, I don't reckon I'd have much chance of finding you until morning."

He chanced a glance out the corner of his eye. Royal gave no indication he was listening.

Burrell continued. "Of course, by then you'd likely be in the next county and wouldn't be back here so I wouldn't have any chance to lock you up. They wouldn't have a chance to hang you."

Royal looked up. The jail was getting closer but he made no attempt to escape.

"Damn it, Royal. Don't let this happen. I'm giving you the only chance I can."

Royal muttered, barely coherent, as he walked without looking up. "I... can't. I promised..."

"Promised who? Promised what? Who in God's name would want you to hang for them?"

Royal still had no answer. The weight of his burden had finally beaten him, for he accepted his fate as readily as he had made the promise.

The sheriff opened the door to the jailhouse. "Well you leave me no choice, then. Come on in and let me arrest you proper."

Royal sat in the small jail and stared out through the tiny window at the moonlight. His thoughts carried back to happier times. He recalled days of merriment with Absolon building his house and Anne pretending she didn't know which of them she cared for most.

The sun always seemed to be shining then. All his memories were sunny and bright and everyone he saw was wearing a broad smile. He remembered Anne walking around his house criticizing the Spartan decor. She told him how desperately he needed a woman's touch. He felt a twinge at words spoken but allowed her tease without response. She grinned broadest when she stood at the top of his stairs and dared him to dare her to peek into his bedroom. He refused and she brazenly opened the door and looked in anyway. He would never forget that smile she wore as she poked her head in his most private of sanctuaries. He came slowly up the curved staircase but refused to go onto the second floor until she promised to abandon her shameless teasing. She laughed with the naughtiness of it. Everyone in his memories seemed to be smiling. But when he looked into the mirror, his own face was nothing but pain and sorrow. Had it always been so? The moonlight shining through the tiny window had no hope of bringing any gladness to him this night. It was as if he was relieved to see it finally over.

By noon the following day, the whole town had heard of Parnell's death. The men had gathered in the saloon to plan their next move. Losing two men required a strategy and those few friends of Parnell were most agitated, stirring the crowd to a raucous, lynching mentality.

The sheriff tried to gain order by shouting but he became just another voice to shout over as the volume rose. A man next to him started ringing a school bell loudly and kept ringing even after he had the attention of everyone in the room. Finally he stopped and smiled at the sheriff.

Burrell returned his smile before addressing the group. "Now I know you're all concerned about what's happened in our town. But we ain't got a judge in town and the circuit judge won't be around for a few weeks. Nothing's going to happen until then."

Sam Gottwick was at the front of the group. "Well we're going to need a new captain for our militia at any rate." The crowd seemed to agree.

Charlie stood up and flexed his suspenders. "I'll take a crack at it."

"Now we got to vote on it," said another man.

"I nominate Sheriff Wilson!" said Sam.

The sheriff shook his head. "You know I ain't got time for it."

A man in the back was heard over the nominations. "I say first things first! What are we gonna do with that killer?"

With that, the crowd chimed in. Sheriff waved his arms to still the rising tumult. "Now I just told you. We aren't doing anything until the circuit judge gets here."

"There's a war on, Sheriff. We don't have time to do things the old way. Desperate times call for desperate measures."

As the sheriff held on to the law in the room, he saw Doctor Perciful push through the swinging doors of the tavern. Studying the crowd, the doctor made his way to the bar and the sheriff's side.

Charlie agreed. "Yeah! And there's an enemy out there hoping we won't be ready for him. We need to do something now!"

"I think that's a very good point," the doctor said in a loud, clear voice. "There is indeed a war on. We need to know who our friends are. And our enemies. Am I right, Gentlemen?"

Burrell looked down at him from his perch on the bar. "What are you going on about, Herman?"

"I had a chance to examine Parnell to be sure he was dead and I found something interesting. Anyone know where Parnell would come up with a double eagle?" He spoke loud and held up a twenty dollar gold coin for the room to see.

"Parnell ain't never seen that much money all at once in his life," Charlie said.

"Well I found it in his pocket alongside this," Doctor Perciful continued, holding up a folded piece of paper. Handing it to Burrell, he said, "Would you do the honors, Sheriff?"

The sheriff held the note at arm's length to adjust his eyes. Studying the paper, he spoke just loud enough for the room to hear.

"This has the names of our militia leaders. It shows how many we are and when the army comes around. It even says here that our only cannon is hid in Sam's barn.

Amid the instant widespread murmuring around the room, Sam was most quickly outspoken. "What the...? If the Yankees got a hold of that, they'd burn me out for sure!"

"All of us, most likely," another agreed. "Hey Sheriff. Are you saying Parnell was a spy?"

"Looks that way," Burrell said, still studying the note.

"If he'd given that to the Yankees, we'd all be good as dead," the doctor added. "Looks to me we got us a hero locked up in our jail."

Burrell looked at Sam. "Well, Sam. Still think we need to do something right now?"

Sam nodded. "I do, Sheriff."

It was less than an hour of assurances and agreements later that Royal was reapplying his personal effects at the jailhouse. Burrell sat behind his desk with a smile of satisfaction while Herman Perciful sat on the edge of the desk.

"Well how's it feel to be a free man?" Burrell asked.

Royal was less than enthusiastic. "Not sure. Hard to believe, really. I was just coming to terms with the thought of that noose."

Burrell was relaxed and composed as he rolled a cigarette. "Could've happened, Royal, just as easy as not. Mind if I ask why you didn't run?"

"I made a promise to a friend. I had to stay."

This brought Doctor Perciful to sit erect. "Even if it got you killed?"

"I'm bound to stay. Let's leave it at that."

The sheriff got out of his chair as Royal buttoned his coat. "Well I'm glad it didn't come to a lynching. How bout I buy you a drink?"

"No thanks," Royal replied. "I think I need to stay out of town for a while. There's a lot to forget." With an unemotional nod of appreciation to both his loyal friends, he left them.

The doctor exhaled in relief. "Well thank God it worked out. Royal is like family to me."

"Yeah. Thank God is right. It's kind of a miracle when you think about it."

"What? That I found the note or that they let Royal go?"

The sheriff fell back into his chair and lit a freshly rolled cigarette. "That there even was a note. I happen to know that Parnell couldn't read or write a lick."

Doctor Perciful turned back to look the sheriff coldly in the eye. There was no surprise in his tone as he calmly replied, "You don't say?"

17

Victoria sat alone and watched the flickering campfire. The absolute darkness of the summer night left her little else to look at and sleep hadn't come to her just yet. She had selected a spot well off the traveled roads and in the base of a dry creek bed to make her camp. It was less likely to be chanced upon and the fire was not easily seen from a distance. Here and in the privacy of her natural surroundings, she took her boots off and dared sit in semi-feminine position. The slightly oversized boots lent to her masculine disguise but were padded to keep her in the saddle. This made them hot in the warm summer days and a pleasure to kick off in the cool evening. She held her bare foot up and pulled the pant leg down to expose her muscular calf. Posing her foot in a dainty, pointed toe position, she recalled Virgil Porter's words. "Pretty as a picture book lady" he said of her. So rarely afforded the femininities of society, she could at least stop reminding herself to talk low and avoid eye contact. At these times, she enjoyed being a woman, if not a lady.

Stretching at full length, Victoria allowed the white shirt to reveal the shape of her breasts. She spent much of her time bound around her chest. Though not as buxom as some women, her breasts had never endured breast feeding a child or the depletion of childbirth. They stood well supported from her toned frame and with distinctive form that was visible even through the thermal underwear and heavy double breasted blouse. When in uniform, she bound them close to her ribs with a long sash of sheer cotton gauze. This gave her the appearance of a young man in good physical condition. No more.

As she sat on the ground, contemplating her situation, she reflected on times long since forgotten. She looked about the clearing and recalled a room about the same size. It was the very room her mother led them into years earlier.

"Tell me you're joking, Myron," Davila Jacobs said as she looked around the lobby of the hotel in Bentonville.

Myron followed her in, closely followed by the well dressed teenage girl and boy. "Now don't jump to any conclusions, Davila. Let's look around a bit."

"Look at what? This is clearly beneath human standards."

The girl looked about as she held her younger brother's hand tightly. "It isn't bad, Mother. Where will we sleep?"

"Isn't bad? Did you see anyone tend to our luggage? And I have no doubt the food is inedible."

"What do you say we go find out?" Myron said, smiling at his children. "Who's ready for supper?"

"I am!" shouted young Daniel.

Davila Jacobs seemed afraid to touch anything as she peered about in disgust. "Eat? Myron, be reasonable. We just can't stay here."

"We can and we will. Just give it a chance."

"I'm not concerned for myself. I'm thinking of the children. How is Victoria expected to learn etiquette in this wild west ... ho down? What of her ballet?" She scanned the lobby and caught sight of the hotel clerk staring blankly at her. She offered no apology.

"I like it, Mother," Victoria maintained with a smile.

"And we're south, not west," Myron added. "Now I'll get the bags up to the rooms and meet you in there. Go on in and order a plate for me."

Davila looked at Victoria. "Darling. Don't worry about adjusting to this rural environment. We'll be back in the civilized world soon and, with any luck, you'll never be subjected to these atrocious conditions again."

As Davila held a lace handkerchief to her mouth and looked around for a tolerable place to sit, Victoria viewed the room and surroundings in amazement. They truly seemed inviting to her and she wanted so much for her mother to see what she saw. As the memory of her mother's words faded, so too did her memory of the rustic hotel lobby. She tried to recall it but all she saw was the wooded clearing and the absolute absence of even those luxuries her mother deemed below human standards.

What she wouldn't give to sit in a chair or lie in a bed. Just one night, she thought, of the life she left behind. She tried to remember the times when things were better. It seemed like a lifetime ago. Mason working and smiling and letting her know how much she was loved. He had a way of showering her in love with the most subtle of acts. It was in his absolute devotion to her that he made it felt. He never missed an opportunity. All wildflowers belonged to her. She sat first always and her opinion ruled unless it would hurt her now or ever. She took none of his love for granted and missed it so badly. When he left, the meaning of her existence went with him. Neither of them could have realized how much they needed each other. True soul mates parted and the tragedy ached.

Two Union soldiers crept stealthily toward the campfire. They had spotted the glow from the trail and smelled the food and coffee. As they drew cautiously closer, they saw it was a lone camp. One or two men at best, they thought.

From the cover of brush and darkness, they watched for several minutes. The fire burned but no one came near. At the edge of the small clearing, they saw the head and outline of a tall brown horse. Someone had to be near and the only smart move was to wait and watch. But the aroma of the beans and meat cooking was still in the air, wafting from the unwashed cookware. Burl and Lou were the only remaining members of the five deserters that had been hiding out for so many weeks. They were hungry and they chanced an incursion into the open.

The heavy set, unshaven Burl ventured out first. Pistol in his hand, the grizzled corporal stood in the clearing and looked cautiously around. Sensing no one, he gestured to the brush and a tall, slender private came out. They both looked around, wary of dropping their guard as they moved toward the fire.

The heavy set man looked at the horse, then at the saddle and saddlebags on the ground. He turned to his friend.

"Looks like just one, Lou. He's Army."

"Theirs or ours?" the other asked in just above a whisper.

He looked around and saw the gray jacket hung from a tree branch. "He's a Reb."

The tall, slim man looked at the tin pan near the fire. "Well he's a

Reb what just ate, Burl. Looks like he left some for us."

They both moved toward the food. As they bent to taste it, they heard the distinctive click of a hammer being pulled back. Wiley as they were, they knew to freeze.

"Ain't no need for that, Reb," the corporal said from a half bent position. "You got us."

Victoria stepped out of the bushes with a rifle trained on them. She had her hat on but now missed her jacket. The white shirt hung loose enough on her to conceal her bosom, but her thin neck and jaw line were exposed. "Drop the guns near the fire and step back," she said softly, rasping her voice for fear of sounding feminine. "Let me see your hands."

They instantly complied, dropping two pistols and a rifle on the ground. Both men put their hands on their heads as they slowly turned to face their captor. She stayed well back, head lowered and chin pushed into her drawn collar. She gestured with the barrel of the rifle and they moved away from the guns.

"Sit," she ordered.

"Yessir," the skinny private said. "Don't get trigger happy or nothing."

"We surrender," said the corporal as he lowered himself to the ground. "You got a couple of deserters here."

"Uh huh," she said in little more than a grunt. "Just get your butts down. Stretch out right there."

"Okay. Just relax, Reb. You got us prisoner, sure as anything."

Victoria sidestepped toward the guns. Squatting toward them, she tossed the pistols toward her horse. "Sorry, Yanks. You're going to have to move along. I'm not taking prisoners."

Burl looked at her. "That a fact?"

"Now belly down in the dirt," she ordered.

Lou immediately started over, but the older, more cynical corporal remained upright. "Not taking prisoners, eh?"

"Face down." She sensed she was losing the tone of authority. Fearing he would hear more than doubt in her voice, she tried to impress him with a move. She stood upright and stepped toward him. "Do it now!"

Lou was lying down with his hands on the back of his head. "Better do it."

Burl still sat defiantly upright. "Just seems funny. You knew you weren't taking prisoners, you knew we were Yankees, but you didn't shoot. Now I'm a wondering why?"

A shock surged through her with the realization that he was about to call her bluff. Until this second, she didn't know she was bluffing. She had to try again to regain control.

"You can wonder while you and your friend are lying down. I want to see your hands behind your back. Do it now!"

"Burl," breathed the thin man. "Do what he says."

There were many reasons a man might turn to desertion in wartime. Lou was a coward, plain and simple. He was afraid of being killed. But Lou was no coward. He had a problem with authorative figures, taking orders or doing anything that he didn't directly benefit from. No soldier could prosper from such initiatives and he found it difficult to let go. It was easier to go where he could decide for himself what was best for him. He preferred to examine his options, consider the possible outcomes and do what seemed the most prosperous or least hazardous at the time. Now he studied her. He looked at her hands. She had not had the chance to put her gloves on. Even though she held the rifle with a firm grip, her fingers were thin and delicate. He noticed the narrow shoulders then her overall look seemed to line up with the voice. She saw him smile confidently with the chilling realization.

"Seems like we got us a situation," he sneered. "I'm thinking you ain't quite the soldier you want us to think you are."

Lou, taking notice of the fact that his friend's defiance had gone unchecked, dared to look up.

"And I'm thinking if you planned on shooting anybody you'd have done it by now." As his friend watched, he started to slowly stand. "Any other secrets you'd like to share with us?"

Lou sat up and looked as his friend moved. "Easy, Burl. We already surrendered to him."

Victoria had the rifle trained on him and was trying her best to remember what she was supposed to do next. The fear in her eyes strengthened his conviction as the ominous looking ogre of a man moved toward her.

"Let me tell you something about men, Missy. Even colored men don't usually pull a gun unless they plan to use it."

"Missy?" the Lou echoed, now coming to his feet. He looked at her and saw what his cohort had already spotted. Victoria took her first step backward.

"You ain't got it in you," Burl grinned as he closed the distance on her. "I'm thinking I'm gonna be real glad I surrendered."

"You sure she won't shoot?" the thin man asked, following Burl closer to her.

Burl nodded with a sinister grin. "Oh I'm sure."

Lou smiled a virtually toothless grin. "That's real good. I ain't seen a woman in a good long time."

"Now just take your pretty little finger off that trigger, Missy. We're all going to get along just fine."

Victoria took another step back, still holding the rifle trained on him. She suddenly realized that the rifle they had dropped was now between them. She saw him realize the same thing and knew her time was over. He was about to bring to her a terror beyond what she had prepared herself for. This was not war. These men were not soldiers or the enemy. She was not going to be stopped. Not by them. Not now. Not after so many weeks and months without Mason. Mason. What would he say of her? Would she even be allowed to find out? These cowards intended to steal the rest of her life from her and from Mason and for that, she squeezed the trigger. Not to kill him, but to keep her hopes alive another day.

The corporal doubled over and fell, thrashing in agony to the ground. Lou watched him in shock. Then he looked at her. Victoria did her best to study him in the instant allowed. Did he know whether or not she had a pistol? Did he realize the rifle was a breach loader and now spent? Would he run or attack?

His thoughts went around the same cycle. Then he did as the situation called for. An unarmed woman was before him. She was stunned and afraid and he lunged toward her. She tried to pull away but he grabbed her and pulled the rifle from her grip.

She never took her eyes off him as he tossed the rifle to the side, his left hand tightly clutching her arm. She saw the shock in his widened eyes as her knife plunged into his ribs. She was deathly cold as he fell back away from her.

He tried to turn and run, clutching his bleeding chest. He fell into a tree and found the pain and shock so draining that he could not push away from the tree before the bullet from her pistol struck him in the back. He fell into the brush and died.

Victoria knelt on the ground holding the smoldering pistol in one hand and her knife in the other. As she watched the two men fall silent and still, she was overwhelmed with the realization of how surreal her life had become. Slowly, stunned and in shock, she came to her feet. She struggled to remember why she had come. Why was she not in her home? Why was she alone in the woods, hundreds of miles from home, dressed like a man and surrounded by dead men?

She dropped the weapons to the ground and started weeping uncontrollably. "Oh my God. Mason. Where are you? I can't do this." She looked up into the summer stars and felt the tears stream down her face. She wanted only to go back, to give up. She wanted her life back. But in her life, there was a man. It was there that she found her motivation. In her conceding to the torture of her quest, she found the only path that remained before her. She wanted now what she wanted from the onset. She needed Mason. In the acceptance of her inability to go through life, this or any other, without him, Victoria surrendered to her fate.

The Confederate camp readied to move. As the men broke down tents and dowsed fires, a soldier walked through the camp calling names and handing out letters.

"Caldwell!" he shouted, reading from the letter on top.

"Over here, O'Donnell," Caldwell shouted excitedly. He ran over to grab the letter from O'Donnell's hand. "This is from my dad. They said we were cut off. How'd you get this?"

"That fella they call the Magician brought a batch of mail. Nobody knows how he keeps getting through. Yanks can't seem to touch him."

Caldwell opened his letter. "The man is possessed or something. I don't honestly care if'n he sold his soul to the devil. Long as he keeps doing it."

"I think he just loves what he does. A man'd have to love something to be that good at it. Hey. You know a soldier named Corbel? Mason Corbel?"

North of the camp, the lone rider slowly drudged along the darkening trail. The skyline showed rain approaching, but Victoria kept moving forward.

18

April 20, 1863
Fredericksburg

The rain fell as it did in Virginia. Serious and heavy. It rained as though it meant to stop something. This was the spring rains as Virginians knew them. But the torrential downpour failed to dampen the mood of one animated man waiting impatiently at a small railroad station twelve miles south of Fredericksburg. He had seen harder rains. He had seen tougher conditions. The stone-faced man nervously flapped his arms against his lean frame and paced like a caged cat as the train pulled into the Guinea Station because he knew it carried a very precious cargo. This was a cargo he had not seen in months and the cargo carried something he had never before set eyes on.

General Thomas Jonathan "Stonewall" Jackson did not wait for the locomotive to stop. It was still grinding to a halt as he vaulted onto the first car and excitedly scanned the occupants. The civilians stared back at the grim looking, bearded soldier. None looked familiar and he hurried to the next car. By now they were starting to stand as the train was nearly at full stop. As he quickly took census, he heard a man behind the standing passengers speak.

"Can I help you, Ma'am?"

"No thank you," replied a woman's voice. "I can manage."

It was her and he politely forced his way between the others to come to the side of his beloved wife. Without a word, he looked at her and let his usually stern face crack into a nervous smile. Then he looked down to the tiny bundle in her arms. It was the first time he had seen his infant daughter.

General Jackson was a fighting man of legendary prowess and the war needed him. Lee needed him. The Confederacy needed him on the battlefield. But they would wait. For the next nine days he and his young family enjoyed a domestic bliss that would last his wife a lifetime. It would have to. Three weeks later General Stonewall Jackson would be dead.

April 23, 1863
Tennessee Hills

Absolon hunkered next to Window in the shrubs a safe distance from a small farmhouse. Smoke billowed from the stack and chickens pecked the ground near the front door. This was clearly a poor but working farm. They hesitated because the farmer was nowhere to be seen.

From behind them, Dooley whispered as loud as he could. "What do you see?"

"How many of them are there?" George chimed in.

Absolon waved at them to keep quiet as he and Window scanned the surroundings for a head count. So far the only person they had seen was the heavy set old woman who had gone into the house twenty minutes ago. They were wary of approaching to find a group of defensive farmhands, sons or anyone who might take exception to Yankees. Deep in these hills, too far from anything remotely resembling law, people learned to protect themselves without hesitation. Horse thieves, chicken thieves and wandering minstrels had been known to meet their maker for simply coming into a campsite unannounced. This house was worth protecting and likely had been up until now.

The seven soldiers could surely take the farm by force but that would make them no better than the rabble they shunned whenever confronted. They had become selective in the men who joined them. No pillagers, deserters, cowards or trouble-makers found welcome with these guerillas. They could take the farm, but not if it meant murdering innocent farmers.

"You got any ideas, Window?" Absolon asked.

Window had been watching the door and windows of the farmhouse for nearly an hour now. "I think she's the only one in there. Don't mean no one's comin' and don't mean we should rob her."

"But a couple of those chickens would sure go down good."

"She got a smoke house on the side, too. Bet she got her some bacon or jerky in there."

"So what do we do?"

"We could try to sneak it and maybe get shot. We could just charge down there and maybe get shot."

"We could trade for some food."

Window turned to Absolon. "What we got a farm woman needs?"

Inside the farm house, the weathered old woman tested the pot to see how her stew was coming. The roadmap of a hard life shown in the wrinkles of her leathery face. Juanita Pickering walked with the hunched over posture and hay-colored bird's nest hair of a woman in her sixties. But that was her life. In actual years, she was less than forty and her age meant far less to her than the fact that her stew was nearly ready.

From outside, she heard a man call out.

"Hello in the house! We're friends."

Juanita peeked out the window to see four men standing outside. They stood in plain sight with their hands held out and open to show they had no weapons. Two of them wore blue trousers but none wore complete uniforms. Window stood behind Absolon, Dooley and George and quietly watched.

They tried to keep the forced smiles on their faces as they awaited the response. Dooley's smile was ridiculously fake looking but he held it nonetheless and whispered though it. "What if she don't believe us?"

"What if she ain't alone in there?" George added.

"Don't worry," Absolon reassured them. "Just stick to the plan and let me do the talking."

"I hate this plan," Window hissed from behind them.

The other three hid in the bushes to watch their backs should the suspected farmhands return. They also felt the fewer numbers would be less intimidating to the lone woman.

As they stood in plain sight grinning and waiting, the door finally creaked open and Juanita stepped onto the porch. As they anticipated, she was brandishing a shotgun and nothing close to a smile.

"What you want?" she barked.

Absolon took a cautious step toward her. "We don't mean no harm,

Ma'am. We're just hungry. Wondered if you could help us out."

"Got nothin' to spare. Off with ya." There was no doubt in her tone.

"We ain't askin' for much, Ma'am," he continued. "And we're willing to pay for it." He used the comfortable southern accent he'd spent most of his life among the aristocrats trying to hide. This woman of the Old South would surely be less likely to shoot a fellow Confederate, he hoped.

"Got no need for money. No place to spend it around here."

"You work this farm yourself, if you don't mind my askin'?"

Juanita squinted ominously at him. "I do, and don't go getting any funny ideas. Last fella ain't here no more 'cause I shot him dead, right about where you're standin'. I may be a woman, but I'll shoot you quick as I did him. Count on it."

"We do. We will. I was just thinking about a fair trade. You got something we need and maybe we got something you need."

"You got nothing I need, young feller."

"What about help around the farm? Wouldn't you find use of a farm hand?"

"You mean you?"

"No Ma'am. We got this here nigger and we don't need him." They parted and Window reluctantly stepped forth. "He's a good worker but we lost our place to the Yankees. Got nothing for him to pick."

Juanita finally lowered her shotgun and leaned on it like a walking stick as she studied the offer. "What makes you think I need a slave?"

"He could do things around here for you. Tend to the chickens and pigs, work that there garden, fix your roof. Lots of things. He's smart, too. Ain't you, Boy?" He poked Window to respond.

Window tilted his head to make sure only Absolon saw the sneer as he allowed an answer. "Yessah."

Juanita cocked her head and studied Window a bit closer. "He looked older before. Bring him a bit closer. Just you. The smartass. Rest of you stay back."

George and Dooley stayed back and silent as Absolon walked his offering closer. She looked him up and down. "I have to admit I could do with some help. Army took all the able-bodied men. Killed most of them. What do you want for him?"

"Just a couple of those chickens, some fatback and some coffee."

"That cornbread I smell?" Dooley blurted.

She looked up at him with surprise. "You must be hungry. I took that bread out of the oven hours ago. Was gonna have it with my stew."

"We are for true, Ma'am," Dooley finished, clutching his hat in his hands in a humble manner.

Juanita studied the men, then their offering. "Will he do what he's told?"

"I guarantee you Ma'am, you won't never tell him nothing twice," Absolon assured her, allowing the first smile of the confrontation to cross his face.

A short while later the three were walking away from the farm with four dead chickens, a poke of staples and a slice of cornbread. Juanita stood on the porch and watched them until they were well away. Not once did they look back or say goodbye to a scowling Window. He stood next to her and obediently watched his comrades abandon him.

"Well, Boy," she turned to him. "Come on in and let's see if you're worth it." She gave him a subtle wave as she went inside the house.

Window followed without enthusiasm. He entered the front room of the farmhouse and looked around. "What you want me to do?"

Juanita stepped up to him and looked at his teeth like a horse on the block. She patted his shoulders and poked his chest, seemingly satisfied with the healthy young buck. Window was assuming she was assessing his physical ability to work right up until she grabbed the front of his trousers and shoved her hand straight down the front. His eyes turned big as saucers as she took a firm grasp of his manhood and harrumphed.

"You'll do," she said in her gravely, farm voice. As she turned away and walked toward the bedroom doorway, "Supper can wait a bit. Come on in here, Boy. Let's pay the rent." She swung the creaky wooden door open and looked at the unmade bed without shame. Juanita turned back as she ordered Window, "Get shed of those britches, Boy. I got..." She looked back at an empty room. The front door was still closed but the side window was open enough for the agile young soldier to make a hasty escape.

"Damn it!" she growled. She scooped up the shotgun as she ran out the front door.

Window was sprinting down the path with fleetness born of a fear hitherto unknown to the veteran soldier. As he turned the first bend away from the house, he slowed to a walk and gasped for air. Glancing back, he saw her coming. The shotgun in one hand, he did not see the anticipated crotchety stagger of an old woman but a healthy sprint more than fast enough to match his own. Juanita was clearly not one to be trifled with and less to be easily outdistanced afoot.

"Dayum!" he gulped and took off at a high gate. It was a footrace as unexpected as it was bizarre. The heavy woman was shockingly fleet and determined and the swift young man gave his all to escaping her. She ran of anger and will while he was propelled by fear and shock.

As she looked ahead with the same natural determination that had kept her alive while the war and destitution claimed all others within miles of her, she could see the distance between her and her quarry narrowing. She would not be lost. He made his way around the next bend but she knew the trails and would get him soon.

She turned the corner and came to a halt in the face of six guns aimed at her. Window stood behind his friends gasping for air, drained from exhaustion and amazement.

"Sorry, Ma'am," Absolon said to her in a tone absent of hostility or malice. "You weren't supposed to catch him."

She was anything but afraid, though she knew she'd been trumped. Looking down her nose at the guns, she spat on the ground. "Mighta known you was Yankees."

Window managed to stand upright and point an accusing finger at her. "That woman ain't right!" At that she made a threatening half-step at him without raising the gun and he ducked behind Absolon. "Watch her!"

"We'll be havin' our supper now," George said. "You should be moving along."

She scowled at them and finally turned to walk away.

"G'night, Ma'am," Dooley called. "And God bless."

Absolon watched her disappear around the bend. Then he turned to

Window. "What was she having you do that was so terrible?"

"Seems like anything would be worth some of her cornbread," Dooley added.

"Yeah," Absolon continued. "You could've had a nice night's sleep in a nice warm bed."

At that, Window pointed a warning finger in his face. "Nothing... is worth that. Nothing."

Juanita came back to the house, so angry and dejected that she failed to notice the riders that came up to within twenty feet of her. She slowly raised her eyes to see three uniformed Confederate soldiers.

"What the hell do you want?"

The soldier in the middle spoke. "No harm, Ma'am. We were just hoping to water our horses and maybe get a taste of whatever we smell cooking in there."

"And that's all, I suppose."

The soldier on the right spoke in a strong Georgia accent. "Well Ma'am. If you're a'feared we might take advantage of you, I can assure you you're safe."

The third man finally broke into laughter. "I can pert near guarantee it!"

The three had a laugh at her expense before composing themselves. The middle one spoke again, doing a poor job of repressing his grin. "Sorry Ma'am. But you ain't exactly... I mean you don't look like a ... Well let's say you've got a rustic charm about you that should keep you safe."

Juanita stood silent while they had a giggle. Then she found a bit of a smile, herself. "Tell you what. You fellas willing to earn your vittles?"

The man in the middle looked at her suspiciously. "Maybe we are. What you got in mind?"

"My slave done run off. He just got away from me down that trail there. You boys run off and bring him back and I'll have beef stew and cornbread waiting for you."

The men perked up. "Warm stew and bread? Lady you got yourself a deal!"

"Which way did he go?" the one on the left anxiously demanded.

"Straight down there just five minutes ago. Hurry up now."

The three men howled with delight and spurred their horses. They galloped away and out of sight, whooping and calling out to the runaway slave and everything short of keeping quiet. They would surely be heard approaching.

Juanita watched the trail for a moment then shook her head and walked into the house. As she crossed the threshold, she heard several shots ring out from the woods. The shots came from the direction she had last seen the Yankees.

"That's a bet I can't lose," she muttered as she went inside to finally taste that stew.

The Carmichael Mansion was quiet and darker than the encroaching night, save a single candlelit corner of a bedroom. Anne sat alone in her bedchambers and quilled a letter to Absolon.

My Dearest Absolon,

So many things have changed here. Your trusted friend Royal is only now safe from the wrongful accusation of killing a man. He was acting, I dearly regret, in defense of my honor. To this, I must tell you many things and you must know how this pains me. The honor Royal defends is no more. I have fallen, more than once from grace and in my desperate hour I sought the hollow comfort of others. Royal naturally remained loyal to your friendship and a gentleman but few men have such integrity. He defends me for you and I must now tell you that it is no longer needed. As I am not the lady you proposed to and no longer deserve you or your dear friend at my side, I do solemnly release you from your vows. Please accept this word and allow me my solitude and solace.

As ever, I pray this letter finds you well. May God spare you in his mercy.
Anne Carmichael

She dropped her head to sob as the candle flickered out.

It was late in the evening as Royal opened the front door of the Carmichael Mansion to find a dead Union soldier at the foot of the stairs. Stepping over the body, he cautiously climbed the stairs and pushed open the door to Anne's bedroom. A man clad in a blue uniform lay dead against the door. Pushing him clear, Royal stepped into the room. Several dead soldiers lay strewn about the floor and Anne stood in the middle of them looking at him. The moonlight from the window shown indiscreetly through the sheer white fabric of her dressing gown. Royal could see all but the detail of her delicate figure.

She seemed strangely calm. "Thank God you came." She opened her arms to him and Royal moved slowly toward her. The soldier at her feet suddenly grabbed his pant leg and gripped him tightly. Royal pulled against the dying man's grasp, looking down into the blood drenched face of Absolon. Absolon looked up at him in anguish, his eyes pleading though he said nothing. As Royal watched in horror, his friend closed his eyes and died. His grip on Royal was released.

Anne still stood with open arms waiting for Royal. He stepped over his friend's dead body to take her in his arms. Feeling her softness against him he fell with her to the bed in a lover's embrace and he kissed her lips and face passionately. Opening his eyes, he stroked her hair and found his hand dripping with blood. He tried to wipe it from her head and it only grew.

He pulled back to see that Anne was covered in blood, her hair matted to her scalp as she lay on the blood drenched sheets. She didn't seem to notice or mind and pulled him back to her. With a smile, she pulled his lips toward her blood covered face.

Royal sat up in his own bed and gasped in the darkness. Sweat dripped from his tortured brow as he looked around his bedroom. It was only a dream. Just another nightmare, he told himself. Dropping his head into his hands, he wept silently.

April 28, 1863
Rappahannock River North of Fredericksburg

Fighting Joe Hooker's Eleventh Corps had been crossing the river for a day and would for two more before the forty thousand infantrymen had splashed to the other side. More would come later, but the plan was coming together.

"This is the plan, Joe?" queried one of his commanders. "You know we've already been spotted." Major General Daniel Sickles was one of Hooker's most trusted officers despite being even more controversial than Hooker himself. The flamboyant Sickles drew all manner of attention to himself by his reputation for drinking and womanizing as well as prowess and courage on the battlefield. Hooker absorbed the victories and let Sickles draw negative attention away from him. It worked to some degree though few knowing them both would dare guess whose elbow bent the most.

"Only what they could see, Daniel," Hooker smugly responded. "They didn't see the cavalry but they don't know they're on their way to Richmond to cut off Lee's communications."

"That magician?"

"Those magicians. We need to cut them off for sure. And they haven't spotted Sedgewick's corps yet. He won't cross until we're ready."

"And what if they're ready for us?"

"That's the beauty of it. They think they are. Their complacency shall be their undoing. They have no idea how vulnerable their flank is." Hooker took a long swallow from a silver flask. "My plans are perfect. And when I start to carry them out may God have mercy on General Lee, for I will have none."

Sickles smiled at the quote-worthy statement. "The newspapers aren't here, Joe."

"Translation, Major? I'm going to whip Bobby Lee's Confederate ass and there isn't a damn thing he can do about it."

Sickles chuckled with the brazen quip. "Now that's one I can get on board with."

Hooker knew that he had the advantage of superior numbers. Lieutenant James Longstreet, a formidable Confederate commander, had taken two strong divisions with him in to gather food and supplies from the southeast. Lee wouldn't launch a major offensive until Longstreet returned and Hooker meant to hit him while he waited.

Major General John Sedgewick erected pontoons and his full force crossed the river in a fraction of the time it took Hooker. Now both wings were on Lee's side. Hooker's plan was coming together. He moved calmly forth, enjoying the imaged sight of Lee's fear of the overwhelming numbers coming down upon him. "Oh how he will run," Hooker thought. "Like Bull Run never was, I'll run them." To date, he had told no one that he was among those leading the panicked retreat at the first Bull Run but he carried that disgrace with him always. Payback was due and now eminent.

"They've got us outnumbered at least two to one," General Jubal Early told Lee.

"I can read, Jubal. I'd hoped to sit for a while but looks like they've got other plans."

"We can outrun them. They have no cavalry that we saw."

"Well that would certainly be the right thing to do," Lee said in an almost joking tone. He studied the maps and notes about the terrain Hooker was crossing. "It would surely be the safe thing to do. But then..."

General Early found himself and ten thousand troops digging in at the Old Fredericksburg entrenchments to meet Hooker head on. Lee was anything but afraid of Fighting Joe.

It was mid-afternoon when Hooker's fifty thousand men and artillery met at a junction in the roads. All around them was dense wilderness but here at the intersection of Ely's Ford and the Orange turnpike stood a large brick tavern named Chancellorsville. It was a perfect headquarters for Hookers perfect plan.

"This is splendid," exulted one of his commanders. "Hurrah for Old Joe!"

The cheer was echoed and they settled in. They had scarcely hung their hats when the eager commanders began to get anxious about Lee's position and vulnerability. They had encountered no opposition yet and knew it was ahead.

"We need to move out, Joe," Major General Couch demanded. "Press east and get clear of this God forsaken brush."

Joe seemed a bit too at ease. He sat in a comfy chair and put his feet up. "No need to rush, Major," he said as he signaled his aid to bring the bottle. "We can wait for the rest of the Eleventh and hit Bobby Lee full force, assuming he doesn't turn tail and run or surrender straight away."

"Lee isn't likely to surrender."

"But he'll surely run. The man knows when he's outnumbered and outmaneuvered."

None of the officers in the room could put on a brave face to this. Even Sickles, usually happy to sit back and share a drink with his commander, was taken aback by the orders. "We've got momentum here, Joe. We can't just stop. Just give it up."

"We have stopped, Gentlemen," Hooker said in a calming tone. "Relax. This is all part of the plan."

Two divisions of Confederate infantry held a prominent position on a ridge covering the Plank Road and Turnpike. Majors Anderson and McLaws and their troops were camped at the Zoan Church and well dug in when Stonewall Jackson arrived. He had been advancing since 3:00am and was not about to stop or waste the advantage of surprise. He ordered the Majors to drop their shovels and fall in with his troops. The now greater force pushed on through the dense wilderness. Most of the winding trails they trotted relentlessly along were too narrow for three men abreast.

It was late morning when Hooker stretched his well rested muscles and ordered A.P. Hill's division to advance up the river road and clear out the rebels. He sent another division toward the Turnpike. Then he ordered breakfast. It was not long before he received word that the second detachment was hit hard by a surprise attack from Jackson.

Finally the fight had come to them and the officers in the makeshift command post readied for battle. Maps and plans began to roll for too brief a time. They stood back and could do little other than fume as Hooker sent orders for the engaged troops to fall back and take a defensive stand in the dense brush. Hill had marched almost to Bank's ford without seeing a soul. The advantage they had slept with was gone.

Fighting Joe ordered the returned and greatly annoyed Hill and the rest of the infantry to dig in around Chancellorsville and wait. Major Couch again was on his hip when Hooker outlined this new strategy of waiting.

"Joe," he started. Then he took a cleansing breath and added a note of military respect, hoping it would ignite some fight in his commander. "General. I must protest to this defensive strategy. We're on our heels before the first round. We need to go out and hit them before they pick off another division. We need to regain the momentum here."

"It's all right, Couch," Hooker reassured him. "I've got Lee right where I want him. This way he has to fight me on my own ground." He smiled and lit his cigar as Couch reeled.

Unable to believe his ears, Couch stormed out of the room. He knew his place as a subordinate officer but his next words would surely be mutinous. He had lost all faith in Hooker. He managed to bite his tongue until he was at least thirty feet from the door and behind a broad tree. Only then did he growl out loud, "You blithering idiot!" He butted his head against the tree in hopes that the bark would absorb some of his pent up frustration. As he gently tapped his forehead against the tree, he mumbled, "You disgrace to the uniform. We're all going to die. You moron. You coward. You imbecile."

As the Federals dug in at Chancellorsville, Lee and Jackson were a short distance away lining the Plank road. Their scouts had given them the news about the Union entrenchments and it seemed a frontal assault was not feasible. The great military minds turned over some empty Federal cracker boxes and thought. With the enemy dug in "Tighter than a tick on a dog's back", they would have to either draw them out or wait. This was tempting as Longstreet would eventually return with supplies and reinforcements. Some among them still pressed for slipping out to the south while Hooker's trap had stalled. Lee knew there was a way to bring Hooker down.

It was late that evening when Cavalry leader Jeb Stuart rode in with an exciting intelligence report.

"Their right is in the air," Jeb announced excitedly as he leapt from his mount.

"Are you sure?" Lee asked.

"We can hit them. I know we can."

The term 'in the air' meant they sat in a position with no natural or artificial obstacles. Their right flank was, for the moment, exposed and vulnerable. They had a shot and had to take it.

On May second, Hooker's forces finally exposed themselves to a greatly diminished Confederate front. Reconnaissance told him it was indeed Lee he faced, but he was told that the rebels had been slipping out in waves and retreating. This was what Hooker had expected. He did not expect the remaining force to fight him head on. As he commanded from Chancellorsville, he was stunned by reports that the brash rebels, outnumbered better than three to one, were not running and were actually daring Hookers regiments to advance on them. Less than fourteen thousand rebels defended the Confederate front and Hooker sent orders laced with caution and hesitation.

"They'll run," he muttered. "They better run." He showed his hand as the eleventh Union corps emerged from the thick brush and showed their strength. Hooker waited for the news of Lee's terrified retreat from the overwhelming might of his adversary. No such word was carried. He was instead told of how the rebels were holding their own and refusing to budge. Hooker tried to console his staff by stating they had no choice left and the day would soon be theirs.

His officers again reminded him that if they had pushed harder before Lee had a chance to dig in, the fight would be over. His men were out there dying for his brashness and overconfidence.

The open fighting was going comfortably according to plan, though Lee's vastly outgunned army was putting up tenacious resistance. The Bluecoats were slowly gaining ground and confidence. Suddenly a bugle rang out from the woods. From all along the densely wooded right flank, one bugle after another echoed the call. The stunned Union forces saw waves of Confederate troops emerge from the brush with a bloodcurdling rebel yell.

While Lee courageously held the focus of Hooker's army for most of the day, Stonewall Jackson had spent several hours circling around to the right flank with a formidable infantry. It was his forces ducking in and out of sight that had sparked the rumors of desertion among the Confederate ranks. Lee had taken one of the greatest gambles of the war and Jackson would make it pay off.

The shocked Union corps reeled and turned in chaos. Despite a few honorable stands, the gray forces drove the Union from the fighting field. It was only the coming of sunset that denied Jackson an absolute victory over the confused and outwitted Federal troops. As dusk robbed them of sight, Jackson reluctantly recalled his men.

Hooker was beaten. Saved by darkness, he now listened to his officers warning that Stonewall Jackson wouldn't be deterred by the night. They had to do something. They had to move. He should make for the river under the cover of night and slip out.

"Run?" Hooker pondered. "You'd have me run away? *Me?* Gentlemen, I will not run. Not from Lee. Not from the Confederates. Not from..." He hesitated to gratefully accept the tall glass Sickles offered him, rivaling his own. "We aren't licked. Not by a long shot."

"What do you propose to do?" asked General Rhodes, one who narrowly escaped his death on the field that day.

"Do? I intend to fight." He took a long swallow of whiskey, shuddered, exhaled his frustration and finally looked to Major General Sickles. "All we need is a piece of good news, Daniel. Will you go see if you can make that happen?"

Sickles nodded and matched the deep swallow. "I'll see what I can do."

"Not good enough. Tell me something good."

"We're still here. I'll be damned if they can dig us out of this place. You're still calling the shots, Joe."

"That's a good point." Hooker agreed. They began devising a plan to separate the Confederates again. The drinks on the table gave way to maps and plans as they gathered around to find a means to salvage the front. The officers were able to put behind them the thoughts of what might have been. Now was time to think ahead. Now they had to dig out. Now their commander was in fighting mode.

Out in the night, the Union encampment had been thoroughly scouted by none other than General Jackson himself. Not wanting to squander the day on his misfortune of nightfall, Jackson and a small band of trusted friends had ridden out in the dark to do first hand reconnaissance. Riding back along the wooded trails, he and his men exchanged views on the stronghold at Chancellorsville.

"We need to cut them off from any supplies and reinforcements," Jackson surmised. "Let them know we did and watch Hooker squirm."

"Too dangerous to hit them now, I agree Jack," spoke his commander. "But let them start to feel trapped in there and they'll feel as helpless as a baby."

"Yes," Jackson echoed lethargically. "Like a baby." His mind trailed to his daughter. Her eyes were so dark. Like his, he thought. But she was spared his stern face. She had her mother's delicate features and she looked directly at him. She knew he was her father instantly. Smart little thing she was. She knew and she loved him already.

A group of Rebel guards in the trees had been staring out into the night and jumping at shadows for hours. Suddenly one hushed the other. They listened. They clearly heard horses coming from the direction of the Union front. One of them pointed silently through the darkness at the silhouette of a band of riders. This was no drill or mirage. They were being breached. In the pitch dark night, the dark, shaded uniforms appeared black, or blue. The first of the terrified guards raised his rifle and the others immediately followed suit. The first round stopped the riders. Two of them ran to the left. The second volley took the rest from their horses as two more dove from the saddles to grip the ground. Only one remained mounted.

The guards came out onto the road to take prisoners should they be alive. Stunned and terrified, they looked into the faces of their own officers. Seated in his saddle, Stonewall Jackson had a shocked, deadpan expression. He wavered slightly, then slumped forward and slid from his mount into the waiting arms of his comrades.

Jeb Stuart looked up at the guard. "My God, Man. What have you done?"

Jackson had been hit three times. His friends struggled to stop the bleeding as he clung tenaciously to the image of his infant daughter. She was warm and safe in her mother's arms. She was looking at him and she was smiling. Though not this night, Stonewall Jackson would die of these wounds. His fight was over.

So engrossed in their strategies were the military minds that only the subordinate Union officers noticed the courier entering the command center with a dispatch in his grip. A captain took the paper from him and his eyes bulged at the message. He looked up and exchanged a few softly muttered words of confirmation with the young courier. Then he approached those at the table and cleared his throat.

"General," he started.

"What is it?" asked one of the others.

The captain knew to whom this had to be directed. "General Hooker, Sir?"

Hooker straightened up and removed the cigar from his mouth. He looked at the captain without a word.

"We needed a bit of luck. I think this is it." He handed the dispatch to Hooker and the others halted their planning. They, too, hoped for luck.

Hooker read a dispatch that advised him that generous reinforcements and artillery were arriving that very moment. He had recouped most of what was sacrificed earlier and now he could give Bobby Lee what he wanted. He had taken the Confederates best shot and come back for more. "What now?" he pondered aloud.

Hooker allowed Daniel Sickles to return to the Furness Road with the Third Corps. His plan was to divide the forces of Lee and Stuart and he executed this part of the plan masterfully. Hooker knew he could defeat each wing separately, provided he could keep them separate.

Lee, too, knew this was possible and would not see it happen. Stuart came around and came at them at Hazel Grove just near Chancellorsville. He found virtually no resistance as Hooker had already ordered Sickles to pull out and surrender this flat. Sickles had fallen back to Fairview, an elevated ground closer to Hookers command.

Stuart was expected to keep advancing on foot and be cut down from the hill. But Jeb stopped at the Grove and set up a line of thirty-one cannons. From there he pummeled Fairview with artillery fire. The federals responded with thirty-four pieces of their own big guns and lit up the sky.

For three hours they battled ferociously. Stuart sent wave after wave against the fortified Union front. Each wave was repelled at a bloody cost to both sides. The Rebels struggled to find their way forward in the dense thickets, pre-dawn light and heavy gun smoke. Those who couldn't find their way back found themselves fighting hand-to-hand with Bluecoats. All were equally disorientated in the wilderness and gun smoke. Visibility became so poor that bayonets became as effective as bullets.

The blazing cannons and muzzle fire touched off fires in the woods. The retreating rebels struggled to drag their wounded comrades out and got cut off. Stuart and his base listened in horror to the agonizing screams of anguish as his men were roasted alive in the tangled, burning brush.

Driven back as they were, the rage grew within them as they witnessed the gruesome fate and courageous sacrifice witnessed. None among them would be the one to turn after his brother had given so much to the cause. The fighting was see-saw throughout the morning and now it was the Confederates praying for luck to turn the tide.

It came as Fighting Joe failed to re-supply his cannoneers. One by one, Union guns fell from the fight and the Rebels grew bolder and closer.

Hooker stared out the front of Chancellorsville and pondered his next move. His commanders were frantically barking orders and pleading with him to get into the fight.

"Listen to that!" Couch demanded of him. "That's our men out there in those woods. *Your* men! They're being burned alive!"

"Our men? Why they shouldn't be in there. The place is on fire. Have them fall back."

Couch stared in disbelief as Hooker took another long drink and studied the woods. Something needed to be done. But Hooker merely stood at the front and listened. He had heard that Jackson had been shot. He dared, for a fleeting moment, smile at his fortune. This was an omen, he thought. He was destined for glory. Nothing could stop him now.

At that moment a Rebel cannonball came so directly at him that it would have surely struck him in the forehead had there not been a pillar directly between them. The shot shattered the pillar and the front of the building, sending Fighting Joe reeling across the destroyed room.

Hooker was stunned, though not seriously injured. It was enough, however to remove him from the fight he had been all but absent from for most of the past two days. General Couch pulled the stunned and flabbergasted leader to relative safety as the others crowded around.

"Is he dead?" one asked.

Hooker struggled to speak but was stunned beyond reason. Couch leaned over the fallen general and put a sympathetic ear to Joe's quivering lips. Then he nodded and rose.

"Right!" announced General Couch. "General Hooker has relinquished command, temporarily, to me and asked that we get the Hell out of here."

The staff looked at Hooker, then at Couch with bewilderment. None among them wanted to be the one to ask how Hooker only now found the ability to make a decision.

Couch continued. "We are to fall back and defend the bridgehead at the Rappahannock. Those are our orders. Go to it, gentlemen."

19

The Union encampment was well off the main road. As was their way, they watched all the roads anywhere near them and especially leading in or out of Confederate towns. The closest road to the camp bent to and away from them as two soldiers stood guard. It was a quiet afternoon and they clearly heard the sound of a horse walking slowly toward them. Raising their rifles, they waited and watched the road ahead. The guards were pleasantly surprised to see the attractive woman riding calmly toward them.

Victoria, dressed in woman's clothes and carrying a cloth handbag, smiled at the men. As she approached, they stepped out, one on each side and addressed her.

"Something we can do for you, Ma'am?" asked the soldier on her right. He was older and boasted two chevrons instead of the left side's single stripe.

"I hope so," she said in her softest, woman's voice. "I'm looking for the thirty-ninth infantry. Is this their camp?"

"No Ma'am. The thirty-ninth is up near Virginia, I think."

The man on the left questioned it. "Is it? I ain't never heard of no thirty-ninth infantry."

"Sure there's a thirty-ninth," the older man said. "Just not around here."

The younger soldier looked up at her. "Mind if we ask your business there, Ma'am?"

Victoria smiled coyly. "It's Miss, actually. And my brother is an officer with them. He sent me a message to come up and I'm having a devil of a time. I thought he meant up here."

The older soldier stepped back to admire Big Willy. "This is some fine horse you got here, Miss." His expression turned to one of concern and suspicion. "Yes sir. Some big, fine horse indeed."

The private on her left continued to make official sounding conversation. "Well now maybe he did. But you shouldn't be riding around these parts unescorted. There's Rebels in these woods."

Victoria noticed the other man's concern with her horse. She forced a smile and response as she watched him out of the corner of her eye. "Oh they wouldn't bother me, would they?"

"Not with us around but..."

The man on the right seemed to be moving far too subtly as he fingered his rifle. "This is one fine horse if I do say so..."

He suddenly reeled and aimed his rifle at her. Anticipating it, Victoria had the pistol in her cloth handbag already aimed at him. Before he could act, the handbag exploded and he dropped to the ground. The stunned private on the left had only time enough to see his partner fall and then look up into the barrel of her gun. She fired again without hesitation.

Two more soldiers came racing out of the woods just in time to see the big horse charge past them. They saw the woman rider and leapt to her defense, turning to face whoever was chasing her. Moving out into the road with their rifles at the ready, they found no one in pursuit. By the time they realized she was not in need of protection, she was well away.

Midday life in Durham was all but nonexistent. Those with homes, farms and families had learned to spend the day with them. The nights were long and fearful as any one could bring the next Yankee division upon them. The tavern stayed open, but the crowd amounted to the precious few not enlisted, at work, or shot for looting.

Turley was one such man. Odd jobs for the price of a drink kept him busy when there was an odd job to do. He came into the saloon and looked about. The only soul there was about the only soul left in town. He approached the drinking, but not quite drunken man at the corner table with caution and respect.

"Captain Pollard?" Royal did not respond. "I think you should know I been asked to do something."

"Then do it."

Turley was uncomfortable. He adjusted himself uneasily but remained at Royal's side. "I'm supposed to post a letter to your friend, Absolon."

Royal looked up at him as though awakened from a dream.

"It's from her. Anne."

"So why tell me?" Royal asked with feigned disinterest.

"Bunch of reasons, really. It's a risk lately since he's a Yankee and all. And you're still in charge of what army we got here. But mostly her state. She don't seem right, Royal. You know. All depressed like. I wouldn't want to be responsible if this had something bad in it. You know what I mean?"

A dozen thoughts, each more terrifying than the last, raced through his mind in the time it took Royal to draw a slow breath for strength. "I believe I do."

"Well what should I do?"

"You should let me deal with it, and never speak of it. Can you do that?" He extended his open hand.

Turley placed the letter in his hand without hesitation. "I was hoping you'd say that."

It was early evening as Lulu hurried to respond to the violent pounding on the front door of the Carmichael Mansion. She opened it to Royal stepping assertively inside.

"Where is she?"

"In her room," Lulu responded without fear of his clear rage. "But she ain't been out in days."

Royal stormed up the stairs and burst into her chambers without a knock to find her sitting on the edge of the bed with her hands behind her back. She seemed startled and rigid. He went directly to her with conviction and presented her with her letter to Absolon.

"What were you thinking?" he demanded.

As her eyes fell to the letter, she became angry. "That wasn't meant for you. Give it to me!"

"So you can ease your own conscience?" he challenged, pulling the paper away. "At what cost, Anne? Think of what this will do to him.

Men are dying out there. If he blinks at the wrong time, if his thoughts fall to this instead of his duty for an instant, he could die."

"I know what's being said. I know what I am now. I couldn't bear the thought of him coming back to… I just wanted…"

"You wanted to make sure he didn't come back?" Royal arrested the harshness in his tone once he heard himself. He watched her struggle against the tears. She had never been strong. Emotionally, she needed Absolon to keep her up. Absolon or him as he once hoped. But her weakness at this time was more than tragic. He looked past her. The drawer of her nightstand was partially open. Knowing what she kept in that drawer for protection, he realized why her hands were still hidden. She held her revolver for the worst reason of all.

"What ever you think now, we can't let that hurt him," he said to her in the calmest voice he could muster. "You're still the same person… *he*… fell in love with. There have been too many sacrifices made for this love. Far too many."

Anne gazed up at him with enlightened eyes. "Yes. I agree, Royal. I don't want anyone to sacrifice for me any more."

"Then hold your words until our Absolon comes back to us. Spare him this and we'll sort it out when it's the only thing left to deal with. Just take some strength in knowing how much you're loved and don't squander it like this. Promise me, Anne."

"I'll try."

"Not good enough. Say you will." She tried to divert her eyes but he would have none of it. "Look me in the eye and swear it on his life."

"All right. I will. But swear you'll be near, Royal. Please don't leave me yet."

Royal did as he had for as long as he could remember. He suppressed the words that he would give his life to speak aloud just once. Governed by his oath, he spoke only those words of the gentleman and friend to Absolon. "My word is my bond." His tone was soft and his meaning clear.

She looked at him and drew all from his gaze. "I know." She truly knew he would always be there for her, but the word he had given, the vow that bound him was not to her.

Their eyes remained locked for seconds that spanned a lifetime and bared souls. In those seconds they silently shared truths that could never be uttered. His heart revealed and soul at long last unburdened, Royal finally pulled away and walked slowly toward the door.

"We're both counting on you to greet him with loving arms when he returns," he said as he left. "Say you will."

"I will."

"And I'm counting on you to refill that drawer. Say you will."

With eyes lowered. "I will."

"We can't change the past, Anne. We can only learn from it... and be strengthened by it."

As autumn turned the leaves on another season of a country at war, hearts were ravished at home. Anne remained true to her promise, though the burden of her guilt weighed heavy as death upon her. She spent the summer months in the black garb of a woman in mourning. She never ventured from her house and no one ever was welcomed inside.

September 15, 1863

My dear friend Absolon,

I pray this finds you well and in some spirits. We hear things of the advancements and it is difficult to call them good or bad for reasons known best to you and me. Anne is well though she misses you terribly. The sooner you are back and with her, the better for us all. She does not venture into town any more as stores are no longer sold. Stocks are depleted and the Yankees have cut off supply chains. But we are prepared and she is seen to. I have trusted men who deliver food and report to me of her state.

For my part, I stay on my own land and communicate with those remaining loyal. Looters and Yankee sympathizers are dealt with cruelly here but it serves a dire purpose. It ensures the survival of our county and we continue to persevere.

As to be expected, she is depressed of mind and may write of her sadness in ways that might concern you. To that I insist you believe me she is well and waiting for you. Your safe return cannot be too soon for either of us. Until then I remain vigilant to my vow.

Your friend,

Royal J. Pollard.

20

November, 1863
Oxford Knob

General George Thomas left General Grant at the command camp and went to join his line officers. Major Waterford was looking out across the lush valley. They were in position along the ridge and ready for battle as ordered. Waterford looked out and counted the Rebel forces poised to face them. Their numbers were less but their position was defensible. The front was a high ridge giving them a natural wall of protection.

"What are we doing?" he asked Thomas.

"Grant wants that hill but he's worried the Rebs will break through if our first assault isn't successful. We're not advancing. Just waiting."

"Smart. Bragg is dug in like a tick on a hound dog. If we move, they'll cut us to ribbons."

"Well Sherman will take the left flank and Hooker will hopefully draw fire on the right. We're not going anywhere, but neither are they."

To their right, the forces of Fighting Joe Hooker were ready to advance. They knew all too well that their commander did not retreat easily and that their lives meant little where accolades or medals were concerned.

General Fighting Joe Hooker was only temporarily out of commission following the blast at Chancellorsville. The impact from the cannonball had left him slightly dazed but all the more determined to fight. None spoke to him of the disgrace of losing to a Union force half the size of his own. He was torn. He needed a victory desperately, but he dare not charge into a losing scenario. One more failure would surely end his career.

Sickles had moved on and Joe's drinking became more noticeable as he was more often the only one doing it to such excess. Denied any chance of glory at Gettysburg, Hooker had taken his forces across the

Cumberland. As they traveled through the rough hills, they picked up stragglers. Some of the guerrillas chose not to join the massive infantry and were shot as deserters. Hooker didn't know of this as he was intoxicated much of the time and left the details of running the advance to his subordinates.

Two of the stragglers they encountered joined without objection, despite having no clear explanation as to where they had been all summer. They had no way of knowing what had happened to the soldiers they had fought with but guessed that refusing this company was the wrong choice. Dooley and George guessed otherwise and were executed.

So it came that, at the front of the column, Absolon and Window stood with rifles in hand. Window had a cloth wrapped over his head as did many of the men. Some did it for warmth. He did it to conceal his skin tone. The men still didn't know he was black and he wasn't anxious to bring it up. Since joining, he and Absolon spent much of the time on watch or at the outskirts of the huge encampments. Now awaiting the order to advance, the men were fidgety and looking around. One of the men inched closer to Window's side, trying to see his face. He looked back and his friends quietly urged him on.

Window sensed him and moved up a bit, keeping his head low. "Told you this was a bad idea," he muttered to Absolon.

"We didn't have a choice," Absolon answered. "It was join or be shot as deserters. We'll be fine. They got a whole army out there to fight."

Window turned his head away as the curious soldier came closer. "Leave the woods, you said. Safety in numbers." He stepped forward just as the soldier got close enough to see his face. The soldier caught a glimpse and turned back to his friends. They exchanged looks and he again advanced to try and look the mystery man in the eyes.

Absolon moved forward and tapped the inquisitive soldier on the back. "Think we'll be moving out soon?"

But the man would not be deterred. Ignoring Absolon, he took another step forward. Window moved again as well and Absolon followed. The other curious soldiers now followed Absolon.

From the back of the outfit, General Hooker sat on horseback and observed. It wasn't long before he noticed the unauthorized advance on his front.

"Who ordered those men to move out?" he asked his captain.

"No one that I know of, Joe," answered the officer. "Want me to go get them?"

Hooker looked back over his shoulder toward the vantage point of General Grant. "Hold it. Don't draw attention to them just yet." Torn between telling his men not to advance, a stigma that had loomed large since Chancellorsville, and explaining the disobedience to Grant, he chose once again to wait and hope the men simply stopped.

His captain stood in the stirrups and watched the movements. "Looks like more of them are starting to move. They were ordered to hold their position."

"They move out any farther and they'll draw fire. That's it. Go get them. Pull them back and dress that front line."

The first curious soldier came up to Window's shoulder. He looked and Window adjusted his scarf, trying to look away.

From the Rebel lines, a rifleman had been watching the advance. Between the small ridges and shallow ravines, he could almost get a shot at the two heads. Looking at the blue cap, he rested the barrel of his rifle on the log in front of him and took careful aim.

The Union soldier came too close for Window to duck and he instinctively pulled his hat down to cover most of his face, forgetting that his hand was now exposed. The soldier looked at the black skin and turned back to his closely following friends.

"I knew it!" he announced almost happily. "We're fighting with a nigger!"

Before anyone could react to the revelation, a shot rang out from the Rebel line and the mini ball whizzed past the soldier's head. They all dropped to their knees in the shallow ravine. From their backs and bellies, the five soldiers looked Window in the face for the first time. Window braced himself for whatever they had as he had no where left to hide.

The men were clearly unhappy but no one seemed to want to make the first move. It was Absolon that finally spoke.

"Fellas. Meet Private Window Graham. The fightingest son-of-a-bitch you'll ever meet."

Another shot landed just over their head. One of the men adjusted his hat and looked at Window. "You better be, Boy. Looks like we got ourselves out too far."

A few more shots were fired and they ducked lower, though Window noticed something different about this volley. These shots seemed to be coming from behind them.

"Hey. Those aren't at us. Sounds like we're shooting back."

Hooker's senior officer stood with his men and looked out over the ridge. He could barely see the top of the heads of the advanced men. He could see only that they were pinned down. The Rebs had a bead on them and were determined to make them the first casualties of this battle.

"Get them out of there!" he ordered to his company. "Give them some cover!"

At that, his men fired another volley to get the Confederates to duck and several more men moved up into the shallow with Absolon. The Rebs tried to return fire but the rolling hills and moguls made it impossible to get a clear shot. They knew they had to adjust their position or the Union might get too close to repel. They could almost see the numbers advancing upon them and some of the Rebs started flanking out dangerously far from their cover in a desperate attempt to halt the advance.

From the top of the ridge, General Grant took notice of the unauthorized advance with concern.

"Who ordered that?" he growled.

"Not us," Thomas said defensively. "I ordered them to hold fast. It must've been Hooker."

Grant lowered his field glasses and studied the positions. "If they breach our ranks, they'll rout us for sure. Find out what the hell is going on."

In the ravine, the dozen union soldiers kept their heads low.

"This was not the plan," said Window.

Absolon looked up as much as possible. "Well where did you think you were going?"

"Just trying to be inconspicuous."

"That was a wasted effort, Boy," said one of the men that had joined them. "I can spot a nigger from here to Chickamauga." He pointed toward the Confederates.

Another that had come up with him pointed back toward the Union lines. "You mean Chickamauga."

"Actually, I think it's...," Absolon started to correct them, pointing to their left but stopped when he spotted the Confederates moving out to flank them. "Uh oh. I think Chickamauga's coming to us, Fellas."

Window looked out toward the enemy with an air of determination as he raised his rifle. "Like hell it is. I say we take it to them."

The first soldier smiled at the gumption of his new comrade. "You *are* a crazy son-of-a-bitch, ain't you?"

A volley of fire from the Rebs landed too close and Window moved out. Seemingly indifferent to the men around him, he muttered as he crouched and made his way out toward the Rebel lines.

"I got your Chickamauga, Reb. Got it right here."

As he half stood and left the relative safety of the ravine, Absolon again did as he'd done a hundred times before and followed his friend. The soldiers with them exchanged puzzled looks but shrugged and moved as well.

Hooker watched the twelve men slowly creep up the hill like a line of ants toward the heavily entrenched Confederates. He was stunned that the Rebs seemed unable to get off a clean shot at them due to the terrain. He saw the Rebs shooting but failing to slow the advance. He saw his own men returning fire and repelling the Confederate flanks.

The officer at the front ordered more men to move out and give them support. The safe route had been laid out by Window. All they had to do was follow and keep their heads down and they were safely below the line of fire. The flanking Rebs fired again and Hooker's brigade again returned fire on them, this time driving them back. As they retreated, the men who fired instinctively gave chase.

From the top of the hill, General Thomas stood with Grant as they watched the unauthorized advance split into two columns as the Rebs seemed to be pulling back.

Thomas feigned outrage. "I'll have them all court marshaled!"

Grant kept the glasses to his eyes. "Maybe you should wait on that, George. This looks like it's turning into something. They just might have opened the door for us."

More of Hooker's men caught up to Absolon and Window. They continued to advance despite the shooting. So far, no one had been hit and they became bolder and more confident with each yard gained. Each time they found another shallow to follow and heard the shots missing them, they gained resolve but did not hurry. They just kept moving slowly and methodically forth. In the absurdity of the slow charge, they found themselves chanting...

"Chickamauga. Chickamauga. Chickamauga."

Hooker sat on his tall horse and stared in disbelief at the apparently successful breach of the enemy line. Two of his officers studied him to know how to act. One looked at the other and decided to take matters into his own hands, spurring his horse toward the front of the advance. The other, not wanting to be outdone, took chase to race the other to the front. One of them would get credit for leading the courageous charge. The other would be thanked for following along.

"FOLLOW ME, MEN!" shouted the first officer to reach the front of the troops. He dismounted to stand safely in the channel the advance had taken.

As the division fell in behind him, the second officer rode past them and dangerously out in the line of fire. "Follow *me!*"

The Union forces poured out onto the grassy slopes and away from the cover of the hills and trees to follow the two competitive officers. The mounted one was too tempting a target and the Rebs opened fire.

He did as would anyone and dropped from his saddle to the ground. But the wave of infantry was already at his heels and the Rebel mini-balls drove them forward into the valley in full force.

As they sprinted toward the Confederate front, Hooker finally shook off his stunned trepidation and, knowing full well Grant was watching from above, ordered the main body of his command to advance.

Window fired on the run and dropped the first Reb to dare raise his head above the ridge. As the Confederates defended their line, Hooker's ranks arrived en masse and the fighting became hand-to-hand.

Grant looked out in excited approval at the turn, though he quickly spotted the desperate Rebs moving out on the right and trying to move artillery into position. Thomas was quick to pick up on his commander's approval and moved quickly to send dispatches to the left and right flanks. Sherman was ordered to advance against the forces of the artillery and infantry.

The fighting became an all out battle and the tide was strongly in favor of unseating the strong Rebel hold on Oxford Knob.

Behind the Confederate lines, General Braxton Bragg looked out across the battlefield, stunned at the devastating turn of the battle. His officers awaited instructions, but he was beyond rational thought. Not known for his quick thinking under fire, he was true to form as he struggled for a plan of attack. Two officers came to his side to demand orders from him.

"Hooker is breaking through our left flank!" shouted his captain.

"Don't raise your voice to me, Captain," he retaliated. "Send the 15th infantry in."

The captain lowered his tone. "Impossible. They're holding off Sherman right now. Cleburne has his hands full."

Bragg took a breath of disgust. "Damn Irishman thinks he's the only one in this war. How long can we hold them?"

"They're through, General! We can't hold them!"

Bragg looked down at the carefully planned assault lying in crumpled maps and diagrams on his table. None would ever come to pass. Reluctantly, he turned to the waiting captains. "Sound retreat. We'll back out and regroup. Cleburne can hold them until we can regain ranks."

In the smoke blanketed valley, the men on the front fired and loaded frantically. Only the furthest out came in contact with the enemy. Absolon had resorted to swinging his rifle like a broadsword, clubbing Rebs before they could take aim on him. Window reloaded frantically, firing from his knee and claiming a man with each ball. He seemed untouchable and the adrenalin pumped through him until he was sure he hadn't exhaled in several minutes.

The trumpet sounded retreat and the confederates turned and ran. Hooker ordered his men to hold their position, still unclear what he had just done. Window finally breathed and Absolon stopped swinging as they watched the retreat. Realizing he had just survived the fight of his life, surely the best of this war so far, Window turned to see Absolon standing exhausted, but also alive. Absolon saw him and, overcome with emotion, started laughing. It wasn't funny. It was simply all he could think of. Window howled his exuberance at the sky in delight. As they gathered their wits, Hooker rode up amidst the troops.

"Men! *That* is why they call me Fighting Joe!"

21

The retreat from Oxford Knob was a slow, arduous trek, mentally and physically agonizing. The column of battered soldiers in General Bragg's forces marched through the mud nearly to their knees. The luckiest among them were those not yet carrying a wounded friend. At the front of the column, the officers rode on equally exhausted mounts.

One of Bragg's captains blew a puff of warm breath into his cold hands. "They need to rest, General. We all do. Bandages need changing. We're stretched out over ten miles."

General Bragg didn't look back. "You saw the report, Jeb. Reinforcements are at least two days ahead and Hooker is right on our tail. We stop and we might as well surrender."

The captain looked back at the ranks. "At this rate, he'll be on us soon. Shouldn't we dig in and make a stand?" As he spoke, he noticed a rider on a tall horse moving slowly along the drudging column.

"We have nothing to stand on," Bragg replied. "If I could get a message to Cleburne to run interference, slow them down. If he could buy us some time to get those reinforcements at Dalton, we'd by God give them a fight."

The captain was still watching the rider. "That's a lot of ifs. There's a courier. Why don't you send him with orders and see if we can make some of it happen."

"Why? What chance has he of finding Cleburne in time?"

The captain watched Victoria draw nearer. She looked carefully at the faces of each man in the long column as she passed.

"I think this one has a damned good chance."

The cloudy, November sky blotted out the moon and stars to leave almost total darkness on the broad Tennessee road. Two Union soldiers were set out to stand the midnight watch. At the edge of the road, they burned a single lantern. This gave them only enough light to see the spot of road the lantern sat on. In the middle of the night they said nothing and did nothing. They simply stood and watched the nothingness.

In the distance, they heard the gaining sound of a horse at full gallop. Bringing their weapons to the ready, they strained their eyes against the darkness, but saw only the darkness. The pounding of the hooves grew louder and louder until it seemed they were virtually upon the fearful guards. They could, by the charging sound all but pinpoint the intruder but still they saw nothing.

Then they both felt a waft of air as the dark rider whizzed past them. They knew only by the sound of the hooves that grew to a deafening crescendo before dwindling again in the opposite direction that they had been breached. Turning, they stared impotently into the darkness behind them as the sound of the night rider faded away.

November 24, 1863

The massive encampment of the fifteenth Arkansas Infantry was laid out across a deceptively calm valley. They had retreated from Missionary Ridge with orders to camp on the east bank of the Chickamauga Creek. So there they sat comfortably on the west bank. General Pat Cleburne had ignored that detail of the orders and had his men camp here. After their outstanding accounting of themselves against a formidable Union division, they deserved rest and food and everything but a cold swim and a night's rest in wet clothes. Cleburne kept them here and comfortably dry, just a few miles from where Bragg would expect him to be. His men were relatively secluded and enjoying a well earned rest.

Victoria rode slowly through the tents and foot soldiers, discreetly scanning the men. She'd learned that a stare noticed generally brought one in return. The scarf covering most of her face, she let only her eyes dart back and forth as she deliberately took an indirect route through the soldiers toward a table with six Sergeants and Corporals seated playing cards.

She pulled Big Willy to halt near the junior officers. "Got a message for General Cleburne."

A sergeant pointed away up the hill. "Officer's tents are up there."

"Thanks, Sergeant. You have a Corbel in your outfit? Mason Corbel?"

He exchanged glances with the others before responding, "Not in my command. Might ask on the hill."

"Thanks. I will." She nodded appreciatively and rode away toward the hill.

At the summit of the small hill overlooking the camp on all sides, General Pat Cleburne sat with his officers. They were in relatively high spirits considering they just come from what seemed to them an indecisive battle.

Major Perkins sipped coffee and wanted for any form of pastry. He stared at the bacon and beans on his plate with revulsion. "We'll have to move soon, Pat. Rations will run out if we stay much longer."

Pat Cleburne still had a thick Irish accent that he made little effort to learn off. Having come to America in forty-nine, poor and unskilled, the niche he had made for himself in the army was well deserved and based on the two things he'd brought from Cork. This immigrant had both the courage under fire to keep a clear head about him in battle and a remarkable instinct for battle strategy. He cared for the fighting men under him and by protecting them through brilliant offensive deployments, made each of them fight like ten. He didn't like pulling out of a fight, but knew when best to do it.

"Soon as the wounded can travel. I won't leave them to the Yankees. Damn I can't believe I missed Hooker again."

"Well we gave Sherman all he could handle. That's something."

"Ah but that Hooker fella really irks me. How can a man in a war call himself "Fighting Joe"? Sure and every man here could be 'Fighting' somebody. Couldn't he? Maybe I'll call meself Fighting Pat Cleburne."

Captain Harrison smiled. "Suits you. Here you go, Fighting Pat. Have some fighting tea."

"I fighting well will. Fight you, Captain. Fight you very much."

"I'll have some of that, Fighting Bill," Perkins said with a smirk.

"Well here you go, Fighting Tom. Sorry we don't have any fighting milk."

Cleburne pointed at him threateningly. "Now them's fighting words."

The light banter was broken up when the courier rode up to them and dismounted. Stepping close to the table, Victoria offered a brief salute that was quickly returned by the general.

"Message for General Cleburne from General Bragg."

"I'll take that, Soldier," Cleburne said, accepting the letter from her with a watchful eye. "How did you find us?"

"Yeah," said Major Perkins. "How did you get through? Did you come from the east?"

"Good horse, Sir," she replied as low as possible. "He goes where he's told."

Pat Cleburne smiled with this. "Aye. That's a fine animal. I've heard tell of you, now that I see him. You've earned quite a reputation. You'd be that one they call the Magician."

"Which way are you heading now?" Harrison asked.

"My base command is reported southeast, Sir. I need to get back to them."

"If we gave you some letters from the men, could you get them through?" Harrison continued. "It's been a while since they've been able to write their families."

Victoria had developed a timer in these situations. Some officers almost never looked at their men and kept their attention on officers and orders. She was comfortable there in the anonymity. But she had become a judge of the character of men and Cleburne struck her as a compassionate man who spoke to people like people regardless of rank. She took him to be the type of man who tended to look a man in the eye when he spoke to him and took note if a man avoided eye contact. This was dangerous. She knew that she was close to being too long here and would be studied too closely should she not get out. The query about mail was all too familiar and her exit was cued.

"I'll take what you've got, Sir. I can't promise more than my best to get them through."

"Your best is pretty damned good," Cleburne responded. "We picked up a lot of General Beauregard's wounded. Folks'll be worried about them. See that you and your mount get fed and rested before you go."

"Thank you, Sir." She saluted in her usual lowered brow style and, accepting the return, started away. She was excused and free to go, but she had to risk it for the question she asked of everyone. She turned back to them.

"Would you gentlemen know if you picked up a soldier named Corbel? Mason Corbel? I've been trying to deliver a message to him about his family."

Perkins thought. "Doesn't sound familiar. But we've got four thousand names out there. Take a look at the dead and wounded list. I wish we could do more."

"Understood." She considered turning, but this time stood curiously before the officers.

"Was there something else, Corporal?" Cleburne asked.

"Actually there is one thing you can do for me, General. If I may."

Cleburne, while reading the message she had delivered, responded. "What's that, Corporal?"

"You called me the Magician and said I had a reputation. That truly isn't making it easier to do what I have to do. It's like a challenge to the Yankees to catch me."

Cleburne looked up from his post. "Point taken. In the interest of the Confederacy and your safety, we need to diffuse this mystique. Make you less of a target. What say we spread the word to our troops and where ever that the so called Magician is actually a network of skilled riders? When one is caught or killed, another takes his place. There is no 'Magician'."

"That might help. Thank you, Sir. I hope I can make this up to you."

They exchanged nods of mutual appreciation before she mounted to ride off. Cleburne returned his attention to the message with a deep concern that Harrison was quick to pick up on.

"Bad news, Pat?"

"Get that map," Cleburne said. "Where are we now?"

They spread a map out on the table. Harrison pointed to a position and Cleburne followed it with his finger.

"We're here. According to this intelligence, Bragg made it to Ringgold Gap and is running south to Dalton. His artillery is here and moving."

"That's a long way off," Harrison said. "Can they reach him?"

"No. He's carrying wounded and one of Grant's divisions is in pursuit... about here."

Perkins studied the logistics. "Then he'll catch him."

Cleburne stood and looked at them. "Thus the message. Our orders are to intercept. We're to engage the enemy at Ringgold Gap and..." he held the paper and read ver batem. "Hold this position at all hazards and keep back the enemy until the artillery and transportation are secure."

"We're not ready for battle yet, Pat."

"I know. But Bragg never was. He wants us to sacrifice our men so he can go get the big guns and reinforcements and look like a hero."

Perkins was still studying the map and notes. "But if we don't go and Bragg gets taken before the artillery arrives, they'll take him and then the guns and we'll have no chance of..."

"I know. We need time to..."

Perkins interrupted them sharply. "Pat. Look at this."

"What is it?" he and Harrison returned to the map.

"Thomas is still back at Oxford Knob with Grant. Sherman went east licking his wounds."

Harrison was getting it. "So that leaves..."

Cleburne's face lit up with the realization. "Hooker! Fighting Joe Hooker is the one we get to cut off."

"Easy Pat," Harrison warned. "He didn't face Sherman. We're supposed to hold off fifteen thousand men with just over four?"

"Last report, he had closer to twenty," Perkins added. "We could be walking into a massacre, Pat. This is suicide. Just like the Ridge. We fight while Bragg runs."

Cleburne had an air of confidence about him as he pondered the orders. "Well first off, if we don't buy Braxton some time, Hooker will run over him and take the artillery as well. With a day or two to get his reinforcements, Bragg just might stop him.

"Might."

"And secondly, Gentlemen. I'm not inclined to commit suicide. We just proved that to Sherman. This isn't Sherman or Grant. It's Hooker. Let's go give him a new nickname. Shall we?"

The hospital tent of Cleburne's division was large and busy. Several partially trained hospital corpsmen walked from cot to cot in pairs. They had been trained in the basics of first aid by the doctors and trained others as they went about the rounds. Cleburne had seen many men die of infections and fever simply because the doctor couldn't be everywhere at once. By this training, the doctor's basic knowledge was spread and he was free to be where he was most needed.

A corporal entered the tent and moved along the rows speaking to the wounded soldiers.

"Mail? Who's got mail? We got a currier leaving soon. If you got anything, give it now."

A man on one of the cots pulled his blanket aside. His arm was wrapped hand to shoulder and his face was half covered in bandages. The half showing was that of Mason Corbel.

"Any chance of them getting through?"

"This one might. It's worth a try, ain't it?"

"Nothing to lose, I guess," Mason said as he pulled a folded letter from his shirt. Handing it to the Corporal, "Can you get that in something for me?"

The corporal took the folded letter from him. "Sure, Cory. Got an envelope over there. Where's it going?"

Mason had been called everything but his name since he was wounded. He was not in spirit or form to argue the point. He simply handed him a pencil. "Victoria Corbel. Bentonville, South Carolina. Can you do that?"

"Done. You rest now."

Victoria rode slowly away from the camp, seemingly dejected and disheartened. It had been so long. Never close or even a maybe. She knew she could go on, but she began to realize this was her life until it ended. The quest was all of him she had and would never let him go.

The canvas sack hung from her saddle horn bumped against her knee, distracting her from her anticipated depression. With each departure, she spent some time brooding over having once again allowing her hopes to rise, only to have them brought down empty yet again. The mail sack was depriving her of her well-earned sulk and she would not have it.

Stopping the horse, she reached behind her to retrieve the saddlebags. Draping the bags over her lap, she opened the cloth sack.

Pulling the letters out of the sack by the handful, "Let's see if we can balance this load, Willie. This bag is just in the way."

She dropped a hand full into the left saddlebag. Then she grabbed another handful and let them slide from her hand into the right. As the letters fell from her hand into the bag, she briefly saw what appeared to be her name slide by. She froze, staring into the saddlebag, terrified to look and again find her own mind fooling her as it had for want so many times. Summoning the courage by telling herself it could not be, she dug to prove herself right. With bated anticipation she thumbed through the letters until her eyes locked on it. Her name on an envelope. Trembling, tears welling, she gasped and stared.

Big Willy never charged harder than this day as he carried her back up the hill toward that camp. She rode through the camp at high gallop and straight to the hospital tent of the wounded. The corporal hurried out to meet her.

"What happened? Did we...?"

She swung her leg over and leapt to the ground. Clutching the letter, she waved it excitedly at him and demanded," Where is he? Mason! Where is he?"

The corporal looked at the letter, then at her. Confused and fearful, he could do little more than point back to a bed and say, "About halfway back on that side."

She ran, then walked and looked. Each bed had a man with some of his face covered by blanket or bandages. She struggled to keep the scarf over her face as she searched. Then she stopped at the foot of a cot. The man's head was covered by the blanket but she saw the sandy blonde hair. She had seen a thousand men with sandy blonde hair. Many were the exact same shade as this hair. But this hair turned just the way Mason's did when it needed cutting. That was enough to put her heart in her throat. She touched the end of the blanket and pulled it toward her. Mason's sleeping face was slowly revealed.

As if the light was suddenly turned on, he awoke and looked up. He stared in disbelief. It couldn't have been a dream. He dreamt of her a dozen times a day and in none of them was his beloved Victoria dressed as a man. He swallowed hard and drew a breath to speak, but nothing came to his lips.

Victoria moved around to the side of the cot, slowly so as not to draw any more attention than she already had. Looking down on her husband, she tugged the brim of her hat to show him it was indeed her under it. Finally she lowered herself to him. Others be damned, their arms wrapped around each other in an embrace of a year's wanting. As if the war would again separate them if they let go, they squeezed until the strength left their arms. A year of embraces not felt, warmth lost, scent forgotten were reclaimed in the desperate, passionate seconds that they held each other.

Finally Mason pushed her back to hold her at arm's length. The realization of what she had done was only beginning to sink in.

"My God, Vic...." He held his greeting at that. "What have you done?"

"What I had to," she whispered, subtly wiping away her tears of joy. "I couldn't make it without you."

"I missed you so much. Did you get my letters?"

"Just this one," she said holding the crumpled letter in her fist.

Mason smiled. "Jeez, Vic. You're the Magician?"

"I'm starting to believe it." She looked at the wad of soiled bandages around his shoulder and arm. "You're wounded."

"Not nearly as bad as it looks. But don't tell them that. As soon as we get to a train station, I could be sent home."

"How long have they been telling you that?"

"Too long. But now I'll remind them."

Behind them, word came around to pack up. The healthy men moved around the medical tent, folding and packing anything they could.

"Looks like we're moving," Mason said.

The doctor came past them as they gathered supplies into a duffle bag. "We're moving to a front. Orders are all able-bodied men are to report to the infantry captain."

Mason looked around the collapsing campsite with worry. He looked to his wife. "I don't know how you got here, Vickie. But slip out. They won't miss you."

"I'm not leaving you again."

"You have to. If they find you out, you could be shot as a spy. And... the baby. The baby?" he finally remembered.

"Oh Mason." Tears welled anew in her reddened eyes. "We have to try again. That's what I came to tell you. I need you to come home so we can try again."

Mason studied her a long three seconds. His embrace was for his own strength, the strength he had always drawn from her. Then he fell back onto his cot, covering his face with his hand. She had known for months how to break the news to him. But she had never once thought of what she would say next. It was as if she never truly expected to get to this moment.

The doctor passed again on his rounds and saw Mason overcome. "Don't fret, Son. You can't fight with one arm and a bad leg. You'll stay back with the wounded."

Victoria turned to him. "I need to stay with him, Doctor."

"You heard the orders. All able-bodied men are pulling out. Big fight. I'll take care of your friend."

"But he's my... brother."

Mason now saw the twist of fate. It was Victoria being put in harm's way. Grasping her sleeve he begged. "Don't leave me. Vic. We can't be split up again."

"He's been called, Soldier," the doctor said. "You know what that means."

As he had prayed since he was first drafted and taken from her, Mason looked at Victoria. "Yeah. I know."

22

November 25, 1863

That night, Fighting Joe Hooker's Division was camped north of the all but deserted town of Ringgold Gap. Absolon sat near a fire, writing. Window sat next to him poking the fire.

"You named from the Bible?" Window asked mostly to break the nervous silence.

"Sort of," he answered without stopping his pen. "You're thinking of Absalom. My grandfather was named after him but they misspelled it. Ma couldn't write too well back then. Pa couldn't write a lick. I was named for Grandad so yes and no to what you asked."

"Damn I almost forgot what I asked. I was just curious about your name, I guess."

Absolon stopped writing. "Speaking of names. Why would anyone name a boy Window?"

Grinning, he leaned back and poked the fire with a stick. "Can't believe you just getting around to asking me that. I was named Winston, but Momma said I was forever in the way. Everything she did, my little head was in front of her. Had to see. She kept telling me, she say... 'Winston. You make a better door than a window,' she told me. Finally she got to just yell *Window* every time I was in the way."

"And it came to be your name?"

"Didn't really care for Winston, as I remember it."

Absolon snickered as he returned to his letter. "So you could have been named Getyerassouttheway."

"In a way, I am," he laughed. "So that's what it feels like?"

"What?"

"Being a soldier."

Absolon looked up from his letter again. "What are you talking about? You've been fighting for over a year."

"Hiding and fighting. You know damn good and well the Army never gave me no gun. Was you done that. All they gave me was a frying pan."

"And now?"

"You saw it. That general looked me right in the eye. Them other soldiers saw me. And there we all was. Fighting like a real outfit. And me leading them out. Man that felt good."

"All things considered, we're lucky we lived through it."

"That's the truth, sho nuff. But truth be told, I wouldn't change a thing. I swear it was the first time in my life I felt free. Doing what I wanted because I thought it was right. Yes sir. Felt real good."

"Well this war is one place where men have to trust each other. It's that or die. Don't think it's going to be like that in the real world."

"What you mean? I ain't earning my way? I'm doing the same and more than any..."

"You're preachin' to the choir. I know what kind of man you are because I fought with you. But I'm talking about later."

"You mean after the war?"

"Yep. This world ain't soon to be changed much. Tough place for a darky. What you said about doing the right thing. You need to do that every time. People'll be looking for something to hate about you. Can't give it to them. Not ever."

"Damn. What I got to do? The right thing, I reckon."

Absolon smiled and returned to his letter. After a moment of reflection, Window looked over his shoulder. "Man you don't write like nobody I ever saw."

Absolon looked at him with surprise. "I didn't know you could read."

"I can't. But I seen letters and books and things. The words usually go across like this. Yours got lines going across and up and down."

Absolon did indeed write across his own lines, as did many of the men. It was a means of making the best of the limited supply of writing paper. "It's kinda the same thing. See I write across in lines like this...," he explained, pointing along the horizontal lines of the paper with his finger. "...Until the page is full. Then I turn it sideways and start over." He turned the paper on its side and showed the new lines now horizontal.

"The trick is to only read the ones going across. Saves paper."

"Pretty smart, I guess. You write anything about me?"

"Oh yeah. I told her all about what a coward you were. So busy running from your own men you ran us right into the enemy and darn near won the war."

Window laughed. "Oh yeah?"

"Yeah. She just asked where you got that stupid name. Now I can tell her."

Window leaned back and gazed outward, into the night sky. "Yes sir. It sure felt good."

The next morning brought an early and determined march. Hooker was bound and determined to catch Bragg before he had a chance to regroup. His intelligence had told him that reinforcements could be awaiting Bragg at Dalton. He intended to make certain that Bragg never made it that far.

As the column marched four abreast through a low clearing at the outskirts of the seemingly deserted town, Absolon marched next to Window.

"Feels different this morning. Feels better," Window said.

"What? Being a soldier?"

"Being a man. Feels good."

"You still on that? What are you now that you weren't before?"

"Don't know really. It's more a feeling than anything. I'm not doing something because my owner ordered me to or because I have to. I have a choice."

"So that's what makes a man? Choice?"

"Yeah. No. It's more than that. Nobody gave me that choice. I took it. I earned it."

"You did that, Mister," added a soldier marching behind them.

As they came to within two hundred yards of the outskirts of Ringgold Gap, the deserted train station came into view at the top of the hill.

Confederate soldiers were spread out across the back of the terminal. They had dug in behind barrels and earthen mounds near the tracks.

Guns ready and bayonets affixed, they waited silently as the Union marched up and into the trap.

On the right flank, Victoria nestled in behind a grassy hill and set her pistols on the ground next to her. She couldn't see the enemy yet, but she had a clear view of the area in front of the station. Mason leaned against the natural wall and checked a powder horn. He had only limited motion in his right arm and the grip of a child so he resolved to reload for Victoria. He bore the pain of marching along with her as the pain of watching her march away would have been unbearable. She had been inducted into Cleburne's regiment for this all important engagement and once done, would have been shot as a deserter for attempting to escape. The Magician might have been able to slip out safely, but her heart was not in it this time. Victoria had earned her reputation through a drive to find Mason. Now in his arms, the drive to leave was simply not there.

So at her side he remained and at his side she resolved to fight and, if need be, die. Mason had a cache of balls and powder and sat ready to keep that from happening. As he counted the shots again, he caught a glimpse of her gazing lovingly at him. He swallowed his fear of the moment and forced a return smile for her sake.

"Just try to keep your head down," he whispered.

"That won't stop them."

"But you're a crappy shot."

She smirked a bit. "I've been practicing."

Mason tried to appear confident, but the thought of another time to be spent without her, or losing her again came to him. He mercifully kept the image of losing her and how from invading his consciousness.

Victoria saw the quiver in his lip. She knew she was his only weakness. She grabbed his arm firmly. "Just keep me loaded. I didn't come this far to say goodbye."

General Hooker rode up alongside the men, believing himself to be an inspirational image. Most of his leadership problems were known only to his fellow officers. The men under him generally thought highly of him. As he scanned his forces, he came upon Window. Window glanced up at him but instinctively tried to look away.

Hooker remembered Window from his valor on the battlefield and smiled. "Not to worry, private. You proved yourself worthy of this outfit. Any man with that kind of grit is welcome and I don't care if he's black, white or blue with green stripes. You'll fit in just fine here. This is a fighting outfit."

As he rode on to join his staff at the lead, Absolon and Window exchanged glances and rolled their eyes at the "Fighting" comment. They had both come to know what that was worth.

Window muttered to Absolon. "Don't think I forgot what you done."

"What? Hid behind you?"

"You was the first white man to treat me like a man. You put a gun in my hand and never took it back."

"I told you. God made you the man you are."

"But you made that man a soldier."

Absolon peered up at the deserted frame of a train station. The windows were shaded and dark but seemed to be looking down at him personally. "Don't thank me for that one just yet."

As Hooker neared the front of the column, one of his junior officers turned back to him.

"I think we should send out a scout, Sir."

"What for?" Hooker replied. "We won't catch Bragg for a day but we aren't stopping until we do. There's only one road and..."

At that instant, two cannons fired at them from inside the train station. The column disbursed as the well-aimed shots struck, landing in the middle of the road. The men tried to take cover away from the open road as the second volley landed in their midst.

Hooker shouted orders frantically to the cowering men on his right. "CAPTAIN! Take your company around. Flank them and take out those guns!"

The captain led his men around the hill and into the relative cover of the woods. With the sound of rifle fire behind them, he rushed through the woods to come up behind and alongside the station, hoping to find a weak point of attack.

Less than two hours before Hooker came into range, General Cleburne briefed his staff on exactly what Hooker would do and what they were to do about it.

"Whenever he gets hit, he stops," Cleburne told them. Leaning over a map of the town and Hooker's approach, he directed the battle plan. "When he gets to here, we'll break his ranks with cannon fire. Have the guns inside the train station so we can hit him straight on. His first move is always to flank to his right. He'll take a division and swing around here to take out our guns."

As the federal division reached the clearing level with the town, they were met by a wall of two hundred Confederate rifles. The first volley took out his main body of men, leaving them to fall back dead weight on top of the next wave. The Union soldiers pushed the dead aside and pushed up and again were repelled by a meticulously timed fire. Outnumbered, and out maneuvered, the captain took what few men he had and retreated.

The cannons fired again and again, claiming a devastating toll. Hooker's captain made it back to him and reported the failure to penetrate.

"They were ready for us, Joe!" he shouted.

"Were they?" Hooker raged. "Do it again."

The captain looked at him in shock. "General. I must protest..."

"Take a minimum of troops. Draw their fire and keep them looking. Major!" he shouted to his next in command. "Take your company around the left flank. Disable those guns and penetrate!"

The officers glanced at each other with grave concern but obeyed as military men do.

"You'll repel him on our left and he'll fake another to that same side with a minimum of force," Cleburne continued. He took the poise of a boxer throwing jabs at his Captain. "Right. Then a fake and a left hook." He swung slow and wide, bringing his left fist to the officer's right cheek.

As Hooker kept his head low, watching his troops inch their way forward along the sides of the clearing, he saw his major approach the woods on the left. Three solid waves of confederate rifles leveled the company before they were able to approach. Hooker watched them fall dead in great waves of blue uniforms.

The captain never made it through the woods. Cleburne's men were so well distributed that no weakness appeared evident. He sidled up next to Hooker as bullets whizzed over their heads. "They got us dead to rights, Joe. Pull back."

"What is his next move, Pat?"

Cleburne smiled. "He doesn't have one. He's not smart enough to take position and too chicken to fall back. He'll launch a frontal assault and try to overwhelm us with sheer numbers." He looked up from the table and out toward the silently waiting train depot. As though he could see right through it, he envisioned the petrified expression on Fighting Joe's face.

Hooker looked out toward the seemingly unreachable depot at the summit. Then he looked back at the captain as if he'd spit on him. "Pull back? Who do you think you're talking to? Bugler! Sound Charge! Fight, men! *FIGHT*!"

It was the only real command left him and Cleburne was waiting for it. The efficient Confederate marksmen had shifted to the front and filled the air with dense smoke as wave after wave of advancing Yankees were laid over each other. They tried by the hundreds to advance against the brilliant defense with Hooker's commands ringing in their ears. The Confederates fired again and again, visibly depleting the blue hoards in body and spirit with each release. Cleburne's cannons had been directed to the perimeters to force the main body toward the center of the battlefield. The Union forces driving up the center had been so regularly hit at the spot of attack that there now came a pile of bodies strewn across the battlefield. The next wave climbed over them to advance and the Rebels picked them off the top, leaving them to fall back and add to the pile of dead. It looked to all as though Cleburne was shingling a roof with dead Yankees.

Victoria fought ferociously from behind her barrier. She had been positioned behind a mound of earth to the right of the depot and remained stationary during the second wave when the main body shifted. Two divisions ran behind her to spread out and await Hooker's second failed charge. Next to her, Mason loaded weapons and guarded her flanks. As she emptied her rifle and grabbed a loaded one from him, Mason had a half second to gaze at her with unexpected admiration. She was too busy shooting to notice.

From the other side, casualties mounted to horrific numbers. Hooker kept ordering charges as his men were literally piling up on each other. He was vested now, like a gambler that had lost his home but was still in the game. He couldn't stop. He dare not lose. Again his captain appealed to him.

"Pull back, Joe. Sound retreat while we can!"

Hooker peered again through the carnage and up into the town. The dense gun smoke made even the depot difficult to see. But he stared as though he were locking eyes with General Cleburne himself. He could see the wily Irishman leering back tauntingly.

"Never!"

"We're getting wiped out!"

Hooker stiffened his resolve. "We're taking casualties. So are they!"

The captain looked out past the growing pile of dead soldiers, all in blue uniforms. "You're wrong, Joe! They're picking us off like fish in a barrel! Get them out of here!"

Hooker turned to his captain in near rage. "I tell you they're taking just as many casualties. Maybe more! We'll overwhelm them with our resolve! CHARGE!!!!"

Deep inside the town at the command center, Pat Cleburne received continual updates on the battle. At the point of Hooker's decision, he looked out. He knew it was time and he knew Hooker was out of options. He knew Hooker was feeling his presence at that very instant. Out there, through the smoke and violent action, Hooker was looking to him for a prayer. He sent none.

From his position behind a fallen log, Window fired and fell back against the log. Next to him, Absolon fired and dropped.

"I can't even see what I'm shooting at," Absolon shouted over the thunder of gunfire. "Still glad I made you a soldier?"

"I'd be gladder if'n I could see past that pile of dead Yankees!"

Window fired again and fell back to reload. As he shoved the ramrod into his rifle, he felt a bump from behind. He turned as Absolon slumped into his arm. Carefully, Window laid his friend down in his lap. The mini-ball had opened a small hole in his chest but, as Window cradled him he felt the large exit wound in Absolon's back. The lead ball had flattened as it passed through him and took his ribs and shoulder blade off. Window had time to wonder if his heart was still in his chest.

With a trembling hand, Absolon reached into his blouse and pulled out his last letter to Anne. Gasping and coughing, he handed the blood stained letter to Window.

"See she gets this."

Window felt his eyes begin to tear. "Give it to her yourself. I ain't your nigger."

Absolon smiled, seemingly trying to laugh at the joke. As Window cradled him, Absolon shuddered from a private chill, then died in his arms. There was, for this second, no guns, no enemy, no families left or battles lost. There was nothing but the warmth on his arm. There was only the best friend he knew gone. He hugged him tightly and sobbed his goodbye to Absolon.

"Thank you. Thank you."

The guns thundered back and the fighting more evident than before. Window laid Absolon down and dried his eyes just as another volley dropped two men dead around him. Surrounded by death, Window felt a new rage welling within him. He grabbed his rifle and affixed the bayonet. With a moan of rage and terror, he stood from his protection and charged at them, screaming like a Rebel. Some of the Union men saw him and, with Hooker screaming in the background, followed Window. The screaming assault led around the pile of dead Yankees instead of over the summit. He ran to the left and charged fiercely up the hill with a company behind him.

At the first sign of a gray uniform, Window fired and a Rebel fell. Another jumped on him and Window held him away by bracing his rifle against the man's chest. The Union company passed in attack as they looked each other in the eye at close range. Window, wide-eyed, suddenly saw the menacing face of Tom Bridger on the Rebel soldier. He heard the overseer's voice say:

"You're a dead nigger."

The soldier reached out and grabbed Window by the shirt, nearly pulling Absolon's letter out. It was the incentive needed and Window screamed and threw the man to the ground. With maddened rage he thrust his bayonet down into the man, pinning him to the ground. He saw the whip in the man's hand change back into a rifle as the hand stopped twitching.

Pushing the letter safely back into his shirt, Window looked back and saw the pile of dead Union soldiers behind him. To the right he saw the log where he'd left Absolon. Then he turned again to face the enemy. He saw his men still trying to advance. A soldier climbed up onto a grass covered mound and fired downward. The man was instantly shot and fell back. Window raised his rifle and charged the mound.

As he charged, his mind drew all from his past that brought him here. More rage than any man could endure was in his heart at that instant. He saw Old Nate tied to that tree. He saw Bella thrown to the ground. He saw his father on the auction block in Charleston being sold. He saw his father look back at him one last time as he was pulled away like a plow horse, the buyer slapping him for hesitating. He saw all of the torment in his life and embraced it as he attacked.

He rounded the grassy hill to the left with his bayonet at the ready. Gasping and wild with rage, he thrust the bayonet and stopped the blade inches from Mason's chest.

Mason lay over the other soldier, protecting this body with his own. He clutched a spent pistol by the barrel like a tomahawk. Window looked into his face. Mason looked back, slowly recognizing his attacker. Window's eyes narrowed. He grit his teeth and blew rage from his nostrils. Was this another vision, like the overseer? Then he suddenly relaxed a bit and lowered the bayonet.

"Mister Corbel?"

Mason was stunned. "Window? My God. *Window?* Is that you?"

Window knelt next to him, ducking his head behind the mound for cover. "Yessir. You wounded?"

"My leg. And my arm from before. I can't move."

The sound of gunfire and anguished screams was less in their ear as the battle moved on. Still it was evident there was fighting left to do. Window looked at Mason and squeezed his rifle tightly. Slowly he lowered it to the ground and reached for Mason with open, empty hands. "We got to get you out of here."

"No. I can't leave..."

As Window looked on, Mason lifted the hat of the soldier he had defended with his own life. Window looked down into Victoria's face. Her eyes were closed and her chest was matted with blood.

Window gasped, shocked to find her here, mortified to see the wound on her. "Oh Mother of Jesus. What you two gone and done?"

"She followed me out here. We tried to just survive but..."

Window studied the wound. It was higher than Absolon's. It surely missed her heart and lung but the hole was bleeding badly. "She needs a doctor."

"Ours is dead. And if they find her out, they might think she's a spy. We need to surrender."

"Oh no you don't. Don't do that, Mister Corbel."

"They'll give her medical attention."

"I seen what they give prisoners. And I know what they'd do to a lady like her. No sir. That ain't a option."

Mason half smiled. "You know a better way, Window?"

"You need to take her home. All the way home. Git her out this war. Dress that wound when you're away from here and just take her back to where she should never have left."

"I can't. I can't even take myself home."

Window looked around, daring to hold his head above the cover to see where the fighting had lead. "I ain't leaving you, Mister Corbel. We'll get her out of here."

Pushing his arm under her shoulders, Window started to lift Victoria. Mason looked at him with an expression of stunned admiration. He knew too well and full he was witnessing the greatest act of selflessness he had ever seen. Window's devotion to decency surpassed all else and Mason felt humbled in the presence of him. Collecting himself, he struggled to his feet to help.

The fighting pushed south and into the streets of Ringgold Gap. Amid the wounded and dead, the valiant and the feared, none noticed the spectacle of the soldier helping another along. None noticed the man in the middle was black, or that he held a white woman in his arms. It went without a glance that the Confederate soldier leaned on the Union man like a brother. There was, in this trio and amid one of the bloodiest fights in history, only love and respect. No more fighting was in them. Not these three. They left the battlefield and the war that day.

The fight continued without them for an hour. When Cleburne gave the order to retreat, they took with them a great victory on many levels. He had faced Fighting Joe and taken him to task, stopping Hooker's forces by brilliant strategy and furious defense. By this, General Bragg had made it to Dalton unmolested and gained reinforcements.

Pat Cleburne lost two hundred and twenty-one brave men that day. Joe Hooker reported twice that in casualties, though none including Grant believed it for a second. It was evident he had lost nearly ten times that and failed in his mission to boot. His reputation as a military strategist and leader was already unenviable. His reckless abandon and disregard for human losses in battle led to more and repeated controversy, though Lincoln's need for fighters allowed him to remain in command. The president, in response to the sheer number of deaths Hooker amassed in a conflict was quoted to gasp, "My God. What will the people say?"

Joe Hooker later maintained the dub 'Fighting Joe' was given by a newspaper man hoping to hype sales and propagate the war. He claimed he never liked the name. But he also claimed to live a good life despite the entourage of revelers and prostitutes that seemed to appear and every civilized settlement along his campaigned trail. He and his now renounced nickname were responsible for prostitutes eventually being called 'Hookers'. His career had every opportunity for greatness, but Joe Hooker was remembered only by seediness and negativity.

23

———

November 25, 1863

Dearest Anne,

I pray this finds you well. If the rumors hold true, I look for some end to this ware soon. The Rebs are said to be buckling, though you can't tell it from the fight in those left. We just won a great victory over a big outfit. My negra friend Window led the charge and fought like a real hero. The men seem to have accepted him as one of us and he pears happy as I've seen him. We were feeling our oats after the Rebs ran off but then that General Hooker come and told us we were in a fighting outfit. Window knew like me what that meant. Don't worry. We've taken lickings before, me and Window, and we can take as well as give. If the worst happens, I've asked Window to see you get this. Most likely we'll just hitch up with another outfit.

I've had time to think back and I realize I asked Royal to stay there and watch over you and he did it without a thought. That was a brave thing as I'm sure he would have been an officer or something. From what I seen of officers, he would be a good one. I hope the locals didn't think less of him for not going.

I now know he said yes out of devotion rather than desire and is the truest of all friends. Please be sure he knows how much we appreciate what he has done for me and for you. He sacrificed more than his life. He gave of his heart and is as much a hero as any man here. As for my heart, you know it is yours still. All my thoughts are of you and will surely be all of my life. Until we are together, feel the love I send.

Yours,

Absolon

Anne sat by the lamp and read the letter. Her emotion was as her garb, still black and without joy.

It was the second letter that she read that told the tale. It came from Royal, delivered by a courier with Absolon's. Absolon's letter was handed to Royal on Christmas Eve. He celebrated the holiday as he did all other nights. He stood watch on the road that forked between the town of Durham and the Carmichael house. He would come no closer, but rarely ventured father from her.

In the cold solitude that had become his life, he was approached by a band of travelers going home from the war. The man, slumped over in the saddle of the big horse, seemed ill, but alive. The horse pulled a rustic litter carrying a woman. She rested comfortably and, like the man, would survive her wounds. The tall negro leading the big horse assured him with absolute confidence that they would make it.

He had brought them this way to ask directions of Royal. As it happened, Royal knew the way and did accept the post. There, on that frozen, moonlit road, the two strangers spoke briefly, and Royal's head fell to his chest in grief. It was over. For months and years since Absolon left, and before that he was sure, Royal had fought with all the decency in him to suppress thoughts of this moment. He had caught himself at times of want, imagining the time when his dear friend was no longer between him and her. He would approach her and finally tell her what she surely must have known. They would mourn Absolon, then bond by their common grief and he would find reward for his loyalty. That was the thought he wrestled with for so long.

Now it was handed to him in earnest. He shuddered with the thought of ever speaking the name of his friend to her. The guilt in him weighed heavily and he struggled to hold the thoughts and tears and grief overwhelming inside him. The Negro shook his hand and led the band on toward the west. He had fulfilled his promise to a hero. Now he went toward the uncertainty of his course, knowing that the punishment for escaping was to be beaten nearly to death and the act of enlisting was surely a death sentence. His master was alive and behind him and only in that did he find hope of salvation.

Miles stretched out before them and were crossed one at a time. Each day was a slow, drudging march toward home. Each night was a much needed rest for Mason and Victoria. Window sat most of the night watching and tending to them. He slept as much as he dared, but Victoria grew steadily weaker and he grew increasingly fearful of their chances.

By noon the fourteenth day after leaving Absolon's letter with Royal, Mason felt the horse stop. He looked up to see Window off the road peering over a hilltop. Gathering his strength, he slid from the saddle and stood on his own for the first time in a week. He went back to check on Victoria, sleeping uneasily in the litter. He felt the fever in her and her pallor frightened him. She had begun to improve and was even speaking only days before. But a snap of cold and freezing rain took a heavy toll on the unprotected travelers. Window had been torn between seeking shelter or pushing on to the relative safety and hope of the Corbel plantation. Only in the direst of conditions did he dare stop. The war was still out there and would not treat them kindly should they be found. He assured Mason time and again that they would be home soon. He would not fail them. The sicker Victoria became, the more driven to continue Window seemed.

Why, Mason now wondered, had they stopped? How far had they to go? He left her to go to Window for answers.

Window was watching a small shack just off the road and seemingly deserted. As Mason came up behind him, he saw the object of Window's attention and whispered in a gravelly voice used for the first time in a week.

"Is it empty?"

"I think so," Window responded without turning. His voice was equally, though deliberately soft. "I need to be sure before I shows us. Look over there."

Near the south side of the cabin lay the prone, lifeless figure of a man in what appeared to be a Confederate jersey. The weather and dirt made it difficult to be sure from this distance that the man was anything but dead. The awkward position of the arms made this point irrefutable. Another victim was spotted on the other side near a window. Equally dead was he.

"We can't stay here, Window. Vickie needs a doctor."

Now Window turned to him. "If we don't get some fresh bandages and some alcohol for her wound, she won't make it to no doctor. That sick hole in her is doin' nothin' but pumpin' poison around in her. We needs to clean it proper and that means I needs to see what's in there. But first I needs to know who shot them fellas."

Mason nodded. Window's logic was as impeccable as his motive.

"What do you want me to do?"

"You need to stay out here with Miss Corbel. Back her a good ways off and wait for me. Anything happens to me, you get her out of here."

He started to rise and Mason grasped his shoulder. "How many times can I thank you?"

Window clutched his wrist. "One'll do. It's comin'."

Window helped Mason lead Big Willy into a clump of woods for cover, safely away but close enough to hear a shout or a shot. He left the Corbel's here and made his way in a broad circle toward the little cabin. Should someone see him approach, they'd be less likely to find the Corbel's.

As he approached the house, he found a third man laying dead in the trail. This man was well away from the cabin and in civilian clothes. Leaned against a tree, the ax in his hand was the closest thing to a weapon found. Window felt the cotton shirt and made note of it. Other than the blood matted-breast, the shirt was suitable for bandage material. He would pick it up on the way back. Drawing his pistol, he moved on.

The dead man near the side window was indeed a Confederate soldier. He was slumped face first against the wall and as Window crept past him he could tell that the top of the man's head was torn away. Window surmised this Reb had peeked into the open window and been shot in the face by the occupant. The only good sign drawn here was that the body seemed to have been laying here for several days, if not weeks kept by the cold. The shooter could be well away.

Coming around in the slowest, most cautious step of his life, Window was on full alert as he approached the second dead soldier. This man lay chest down with his head tilted funny. Window knelt next to him and poked the head with the barrel of his pistol. He was definitely dead. He lifted the man's head and found the underside of his head blown open in a gaping hole. Window had seen exit wounds before. The man had been shot in the head at close range. A second look at the thick hair on the upper side of the head revealed the .54 caliber hole just behind his temple. He was dead before his knees buckled.

Victoria shuddered. "Mason," she moaned without opening her eyes.

He was at her side already. "I'm here, Vickie." He stroked her brow and pushed her bangs from her face with his good arm. The blankets around her kept her warm but his hand was like an ice pack on her fevered skin. He laid his open palm on her forehead as he tried to calm her. "Hold on, Sweetheart. We'll be home soon."

"Home? We're really going?" She forced a weak smile.

"Uh huh. Window's off finding some food and bandages. We'll be home in two days. Three tops. How's that sound?"

Her face grew solemn. "It was such a dark place, Mason. I hated it there without you. It was so lonely."

"It's going to be all right." He did his best to hold the reassuring smile though she looked so very weak. He had never thought of her as being anything but indomitable. He was always willing to care for her and protect her. This was the first time in their lives that she needed him to. As he felt the pain in his wounded arm, he prayed he had the strength.

"I'm sorry, Mason."

"Sorry? For coming out here? I guess I should have known you'd..."

"No," she cut him off. "I mean about the baby. I'm so sorry."

"He looked her evenly in the eye this time. His smile was sincere. "We're still here. We'll try again. Don't you dare apologize. Not for that. Not to me. Not ever."

"You don't think I'm a failure? Not on some level?"

"I think you're my wife. I think you're the bravest person I've ever known. And I think you're already a mother. You just haven't got a baby yet. It'll happen. God wouldn't do that to you."

Her smile seemed to come with the last of her strength and she closed her eyes. He stared fearfully for a long second until he heard her breathing. She was merely sleeping. He exhaled his relief and watched over her.

The door of the cabin was closed, but unlocked. There was no lock that Window could see as the rustic wooden door creaked open with little more than a touch. The two room shanty seemed deserted but he sensed a presence. Possibly not long empty, he thought, and hoped. People left a bit of themselves in a home, he was taught. He kept his wits about him as he looked about for anything he could use.

There, in the corner across from him, he saw a washbowl and a pitcher. There were white cloths next to it. Not bleached white, but they looked clean enough. On the dusty shelves behind the bowl he saw cans. Food, he prayed. And there were three smoked glass bottles. Two of them were corked.

Window crept slowly toward the bottles thinking his luck had finally changed. He kept his head below the window level in case the occupants were outside. He held the pistol because it was already in his hand, but his attention was increasingly drawn to the bottles as he got closer. It was at the precise moment that he found a prayer of hope that he heard the distinctive click of a hammer. The unmistakable sound of a rifle being cocked just behind him.

He froze, expecting the fatal ball to come any second. The image of those fallen outside played his thoughts as he felt the touch of the barrel on the back of his head. He had only a second to silently curse himself for never checking behind the door.

Gathering what he could of composure, he attempted to speak. "Now easy there, Mister. I didn't mean no harm. I thought this place was empty."

"It ain't," was the reply. The soft, monotone voice was that of a ten-year-old girl.

Window didn't know how to respond. She wasn't a soldier, but she wasn't a reasonable adult either. What was he to say? As he was still alive, he dared try.

"Now I ain't your enemy. You don't want to kill nobody and I sho don't want to be dead."

"Put that hog leg down."

"Yes, Missy. Doin' it now." He slowly obeyed, lowering the pistol toward the floor. He chanced a slow glance back as he moved. She was blonde and filthy and stared at him emotionlessly down the length of an old musket. "There you go. You got no need to be scared of me, now."

"Ain't scared."

"Where's your Ma and Pa?" He kept his voice low and unthreatening as he attempted to gain her trust.

"Gone. Pa off to the war. Soldiers kilt our Ma. Now I'm the Ma and Pa."

"What soldiers? Them outside?"

The barrel was still trained on him as she coldly responded. "Others. They left. These came later."

"You killed them?"

"I killed 'em."

"Was it Rebs what killed your ma? Rebs like them outside?"

"Don't matter. It was soldiers. We cain't trust nobody now. I'm the Ma and Pa."

Window dared turn a bit toward her. There was still no emotion in her. No trust. But he wasn't dead yet. That had to be a good sign. He tried to keep his wits about him. His right shoulder was nearly close enough to push the gun aside. His left hand was nearly close enough to grab the pistol from the floor. He would chance it but for one thing.

"Who is 'We', Missy? Who else is here?"

He had to ask, but at that, he saw her young, pained eyes narrow angrily. It was clearly the wrong question.

Mason softly stroked Victoria's head. Window had been gone a while, but he had no choice but to trust him and wait, so wait he did with resolve. In the distance he heard a shot. It was muffled and well away but clearly gunfire. He looked down to see Victoria still sleeping soundly. He wanted to run toward the gunfire in case Window needed help, but this sleep seemed different. Victoria seemed almost too restful now. It was as if the unburdening put her more at ease. Was she letting go? Had his precious Victoria given up the fight for the first time in her life? Was that apology her death bed confession? No!

Shaking her by the shoulder, he forced her awake. "Vickie! Vickie. Wake up."

She stirred. "What? What is it?" Her voice was groggy and her eyes were glazed over. She started immediately dropping back into the slumber that so terrified Mason.

"Keep awake, Vickie. Look at me. I need to know you're still fighting."

"Can't... Just let me rest. I can make it."

"Vickie. I have to go after Window."

She forced her eyes open. "Don't leave me, Mase. Don't leave me again."

"Just for a minute. I'll be right back."

From behind them the dry bushed parted with a less than subtle rattle. Mason reeled and aimed his pistol directly at Window, who stood fearlessly in the mouth of the same trail he left from. In his arms was a large wad of cloth and bandages.

Mason lowered his weapon. "Thank God. What did you find? Bandages?"

Window soberly approached. "Yessir. Bandages. Alcohol. Some canned meat and something else."

He handed the bundle to Mason and Mason gasped at what he held. He couldn't draw from the odd expression on Window's face if he had any idea what this meant. Slowly he tuned and knelt next to Victoria.

"Vickie. Wake up."

She stirred, seemingly unable to muster the strength to open her eyes. "What?" She moaned.

Mason set the bundle in her arms. Victoria opened her eyes and looked at him, stunned by what she felt. His broad grin assured her it was no dream. She looked down into the face of an infant. The boy was no more than two months old and trying to focus on her.

"His name's Aloysius," said the girl. She was ten feet behind Window and no longer armed.

Mason looked at her. "Is he your...?"

"My brother. But I don't want to be Ma and Pa no more. You can do it if you want."

"Aloysius?" Mason said.

"But he don't know it yet. You can call him something else. Don't matter. Long as you feed and tend to him."

Victoria couldn't believe the sensation in her arms. The baby cooed and gurgled as if all was right with the world. They were home and safe and this was his family and there was no war and no death and no wrong anywhere.

Mason hovered over her. "What shall we call him then?"

Victoria. "I was always partial to Mason Junior."

"What about... Window?" He turned to see how Window would react to the gesture, but he saw his friend slumping down against a tree. Mason immediately ran to him. The girl stared without remorse.

"What happened? Are you all right?" Mason asked as he examined Window.

Window coughed and blood came from his mouth. He started to slump over and Mason caught him. As he sat him upright against the tree, he felt a warmth and moistness on him hand. Looking, he found Window's ribs soaked with blood. He looked at him in shock, than to the girl.

"Sorry," she said in her monotone style. "I didn't know he was a good one. I was per-tectin' my brother."

Mason was drawn back to the man in his arms as Window seemed to laugh. "Imagine that," Window managed to say between coughs and grimaces. "I take on the whole Confederate army and walk away just so some little girl can kill me."

"You're not dead, Window. Just shot. We'll get you home. We can make it." He tried to lift him but Window resisted.

"I seen enough of them to know when a man's dying. She got me good." He started to go down and Mason caught him. "Don't you do that to that boy," he warned Mason.

"Do what?"

"Name him Window. That ain't no kinda name. If you going to name him, I gots a favor to ask."

"Anything."

"Absolon. A good name for a good man. Absolon. Just like that."

"Absolon," Mason repeated, looking back at his wife and the baby. Victoria nodded approvingly. He looked to Window. "Absolon it is. Thank you, Window. Thank you."

"She's a fighter, that wife of your's. That baby going to keep her going. She'll make it now. Just you watch them Yankees try to stop her." His voice trailed off, weaker and fading. He shuddered as if cold.

"I don't know if it matters to you, Window," Mason said. "But you're freed. With God as my witness, you're a free man."

As his eyes closed, the right corner of his mouth curled up in the slightest of smiles. "I know that. Thank you."

He died there and then, free in every way.

While the rest of the country and the world saw the war rage another eighteen months, for these soldiers, it was over. Window Graham was buried on the Corbel plantation. His tombstone read: Here lies Window Graham, Soldier, Hero and beloved friend, home at last.

December 26, 1863

Dear Anne,

As mutual friend of both you and Absolon Wilkes, this sad duty falls onto my shoulders. I regret to tell you that our Absolon fell from a Reb mini-ball at the battle of Ringgold Gap.

I'm told he fought courageously and no man could have asked for more than what he gave. I was also told that his last thought was of you. While I loved him as a brother and feel your pain, I must respectfully, in his memory, continue my vigil from this distance. Anticipating your gracious permission, I will call upon you after an acceptable period of mourning.

Yours,

Royal J. Pollard, Esquire

Royal remained that day as Window had found him. Vigilant, steadfast, driven and bound by duty. Standing there on the snow covered road, he resolved not to tell her this night, nor the next. Each Christmas for the rest of their lives would be thus tainted with this bitter memory.

He instead spent his Christmas composing his letter and protecting her from this, the final blow of war.

The most common variety of war hero is the one who never returns. Absolon was buried at Ringgold Gap with the thousands of fallen in both uniforms on the battlefield. The bloody battle was never considered more than a minor historical conflict, all but lost in the shadow of such great battles as Gettysburg. Pat Cleburne and Joe Hooker both missed immortality by other than the most devout historians. But those men who died there and in every engagement from Gettysburg to the farmhouse shootings left someone behind. Each, in his own way, mattered to someone.

True to his word, Royal observed the needed time for mourning before calling on Anne. It was a bittersweet reunion as their meeting wrought the painful memory of Absolon. They had to face it, both of them, and get past it. Their own lives and any prayer of happiness stood beyond it.

He was received and Anne accepted him into her life. More than the pain they shared in their mutual loss, Royal was all but alone in his ability to leave the past behind. Nothing that happened during the war would follow them in their new life together.

The Pollards found little warmth in the Old South after the war. With the majestic charm that had been a part of his life forever gone, Royal took his wife, Anne, and son, James, to San Francisco in 1870. After borrowing all that his charisma and business sense could draw, he struggled for another seven years with orchards and farming. He would surely have gone under had the vineyards not taken off when they did.

The new opulence in California dictated the market and his winery became the family business. When James officially took the reins in 1905, the business was bordering on an empire and he had great plans for international marketing. But the earthquake a year latter destroyed the economy in Northern California and left James Pollard with just enough to buy a smaller, less developed ranch in Arizona. Land came cheap and he was desperate to support his parents, wife and two children.

The Arizona desert proved far less prosperous than the west coast and the horse ranch floundered. The Pollard fortune was finally gone and, while his parents lived comfortably on their retirement savings, James had nothing to leave his children but advice. After fighting the Keizer in WWI, Marcus Pollard returned to Arizona to work for another, larger ranch while his younger sister, Dorothy, remained with her grandparents.

Grandfather Royal died at ninety, one month after his beloved Anne passed away. Dorothy moved to Chandler, Arizona with a few possessions and a wealth of memories. Despite the hop in generations, Dorothy had a special relationship with her grandmother and spent many hours listening to tales of the amazing life spent. She forged her own family but never forgot her history. Dorothy's family history survived in the memory, in the retelling, and in the letters passed down to her from Anne. In that legacy, the sacrifices and losses, the victories and the bonds of friendship, everything that war forced on families and took from civilization, the very emotion of war lived on.

CPSIA information can be obtained at www.ICGtesting.com
Printed in the USA
LVOW11s1728020816

498751LV00005B/203/P